Books by Ki Longfellow

China Blues
Chasing Women
Stinkfoot, a Comic Opera (with Vivian Stanshall)
The Secret Magdalene
Flow Down Like Silver: Hypatia of Alexandria
Houdini Heart
Walks Away Woman
Shadow Roll: A Sam Russo Mystery Case 1
Good Dog, Bad Dog: A Sam Russo Mystery Case 2
The Girl in the Next Room: A Sam Russo Mystery Case 3
Dead on the Rocks: A Sam Russo Mystery Case 4

Follow Ki Longfellow on the Internet:

Facebook Ki Longfellow
Twitter @KiLongfellow
Official Website www.kilongfellow.com
Sam Russo www.eiobooks.com/samrusso

Dead on the Rocks

by
Ki Longfellow

A Sam Russo Mystery

Case 4

Eio Books

Published in the United States by

Eio Books
4436 Steamboat Island Road NW
Olympia, Washington, 98502 U.S.A.

www.eiobooks.com

Library of Congress Cataloging-in-Publication Data

Longfellow, Ki
 Dead on the rocks : a Sam Russo mystery CASE 4 / Ki Longfellow.
   1 online resource.
 Description based on print version record and CIP data provided by
publisher; resource not viewed.
 ISBN 978-1-937819-12-5 (Paperback) -- ISBN 978-1-937819-13-2 (E-book) --
ISBN 978-1-937819-12-5 (softcover : acid-free paper)
 1. Russo, Sam (Fictitious character)--Fiction. 2. Private
investigators--Fiction. 3. Murder--Investigation--Fiction. I. Title.
 PS3562.O499
 813'.54--dc23

                                    2014035866

Cover designed by Shane Roberts
Book designed by Shane Roberts

Dedicated to
Barbara Stanwyck & Seabiscuit

(And to Ty Vivian—here's lookin' at you, kid)

Dead on the Rocks

A Sam Russo Mystery

Case 4

Mrs. Willingford sat bolt upright in bed. The potent scent of *L'Heure Bleue* sat up with her. Perfumed, sunlit and nude, Joker Willingford's wife had skin like peaches, hair like honey, eyes like Nefertiti, and a mouth like Tallulah Bankhead.

"Stop fucking whining, Russo."

"I am *not* fucking whining. I am stating a fact."

"Which is?"

"I don't like boats."

"Exactly. Second day out, second day whining."

"What a load of hooey."

"Even Jane's had enough."

"She has?"

"Only a man who whines as much as you do, could have missed that."

She had me there. I'd missed it. Jane had enough? I looked round my stateroom, the one Mrs. and Mr. Joker Willingford assigned me aboard the good ship Sip o' Sea for the duration of its voyage. Two couches. A desk. A desk chair. A telephone. My own private bath. A closet. A nightstand. An oil painting on one of the walls. I'd need an art expert to tell me who painted it. I'd need whoever painted it to explain why they bothered.

No Jane. Things, already unsteady, were getting rockier.

"I'll stop."

"You promise?"

"No. But I'll try."

Mrs. Willingford traced a long nailed finger around one

of my scars, a pucker of a bullet hole close to my heart. If anything was meant to kill me, it was that particular bullet. Or this particular boat.

I nibbled on Mrs. Willingford's shoulder. Nibbling on Mrs. Willingford's sleek round creamy shoulder never got old.

It was an hour before I whined again.

It was the tipping over of the ship that did it. Did we hit something? A reef? A raft? Another ship!

I grabbed at the padded headboard and held on. "What the hell was that! Was that an iceberg?"

"You kill me, you know that, Sam?"

"Kill *you*? We could be dead! Your boat just hit an iceberg."

"This isn't the Titanic."

"Then it was Moby Dick. I saw *Lifeboat*. Twice. Are there enough lifeboats on this tub?"

Mrs. Willingford and her heady new scent slid off the bed, a big comfy bed bolted to the stateroom's carpeted deck, and all mine for the duration. From down there, she said, "If there aren't, you're fish bait."

The Sip o' Sea rolled hard the other way.

That one did it. I made a beeline for the bathroom, or whatever it's called on a boat. The bathroom had a big round brass rimmed porthole I could open and close. So long as it was my porthole, it was staying closed.

By this time, breakfast had come and gone, delivered on an enameled tray by a smart young man in a smart smoky gray jacket and black pants. Like a lot of things on the Sip o' Sea: couches, curtains, carpets, the tray was that pink you see inside a salmon. Some things were a dark smoky gray.

Fish pink and smoke gray were the Willingford racing colors.

Deck games had come and gone above my head. Someone running. Seagulls yelling. Fellow guests going in and out of staterooms pretty much like mine, laughing, not laughing, bickering. Doors slamming.

My lunch had come and gone. Then come and gone again after the first one got dropped in the passageway outside my door. Gene, the name of my own personal steward, the same Gene who'd brought me my breakfast, had dropped it. It wasn't his fault. It was Jane's fault. She was going out as he was coming in. The sight of a dog and man and lunch collision perked me up for almost a minute.

Less than ten minutes later, Gene was back with a fresh lunch. It included a new fish pink rose.

Although we were only on our second day out, so far I'd eaten in my stateroom more than I hadn't eaten in my stateroom. Whatever was cooking, it was always brought by that same young man in the same smoky gray jacket. For a guy, Gene was as pretty as Montgomery Clift. Having got a load of Gene and most of the other stewards, I'd bet my last nickel Mrs. Willingford did the hiring.

I already knew from a few remarks I'd made and the few he'd made, Gene knew a lot about movies. If anyone liked Carole Lombard as much as me, he did. Finding that out perked me up longer than watching Jane blame the steward for being in her busy way.

And now Mrs. Willingford had come and gone.

As for me, I'd come but not gone. I was still in bed trying to relax by clinging to the headboard and listening to the latest radio episode of *The Adventures of Philip Marlowe*.

Joker Willingford's wife'd showed up after the *Grilled Short Rib with Crimini Mushroom*s—I knew what I'd eaten for lunch because I still had the printed menu—walking in without so much as a knock, wearing some kind of flowing rosy red silk thing, all long droopy sleeves and a Ming the Merciless collar.

No hat. Mrs. Willingford without one of her huge hats

was like the Statue of Liberty without her torch. But there were hats somewhere around. I just had to be patient.

Two hours later she was back in her evil Emperor Ming outfit and out my stateroom door before I was done with my personal toilette.

I got back in bed and steamed.

Jane was gone. Mrs. Willingford was gone. My radio show had signed off the air and I didn't get to know who did it. Without something good on the radio, without Mrs. W. and without Jane, all I had left was staring out my main stateroom window, not a porthole but a big rectangular thing with a great view—if all you wanted to see was the sea.

All I saw was me stuck on a yacht way out in the fucking Atlantic Ocean.

Beyond my door, the rest of the Willingford yacht was crawling with wildlife. Out there somewhere, charming the whole bunch of 'em, was Holly, the girl who lived in her one room next to my one room back in dingy Stapleton on the dingy northern shore of Staten Island. As an island, Staten Island wasn't bad. It had some woods and some hidden ponds and some beaches and some hills. It was only the people on it that spoiled the view.

Also out there somewhere was Jane. Jane was my dog.

Who was I kidding? Jane was her own dog. And she didn't charm anyone unless she felt like it. She felt like it about once in a blue moon.

Shot three times up close by an old friend—my pal Paul Jarrett, once a fellow inmate of the Staten Island Home for Children and now a permanent resident of Sing Sing's Death Row—I still never felt less like Bogart. Bogie at sea was like Bogie on land. He was Bogart. Me at sea was like me at sea. Not Bogart.

The last time I was stuck on a ship, I was being shipped home from the Pacific front. Sam Russo, prize alumni of the exclusive Staten Island Junk Yard for Throw-away Kids, came back in one piece.

A lot of others didn't. Some didn't come back at all.

Four years in the Philippines getting bombed, strafed, machine gunned, mined, starved and sent on suicide missions, I wasn't sure one piece was good enough. What I *was* sure of was, it couldn't get worse.

And then I ran into my first typhoon.

Somewhere out in the gray and endless ocean, every man jack of us sick and tired, all of us in misery and most of us changed forever, all hell broke loose. The sky, already dark, grew darker. The wind, already blowing, blew harder. The waves, already waving, rose higher and higher and higher, high enough to tower over the tallest building on the main street of Stapleton, Staten Island… my home town.

A guy next to me, both of us struggling into lifejackets, claimed they were fifty feet high for sure. He said, "Say buddy, lookit that! That one'd take out the Golden Gate Bridge!"

Brother, did that crack make me gag.

Gripping a ship's plunging rail, staring at a rush of oncoming water, and heaving my supper, I gotta say that trip sure showed a fella what the sea was like. It wasn't good solid earth. Unless someone was lobbing a bomb and you were where it landed, you could trust land to stay land. But not the sea. From one minute to the next, the sea could be anything. As a betting man, those weren't my kind of odds at all.

Ten years old, I'd jump off any Staten Island pier you cared to name: winter, summer, spring or fall. Now I was thirty, just a ride on the Staten Island ferry could give me the willies.

But back then, on the first day of September in the year Hoop Jr. won the Kentucky Derby, falling into deep troughs between high waves, then climbing up their sides before falling back into more troughs, Sam Russo, age twenty five, made a pact with himself. He'd lived through almost five years fighting

Japs in tanks from the back of a horse; if he lived through a U.S. Navy boat ride, he'd never leave solid ground again. No jumping off piers, no getting on ships or boats or canoes, not even a rowboat.

I let go of my bed. Hanging on to it wasn't working. I'd already taken comfort in Mrs. Willingford and believe you me, she could be one hell of a comforter when she set her mind and other parts to it. But I needed more, and two servings in one day of Lois, aka Mrs. Joker Willingford, was the most I was going to get. That meant I had to find somewhere else on the Willingford yacht where I could fight to relax.

That wasn't going to be easy since everywhere I went I'd still be on a fucking boat, but I had to try.

I got up. I washed. I got dressed. I grabbed my book and my smokes but left my gun and my set of lock picks where I could find 'em when I needed 'em. On a private yacht, why would I need 'em? I'd asked myself that when I packed, then stuck them both in my suitcase without giving myself an answer.

Washed, dressed, book under my arm, I went looking for somewhere safe, somewhere alone, somewhere I could pretend I wasn't on a boat.

I also needed to keep away from my fellow passengers.

One look at the bullet tracks cut through my dog Jane's bright red and white coat, not to mention all the scars made by a desperate man with a steak knife up in a pink hotel in Saratoga Springs, and half of 'em were sure I was a one-man Murder, Incorporated.

2

Me getting stuck on the Sip o' Sea in the first place was Holly and Jane's fault. If not for the both of them, I'd be back in Stapleton, lying around in my one room 4th floor walk-up with shared bath. I'd be reading a book in my own Murphy bed using my own chipped ashtray and drinking my own coffee out of my own coffee mug.

I'd of made the coffee myself, just the way I liked it.

Except for the coffee, the cigarette, and the book, so would Jane.

Every once in awhile, when I was sure the drunken troll who'd recently moved into 4-C wasn't home—you could always tell when he was, the noise from his room sounded like all Three Stooges passing wind—I'd use the toilet.

Jane and me, lying around, we'd be waiting for the phone to ring. Maybe it'd be a wrong number like in *Sorry, Wrong Number*. I'd made sure I saw that movie the day it opened at the Paramount on Bay. Sam Russo didn't make a habit of missing something with Stanwyck in it, even if she spent most of it in bed as a hysterical invalid. Or maybe the call would be about a good case. That one was a long shot but it'd happened before so it could happen again. Getting an unexpected call to hop on the Staten Island Ferry and then onto a train headed up to the racetrack at Saratoga Springs to look into why three young jockeys got dead was how I met Jane.

Oh right, it was also how I bumped into Mrs. Willingford.

A heck of a lot more likely, if the phone did ring, it'd be my old pal from the Broken Home for Abusing Kids, Detective Lino Morelli. Morelli'd be calling to try and wheedle me yet again into doing his job when no one was looking.

If Morelli did call, brother, was he in for a surprise. I'd made up my mind. Sam Russo, Private Eye, wouldn't be solving Lino's cases anymore. Morelli didn't know that yet. But give it time. He would.

Turns out, it was me who got the surprise. Nobody called out of the blue with a great case. Lino didn't call. I wondered about that. Staten Island wasn't the murder capital of the U.S. of A. but we did get our burglaries, our muggings, our rapes and our gambling dens. Maybe the island was on a crime sabbatical.

No one even dialed my number by mistake.

The quiet was beginning to spook me.

And then, one lonely Sunday in the early morn when even the girls who worked below my window down in Tompkinsville Park were giving it a rest, the phone finally rang. I woke up to an invite from Mrs. Willingford.

I hadn't seen Mrs. Willingford in two months, not since Holly and Jane and me and Mrs. Willingford were driven out to Belmont Park by Woody the Willingford chauffeur in one of the Willingford cars to watch Middleground, the unexpected winner of the Kentucky Derby—unexpected by me anyway—come romping home in the Belmont Stakes under a sixteen year old apprentice jockey. Middleground took the Belmont after losing the Preakness Stakes to Hill Prince.

As us bettors always said, I woulda made a sweet little bundle if my horse hadda won.

Shoulda, woulda, coulda: that was going on my tombstone if I could afford a tombstone the day came I needed one. Come to think, when I needed one, I wouldn't care if I had one. So forget that.

The horse I bet on for the 1950 Kentucky Derby was Your

Host. I loved Your Host. The battle he fought with Mr. Trouble made my heart race. Where the hell did Middleground come from? But what can you do? A horse race is a horse race is a horse race.

Your Host came in ninth.

I didn't back Middleground. I didn't even notice Middleground until we all noticed him. But I picked right for place and show: Lights Up and Mr. Trouble.

Unfortunately, picking place and show didn't pay off.

Holly liked Your Host as much as I did. But Holly was a looker not a bettor. Being one herself, she was a sucker for oddballs. There wasn't a horse in the Derby goofier looking than Your Host.

Anyway, on the telephone Mrs. Willingford said she and her hubby Joker Willingford were sailing their yacht from New York to Florida. A whole boatload of what I assumed would be swells were going to Hialeah to cheer on Fleeting Fancy, the Willingford's prize mare running in the Old Rosebud Stakes. And I was coming along.

I said no I wasn't. Mrs. Willingford asked why. I said I was too busy. Mrs. Willingford laughed in that deep throaty way she has, the one that does things to me I wish she couldn't just do whenever she wanted. She said she wouldn't tell anyone I was a Private Eye. I said I wouldn't either because I wouldn't be there. I said I wasn't kiddin' around, I meant it when I said I was busy. She said to put down the book, pack Jane's bag and not to keep Woody sitting around twiddling his thumbs down on the streets of Stapleton. She said it was almost 9 A.M. He was already waiting for us.

I thought "us" meant Jane and me.

And then she said I was to make sure Holly was ready too. Holly was also invited so "us" meant me and Jane and Holly. Turns out, Holly'd been asked before me.

Holly was still in the room next to mine: 4-B. Dr. Bloomberg, plastic surgeon to Mrs. Willingford's Park Avenue chums, had fixed her better than new. But before that needed doing, Mickey Cates, a wild Irishman and his wild Irish friends, had fixed the cozy little sex club all set to kill her. After the Irish, Mrs. and Mr. Joker Willingford had taken Holly under their large helpful wing. If she wanted to be, the girl in the room next to mine was in the chips—she could of stayed on at Park Avenue. But Holly wasn't the Park Avenue type. Holly was the Hollywood type… as soon as she had a few acting lessons under her belt. That'd been taken care of too. For over half a year now, five days a week, my friend Holly caught a ferry to Manhattan to study with some serious little Greek in the CBS building on Broadway.

So here I was on some damn boat because Mrs. Willingford didn't know the meaning of the word "no" and because Holly and Jane were the real invitees. I was just the guy on the other end of Jane's leash. Or I would be—if I could keep a leash on her.

Anyway, there was this lug I'd met on my last so-so case, something involving the exciting world of cheap extortion. He was carrying around a book called *The Man with the Golden Arm* but he wasn't reading it. He was using it like a wallet, a single stolen hundred dollar bill flattened between almost half the pages. As a hiding place, it stunk. For one thing, even Jane could tell he couldn't read past the third grade and for another thing, it made the book too fat.

Lino Morelli grabbed the cash. I suppose those bills got entered as evidence. Or a couple of 'em did. In time, I got the book. Now it was me reading *The Man with the Golden Arm*. Only I wasn't reading it in room 4-A where Bay Street met Victory Boulevard. I was reading it on a deckchair I'd dragged up to some sort of top deck near the wheelhouse. This was as far away from the rest of the Sip o' Sea's guests as I could get.

Jane was lying on the warm wooden deck, her rump to the warm wind, her red and white fur ruffled, one eye closed and one eye open. She was asleep. She was awake.

With those eyes, maybe she was both.

First time I saw the eye thing, I thought maybe she was dead. I wondered then and I still wonder—was a Basenji really a dog?

The book was by a writer who was a guy like me, a war vet called Nelson Algren. Algren wasn't Raymond Chandler and the world he wrote about was nothing like the West Coast world Philip Marlowe moved around in, but brother, it was some world. Sunk in Algren's idea of Chicago with Frankie Machine, his junkie card dealer, I began to have real doubts about running around after bad guys. Some bad guys were so bad, they made my eyes water. As for Frankie in his crummy room in a crummy part of his Windy City, he was starting to feel a little like me, or the other way round.

I scratched Jane's chin. I read a sentence or two. I heard a sweet voice from somewhere below. Holly sounded like she was thanking one of the stewards for something he'd brought her on another of the ship's enameled trays. My guess was a Strawberry Daiquiri to go with the decor.

One of the few things made me feel better about getting stuck on a boat was Holly getting the stateroom next to mine.

I wasn't the only one who liked her. The ship's captain, a chisel chinned fellow who'd give Gary Cooper a run for his money in the looks department, seemed to like her a lot. Enough for me to check him out with Mrs. Willingford.

Seemed Captain Eigil Moody was OK. After what happened to Holly in the Willingfords' own building on their very own slice of Manhattan's Park Avenue thanks to some of their very own staff, anybody who worked for the Willingfords now had to pass more muster than Truman's Secret Service. What this meant was that not only every face back at the Park Avenue penthouse but every face on the Sip o' Sea was fresh, newly scrubbed, and inspected down to their skivvies.

All except Otelie Coleman, Mrs. Willingford's cook by

land and by sea.

Otelie was visiting her people in Trinidad every minute of the Blood and Candle caper where Holly came this close to a shallow grave under a lonely Staten Island tree.

I looked at Captain Moody's papers. He'd captained something in the war. He came highly recommended by Joe Kennedy, a friend of Joker's. I wasn't one for Joe, even less for his friend, that all American "hero" Lindbergh, but if Mr. & Mrs. Willingford thought Moody was decent enough, then I did too.

Until maybe I didn't.

We were long enough out of New York City for Cap'n Moody to notice Holly. We hadn't even left the dock before Holly noticed him.

I asked her the obvious question. "What'll you think he'll do when he knows?"

Holly didn't know any more than I did what he'd do. So far, her plan was not to tell him.

I said, "I'd leave it that way if I were you."

"But I like him," she said.

I said, "I don't."

"Why would you? He's not your type."

That one went by like Whirlaway in the stretch. I said, "But if you do spill the beans, pick your moment. One where someone else is there."

"And if that moment never comes?"

"You've got a friend."

"Not much of a friend if he doesn't know the truth."

"True. But better not much of a friend than a guy who might twist your head off."

"Oh, butter," said Holly.

Holly was a girl except he wasn't. Plenty of people knew that, but few of 'em were sailing under Captain Eigil Moody on the Willingford yacht.

3

No job and bounding about on the boring main, I was this close to flat broke. I owed on my phone bill. I owed a bookie. I hated owing a bookie. My ice box was empty. I didn't own a car. I still lived in one room on the fourth floor of a so-so building in beautiful downtown Stapleton with one window. The window looked out over five miles of salty bay water at Manhattan—which was never looking back. But hey, I owned two pairs of shoes, one good trench coat, the perfect hat, a decent gun and a lotta framed pictures of great horses.

My best friend was a humming yodeling dog, and what I did with my spare time was go to the movies—I was loaded with spare time—read mostly dime novels, talk to Holly at least twice a week when we ate together over at Al's EATS on Central Avenue, and pretend I was Bogart.

OK, so maybe that wasn't a clean bill of mental health, but aboard the Sip o' Sea my fellow guests were fruit and nut baskets.

A couple of 'em were famous, a couple of 'em were rich, a couple had talent, a couple were in the racing game, a couple of 'em were smart—but famous, rich, talented, horsey or smart, most of 'em had a screw or two loose in one way or another.

I turned thirty when the last Kentucky Derby was run. Kentucky Derbies were how I told one year from another. At thirty, I was old enough to realize everyone was nuts, but like that big-wig pig said in *Animal Farm*: "All people are nuts, but some people are more nuts than others."

These people were those people. Just like all people.

I wasn't sure, but counting me and Jane and Holly, there had to be fourteen, maybe fifteen nut cases aboard and each of us had a private guest stateroom. The Sip o' Sea had eighteen entire staterooms complete with luxury baths. They weren't all getting used, but like I said, most had some sort of fruit or nut in it.

I thought I was getting used to the Willingford wealth, but on our first day out, two steps off the gang plank knocked that idea out of my head. Us guests had stewards to serve us breakfast, lunch, dinner and snacks with drinks, in our staterooms if we wanted, or on deck if we wanted. There was a well stocked bar manned by a well-stocked bartender who could of mixed at McSorley's, and when the Sip o' Sea bartender was getting his well earned shut eye, the bar was still open but, gee whizz, we had to mix our own. Mrs. Otelie Coleman was a first class chef, good enough for—to tell the truth, I didn't know where she'd be good enough to cook at since I'd only eaten at one or two of those joints: the Colony and Twenty-One courtesy of Mrs. W—but it would be somewhere snazzy. We had enough playing cards to stock a Monte Carlo casino.

Two of the Willingford's guests were actresses, pretty but not as pretty as Holly.

First thing Holly did was check 'em out. So I'd know too, I'd checked with Holly. Both were bona fide females.

One of 'em called herself Clara Louise. A bottle blonde with some kind of a southern accent—not being from the south, I wouldn't know Alabama from Arkansas—Clara was as giddy as Daffy Duck. Every other word she said was some sort of eek or oooh. Clara said she adored animals. Didn't matter if they snorted, barked, honked or blew bubbles, they were her favorite topic, right after the private lives of movie stars. Jane didn't adore Clara Louise. She let Clara pet her, up to a point, tolerated the cutesy names, up to a point, and did her the favor of accepting the choice tidbits slipped off the girl's plate. But that was it. A few snubs and the girl avoided Jane.

Understandable. Jane embarrassed her.

The second actress was a slender brunette. Olivia Powers wasn't giddy or gay or much of anything else in the humor department. She didn't dote on Jane and that was just dandy since Jane didn't dote on her any more than she doted on Clara Louise. Whenever they passed, the brunette never looked down, and Jane—let's just say Jane didn't look up.

But I had to give it to Miss Powers. She was a class act. Not yet twenty, she'd already starred in two first rate Hollywood movies. I hadn't seen either one of 'em. Whether I had or hadn't, Holly said stardom didn't interest Olivia; what Olivia Powers wanted was to be a great actress. This got her out of L.A. and into Manhattan so she could study method acting, whatever method acting was.

Whatever the hell it was, Holly studied it too, and at the same place, the Actors Studio.

"She got in free," said Holly, "and she gets the best roles. There's some who hate that, but not me. Gee Sam, she's so good. Why wouldn't Elia do that?"

"Who's Elia?"

"Our teacher."

"Odd name."

"He's foreign."

"Figures."

Maybe what with the straight face and the method acting, Powers hoped to replace Garbo. Although probably not. I'd heard her speak. She had a dark blue voice. Too bad she didn't say much. I could of listened to her recite Ernest Hemmingway and I hated Ernest Hemmingway, fuck what the besotted Dorothy Parker had to say about the creep.

After meeting all the Willingford guests, I now made a point of sailing in my stateroom. It was them and the fact we were on a boat floating around on the Atlantic Ocean.

Then there were a lot of people not in staterooms.

The crew, the stewards, and the kitchen staff were stuck away somewhere in the front end where when things got rough, they got it roughest. These were the hired folks who all these invited fatheads needed around to tie their shoes.

Otelie Coleman had it better. On Park Avenue's dry unshakable land, Mrs. Coleman had her own small suite tucked away in the Willingford's enormous top floor acreage. At sea, she had her own good-sized cabin next to Mrs. Willingford's stateroom. No crew's quarters for the ship's chef.

As for Joker Willingford, he and his lovely wife not only didn't share a stateroom, they didn't share a personal steward. Joker's man Kenneth was impressive. Tall as a lamppost, blank as a blank wall, useful as a Swiss Army knife, Kenneth didn't look like Basil Rathbone, but he acted like Basil Rathbone. He could also of stood in for any role Boris Karloff ever played. Where Joker found him beat the hell out of me but he ruined Mrs. Willingford's matched set of pretty stewards. I liked him the moment I saw him.

He'd never paid me the slightest mind.

As for Joker's gentleman's gentleman, Daniels was left behind to run the Park Avenue penthouse. This was the very same Daniels who'd served as butler to the late William Ransom Cunningham the Third, but that was before Billy III was tossed off his own fifth floor balcony and wound up making a mess of himself on the sidewalks of Upper East Side New York.

Billy fell to his untimely death in the middle of my last big case, the one where Holly came *this* close to kicking it.

Before Billy went splat, Mrs. Willingford tried poaching Daniels for Joker, she tried wooing Daniels, she tried demanding him. It may of taken a murder—namely, the ridiculous demise of his employer, the ridiculous Billy Cunningham—but Mrs. Willingford always got her man.

If I saw anyone, and I saw as much as I could of Mrs. Willingford, it was Holly. I also saw my assigned steward,

Gene. Gene was in and out of my stateroom tending me as tenderly as if Sam Russo, gentleman in hiding, paid him his wages. Jane was also in and out, but she treated me like she had better things to do. As a star guest, Jane was in demand.

Turns out she also loved boating. There wasn't much we didn't have in common, but being on a boat at sea was one of 'em. The other was rain. She loved it. I didn't.

All I did as a guest was show up for the occasional drink in the Grand Salon. I would of showed up for the life saving drill—a man wants to know where the life jackets are and the lifeboats—if we'd had a life saving drill. Cap'n Chiselchin hadn't bothered with that. Maybe he was waiting for someone to fall overboard so we'd take a drill seriously.

Anyway, here we were, me and a boatload of swells and would-be swells on the Willingford yacht. Holly was happy. Jane was tolerant. She didn't bark but she hummed now and then. Basenjis do that. When a dolphin twisted out of the water alongside the boat, she yodeled. Basenjis do that too. The dolphin must of heard her since it jumped again. And again. Holly, the dolphin and Jane were big hits.

From all I could tell, I didn't exist. Fine by me.

Strolling the shining decks, changing her clothes for every meal, Mrs. Willingford looked amused that half of Joker Willingford's guests hung around the rich old man like the smell in a vat at Joker's Special Blend Distillery. As for the other half, they hung around Mrs. Willingford like most people, men and women, hung around Mrs. Willingford—like bees around honey.

I could whine about sailing but I couldn't fault the boat. The Sip o' Sea was white as shaving cream, as sleek as a close shave, it had an engine rumbling away somewhere below, and it was a—how would I know? I knew diddly about boats. All I could say was it'd picked us and our luggage up off a New York City dock somewhere in the West Side Seventies—I brought Jane and a battered suitcase, the rest brought the Saks Fifth

Avenue Summer Catalogue—and was now chuffing along off the East Coast of who knew where USA headed from Manhattan to Miami.

I'd never been to Florida, never wanted to go—except for the one thing that drew me like a Private Eye to a juicy crime: Thoroughbred horse racing.

As Mrs. Willingford said over the phone, we were all going to Miami to watch the terrific mare Fleeting Fancy—born and bred at Joker's Beeswing Farm back in Old Kentucky—race at Hialeah. That's where the yacht came in and how I was back on a boat far enough from shore there wasn't any shore.

Once I accepted my boaty fate, I realized how much I wanted to be striding around Hialeah breathing in horses again. So the way I finally figured it was: once off the Sip o' Sea, forever off the Sip o' Sea.

The scream made me throw my book in the air. It got Jane on her feet and her teeth showing. The second scream got me off my deckchair and the both of us moving fast towards the back of the boat. The third scream came when we got there. It was Olivia Powers. If she was method acting, you couldn't prove it by me, but that poker face I'd gotten used to was gone with the wind. Anyone could read her hand.

Olivia was shaking, she was pointing, she was building up for another scream.

Practically the whole boat was crowded round her.

No Captain Moody to take charge, it had to be me, Sam Russo, incognito Private Eye.

I put an arm around Olivia's shoulder, I tilted her chin up. I said, "Stop screaming, Miss Powers."

"I can't! I can't!"

"Why not?"

"It's Clara Louise."

"What about Clara Louise?"

"She jumped!"

"Jumped?"

"Overboard."

Fuck.

Kenneth was half over the railing looking down at the wake we made in the sea behind us. Otelie was waving up at Captain Moody and yelling. Everyone was yelling. "Stop! Turn around! Go back!"

Mrs. Willingford was sprinting for the wheelhouse. A clocker clocking Mrs. Willingford from her stateroom to the wheelhouse would of stared at his stopwatch. What a sprinter.

Instead of following her—why bother? if Mrs. Willingford couldn't take care of the boat single handed, I'd eat my life jacket—I didn't sprint and I didn't yell. I was thinking: go back for what? Like Kenneth, I was leaning over the railing. I couldn't see a damn thing behind us except the boat's wake.

If Clara Louise jumped, Clara Louise was gone.

4

If we'd of been on the good and solid earth and the boat was a speeding train or a bus or a car or even a stagecoach, we'd of screeched to a dead halt. There'd be that chance that Clara Louise was only behind us somewhere, hurt, maybe hurt bad, but not dead. There'd be a chance to get back before it was too late.

We were on a boat. A big fast boat.

Little boats don't screech to a halt. Big boats don't even try. They plough on through the waves until the fella at the wheel can bring 'em round in a wide, time-consuming, turn. By then, whatever was behind the boat was way behind the boat. By the time a boat like the Sip o' Sea got back to where whatever happened, happened, whatever or whoever fell overboard wasn't there anymore. The sea had waves and currents and swells. Under the sea swam sharks and giant squid and the Kraken and other unnamable things. There was something else one of the crew pointed out in the melee on deck as the Sip o' Sea made its slow way back. Trying to spot a human head holding its own in a heave of green sea was like spotting a distant green coconut bobbing about on a heave of green sea. It was about as likely as picking every winner in every race in a full week of horse racing at a fair ground. I'd say, less likely.

If my friend Mickey Cates was aboard, the Irish devil who killed for money, the Irish angel who killed for love, he'd say: "Poor lass."

No one saw Clara Louise much less a coconut. The sea we sailed back through was calm enough but calm enough was never calm enough.

Our captain hadn't left the bridge. I saw him up there, spinning his wheel, talking on some sort of device, and scanning the sea with binoculars. I saw Joker up there too. He didn't look well. Tell the truth, he looked pretty bad.

His binoculars were bigger.

I elbowed Mrs. Willingford.

"What?" she said. She didn't say it nicely.

"Look at Joker."

Mrs. Willingford peered up at Mr. Willingford from under a patented Mrs. Willingford hat. I knew we'd be seeing hats. This was some white canvas nautical number, but larger, much larger. "How the hell would you look," she said, "if someone fell or jumped off a yacht you owned?"

No thought needed for that one. "Terrible."

"You bet your ass you'd look terrible. Some lawyer is going to sue us for everything we have."

I guess I looked surprised. Mrs. W. softened round the edges. She said, "I'm rattled. Chalk it up to rattled."

I couldn't help it. I forgave her instantly. Besides, if I'd ever seen Mrs. Willingford rattled, and I hadn't, this was it.

Jane walked over and sat on my feet. She looked exhausted. I knew where she'd been. She'd been looking for Clara Louise.

Half the crew and all of the stewards were also busy searching the rest of the Sip o' Sea for Clara Louise. Jane might be done, but they were still at it. One guy, an engineer—who I'd of called big if I hadn't met "big" on one of my cases, the one where Jane and I saw some Broadway shows and some Broadway shows saw us as well as getting a load of Mrs. Willingford—had herded us guests and the Willingford servants onto the biggest deck.

He'd also herded Mrs. Willingford. No way that could happen if she didn't want it to happen, so what I thought was this: for her it was either sticking with me and Jane and Holly, or it was standing around with Joker up in the wheelhouse watching Cap'n Moody give orders, calling the Coast Guard, and chivvying the navigator.

She chose us. Given the choice, I would of made the same one.

I don't know what they were serving up on the bridge but down where we were there was a permanent buffet and constant chilled champagne.

Seemed wrong to be sipping champagne and nibbling shrimp while the whole bunch of us did nothing else but wait around for Clara Louise to be lost or found—each in our own unique way.

The male half of a well known, well regarded, well rewarded Hollywood writing duo, Carson Kline, said: "Ever think maybe she had some incurable disease? Remember how she was last night, Irma?"

The female half of the Hollywood writing duo, Irma Morton, said: "By golly, you're right, Carson. She went to her stateroom early. She said she didn't want her dinner. I don't remember her coming back. We'd remember if that girl came back… we'd all have to listen to her. Hey you, Merle. Is that right, it's Merle?"

Merle had been trying to get by us. Irma Morton stopped her in her tracks. Of all the stewards, Merle was the only female.

Merle who tended to our three actresses: Holly, Olivia and Clara Louise, was a subdued redhead. A quiet redhead was unusual enough, but even odder, there wasn't a freckle on her, or, not anyplace anyone could see. If Olivia wasn't much of a talker, Merle was almost a mute.

Merle said, "Yes."

"You take… I mean, you took care of that girl."

Carson finished her thought. "Last night? Did she ask for food or something to drink?"

"No, she didn't."

"How about an aspirin or an Alka-Seltzer?"

Forced to speak in front of everyone at once, Merle

flushed right up into her red hair. It made an interesting effect.

"She didn't ask for anything."

Irma said, "Not even this morning?"

"She left a note on her door. *Do not disturb*."

"Aha!" said Carson, "You think she was sick last night?"

"Perhaps, sir. She wasn't chatting or smiling."

Here's where Walter Dew spoke up. Dew was the Willingford's horse trainer. "So once she went down to her stateroom you didn't bring her anything?"

From where I stood, the Morton/Klines were working up the plot to their next movie. Their efficiency was chilling. They were also torturing the poor girl. Walter Dew was making it worse.

But if they hadn't been asking, I would of. Only I'd of done it privately and quietly.

As for Dew, so far as I knew, besides training racehorses, all he cared for was playing cards, roping in whoever he could whenever he could. Like Miss Powers, he didn't do a lot of talking. Clara Louise had done enough for everyone, with Sandrine Brunetti, opera singer, Otto Gerlinger, movie director, King Barton, movie star, and my friend Holly taking up the slack.

"No, sir."

King Barton flung back his head like Barrymore used to, only with less hair. His eyebrows were also rising. "Well, there we have it. All that happy-go-lucky shit was an act. What's-her-name was dying. So today she decided to call it quits."

Instead of anyone pinching the sensitive Mr. Barton, most of us nodded our heads. That made sense. People like to have things make sense. Especially things like a pretty young woman leaping off a ship into the sea and certain death.

Truth was, aside from trying to make sense out of what seemed senseless, there wasn't much else to do. Chatting with Holly about how great she looked after the Willingford's Doctor Jacob Bloomberg got through with her didn't seem right. Although she did look great. Holly'd been a stunner before her "accident" in that big dark house lost in the wilds of Staten Island. Beaten to a pulp and left in a duffel bag to breathe her last by the public toilets in Tompkinsville Park, that was one hell of a memorable case... the one where I got to know Mickey Cates and Mullan's Irish mob and Mullan's Irish mob got to know me. I could call Mickey a friend now, if Mickey was anyone's friend. He for sure was a friend to Sweet Davy Malloy, the kid who almost got bumped off cleaning up the mess I'd found deep in the island woods.

Sweet Davy, as pretty for a man as any of our male stewards, maybe prettier, survived getting shot point blank. Just like me. Both of us were lucky. As for Holly, after the doctor did his stuff to what was left of her, you had to stand back a foot or two to take in all that glow.

So there we were. Eating. Drinking. Smoking. A few of us patted Olivia's head or her hand or her shoulder as she reclined on one of the Grand Salon couches. We looked out to sea. We watched small boats pop up from everywhere to join in the search. Some seemed to come from nowhere, they were on us so fast. Moody'd been a busy captain up there in his wheelhouse. Or the Coast Guard had, wherever the Coast Guard was. Getting closer to where we were, I guessed. But where that was, I couldn't of said. I thought I heard someone mention the coast of North Carolina. Or maybe they said South Carolina. North? South? Even if I could of seen land, I wouldn't know one glimpse of Carolina shoreline from another.

But however they'd heard the alarm, I'd already counted well over a dozen boats cutting back and forth searching, and more were on their way. Big ones, little ones, there was even a tugboat.

Holly leaned in close so no one but me could hear her

say, "If the poor thing's still alive out there, that many boats, one's bound to run right over her."

I'd had the same idea. I bet most of us did. I bet most of us were waiting for a patch of green sea to turn red.

5

Two of "us" were movie stars. Or maybe just one of us was—Holly's fellow student Olivia Powers. The other was a has-been. Before the war King Barton'd been a big deal. You couldn't go to one of those adventure films without seeing his mug in it. A laughing pirate, a no nonsense wagon train boss, the leader of an African safari, the guy who searched for lost islands. Now he was lucky to play the lead's best friend. It took me half a day at sea to see why.

King had fallen in love with the bottle.

Sharing a stateroom across from mine were the Hollywood screen writing couple, a married duo who didn't use the same last name. Irma Morton was a small bouncy big-eyed, white-haired, older woman, sixty if she was a day. Carson Kline was a tall balding chain smoker. If he was fifty, I'd be surprised. He didn't, but she acted in other people's movies, almost always as the comic relief. I knew. I'd seen her in a few. She was good.

Together as Morton & Kline, they'd penned maybe three, maybe four of the funniest movies ever—and they didn't write for the Marx Brothers.

We'd eyed each other up the few times I came out of my stateroom. I don't know what they saw but I saw two people who couldn't look less alike yet act more alike. They didn't belong on a ship. They belonged in the Algonquin Hotel at the Round Table.

A few doors down was the stateroom of the Italian woman, or maybe she was French or maybe German. Still in her prime, Sandrine Brunetti was a little too tall, a lot too wide, and much too loud. For a boat, the low-cut skin-tight red dress seemed less than useful, not to mention the red stiletto heels.

Miss Brunetti said she was a contralto. I was none the wiser.

I did know Mrs. Willingford called her "that woman" and kept out of her way but I didn't know why.

In some other guest stateroom—as I said, the Willingford yacht had eighteen of 'em—lurked a film director. This guy was so hairy he could of shared a cage with a gorilla and people would guess they were married, or at least engaged. Black hair sprouted out of his shirt collar. It covered the backs of his hands. Like grass on sand dunes, little tufts grew on his fingers.

The first time I saw him, he was tugging on Joker's wrist, the bony one with the cane, trying to pull his rich old prize into a corner of the ship's Grand Salon. Being me, I got close enough to eavesdrop. The director's first name was Otto, he was a born and bred German, and like the miracle called Marlene Dietrich, he'd spent his war in Hollywood. I didn't know if that was strictly true but I did know his last film was a stinker. In a thick German accent, he was telling Joker that his new film—something about hunting ghosts in a haunted movie palace he swore Bette Davis said she thought she might do—couldn't lose.

And you could drape me with roses and call me War Admiral.

I knew the two jockeys aboard, one a lot better than the other.

Young Toby Tyrrell rode for the Willingfords. After the three jockey killings up in Saratoga two or so years back, Toby'd picked up the mount on Fleeting Fancy, the mare we were heading down to Florida to see. He'd ridden her ever since and made a name for himself doing it. We'd exchanged hellos a few times. I knew Toby. I knew who he was. He was a decent kid who might one day be a great jockey.

The other jock, Tommy Feather, was an up-and-comer, almost full blood Seneca, and right off the reservation. After hanging around the Saratoga race track, and after I'd learned not only who did it, but *why* who did it would kill three up-and-coming jockeys, I no longer assumed a jock rode because of his love for horses. For all I knew, Tyrrell could of thought they were nothing but meat and a meal ticket.

But I could tell Feather liked horses. So I liked Feather.

Me, I'd won a lot on both of 'em. I'd lost a lot on both of 'em. There were always guys forgot the horse and bet on the rider. When I forgot the horse I usually lost my shirt. Like in '48 when I kept betting against a filly named Conniver. Still don't know why I'd look at who sat on her back instead of at Conniver herself, the one doing all the running. After all, her daddy was Discovery.

As for the older guy the two jockeys kept close to, I'd recognized him right away. Who could miss Walter Dew? Not yet fifty, but with a thick head of hair as white as the Sip o' Sea, and a scar obviously made by a horseshoe denting his noggin, Walter Dew was like the man in the moon… all his features were bunched together in the middle of his big round white haired head. Dew trained for the Willingfords. The trainer they'd had, Scratch Mason, a legend in the sport and a pain in the butt, up and quit when Mrs. Willingford scratched Fleeting Fancy from the '48 Travers Stakes in Saratoga. I knew her reason for scratching the only female horse in the race was a good one, and she knew her reason was a good one, but Scratch never knew why. All he knew was it was the night before the race and there wasn't a thing wrong with the filly. When a horse he trained was scratched, it was Scratch who called the shots, not the owner of the horse. So he walked.

And in walked Walter Dew. Walter Dew'd won everything but the Derby and I'd heard it was killing him. I also heard he'd said if the Willingford's Beeswing Farm didn't have an up-and-coming contender for the race in '51, then no one did.

So far I'd done a swell job of avoiding the radio comic.

Beloved from California to New York and all points in between, the dirty jokes Charlie Dick told by the second day out could fill the Staten Island garbage dump. Funniest thing about Charlie was how he looked telling his jokes. He looked like the nicest guy you could ever want to know. His smile was sunny, his eyes innocent, his voice soft and soothing and warm.

Joker loved him. All Charlie had to do to get Joker laughing was show up. Charlie Dick said he liked Clara Louise like he liked any poor kid trying to make a name for herself in the business. I might not of liked him, but out of 'em all, Charlie's was the only sad face when we heard Clara'd pitched herself into the huge blue Atlantic without water wings.

Last, and to my mind least, was some well dressed, well shod, well groomed plug-ugly lug going by the name of Vergil Sapster. He was a captain of industry. *What* industry remained a mystery to me. Vergil himself was not a mystery. If ever a man was made to poke another man with a short hard finger and yell, Vergil was that man. He smoked too much, ate too much, drank too much, shouted too much, sweat too much, called everyone "buddy" and weighed too little. Vergil Sapster gave off the smell of a fat man but he was short as a match and thin as a matchstick. You could of blown him away with an outgoing breath.

What was big about him was his vanity and his voice.

The way I saw it, whatever industry he was captain of, that industry was full of people sticking pins in small skinny dolls to hasten his early demise.

Then there was me and Jane and Holly and Mrs. Willingford. There was Joker's Kenneth and Lois' Mrs. Coleman. There were the rest of the stewards, one female, the rest male. There was the ship's crew. And finally there was Olivia Powers, the actress with a lot of method who screamed when she saw Clara jump.

She was the only one who screamed and the only one to see Clara pitch over the rail. Or maybe, she was the only one who admitted it.

No shrimp and champagne for Olivia. While the rest of us felt whatever we felt about Clara Louise—who must of felt bad enough to think jumping off a ship far out to sea would feel better—Olivia Powers was like Charlie Dick. She kept to her couch and looked sad.

Jane right behind me, I'd idled up to Olivia and her couch. I'd been trying to feel bad about someone I didn't know beans about but all I'd managed was discouraged. A cute zappy kid like Clara ending it all—for what?

Truth was, my curiosity, never down for long, was up and running. I could thank Florence and "Mister" Zawadzki for that. Any kid like me and raised by those two had to begin by wondering: how did Flo and her Mister come to be in charge of abandoned babies and lost little bundles of ragged hungry faces? How did they keep the job? Didn't anyone wonder what went on in that converted overgrown pile with its four turrets and deep dank basement? Didn't anyone count heads and come up short about once a year? And how could it take more than twenty of those years before the Zawadzkis wound up in their own dark and lonely little cells?

The answer turned out simple enough. No one cared.

Except me. I guess that's why I went into the PI game. I needed to ask questions, and I wanted 'em answered. I wasn't a complete idiot. I knew life wasn't like that, straight questions followed by straight answers, but something in me made me try, and the closest I could figure I'd ever get to understanding anything was to become a Private Eye.

Like why would an actress from some deep southern fried state, young, good-looking, empty-headed and sailing around with a clot of rich people, want to drown herself? They weren't all rich and they couldn't all help her career, but some were and some could. Talk about odd timing.

Maybe she was ill. Or maybe she harbored a secret, one so bad she'd rather not live with it.

"You know her well?" I asked Olivia in my best Joseph Cotton voice.

Miss Powers made a little leap on the couch. It wasn't much, but I couldn't miss it. "Oh! It's you. The guy at the railing."

"Yep, it's me all right."

"That was sweet, what you did. Calming me down." I almost got a smile. "Tell you the truth, I didn't really know her at all."

That stumped me. I was trying to think of something else I could ask, something that sounded like a regular guy just trying to cheer her up and not like some creep looking to hear the gruesome details.

Olivia spoke before I thought of a single thing.

"Ever since I saw her jump, I've been thinking. It's driving me crazy."

"Her jumping like that?"

"Well, yes, of course, that. But before this boat ride where we first talked some, I felt like I'd seen her before. I just can't remember where. Not like your friend."

"My friend?"

"The beautiful girl with the chestnut hair."

"You mean Holly?"

"Holly! Right. She's in one of my acting classes. Everyone notices her."

I made a note to remind myself to tell Holly that.

"I have this feeling the blonde who jumped was in one of my acting classes too. But which one? Why can't I remember? Honestly, who could forget her? What happened to your dog?"

I looked down. Jane was ignoring Olivia as she always did, her tail was as tightly curled. Jane didn't take to too many people and she'd already made herself clear about Olivia

Powers. Usually I agreed with her. But for some reason not now. Probably because the girl was suddenly vulnerable. Her method wasn't working so well. It made me take a better look at the girl who saw Clara Louise jump overboard.

There wasn't a thing about her most would call pretty. She wasn't pretty. What she was, was strangely attractive. She had some kind of magnetism about her. Once I started looking, I wanted to keep looking, watch her do the simplest things… like stand at a ship's rail or lie on a couch. I think I was staring at what made one person a star, and not another. Like my friend Jimmy Stewart. Funny looking guy with a funny voice was a twenty four carat movie star.

I made myself a promise. Soon as I got off this boat, and whatever her two films were, I was buying tickets.

"So, it was just you and Clara?"

"Was that her name?"

"That's what you said. You said 'Clara Louise jumped overboard'."

"I did?"

"Ask anyone."

"Then I guess I did know her name."

"I'd say you did, Miss Powers."

"And then I guess I forgot I knew it."

"I guess you did that too."

"Was anyone there besides me and Clara Louise? I couldn't say. I don't think so. I think we were alone. I don't mean together. I wasn't with her. I was alone. She was alone."

"Did she see you? Did she know you were there when she jumped?"

"I don't know. If you mean did she look round and wave? No. She had her back to me the whole time."

"So you saw her climb up and jump? You didn't try and stop her?"

I was pushing a little here. I could even lose her if I pushed too hard. I didn't want to lose her. I wanted her to trust me, to tell me what she knew. You might think that's easy, but it isn't. Even honest people get muddled and tongue tied when put on the spot. And if I was doing anything, I was putting poor Olivia Powers on the spot.

"I had no idea she'd do that."

I kept my voice low, my tone gentle. "What did you think she was doing, Miss Powers?"

"I didn't think. It was too quick. One minute she was walking fast across the deck. The next minute she'd leapt up onto the railing and was gone. She didn't look at me. She didn't look at anything. And she didn't say a single word. Not one."

6

I wasn't officially working a case here. No one hired me. Lino hadn't lured me into anything. Without a case, Sam Russo was just another guest bobbing about on the sea. But case or no case, I was who I was. Asking questions, not believing any of the answers until they were set in stone, wondering if how a person looked was who a person was—I couldn't help it. Paid or, more often, unpaid, I was born to be a snoop.

This was a case of some sort. It wasn't my case but it was a safe bet I was the only PI for miles around. When the Coastguard showed up, I'd try'n back off, but until then I was Sam Russo, Private Eye, and Jane was my good right hand. As for Mrs. Willingford, if I knew Mrs. Willingford she'd do what she always did: get in the way, find things I hadn't found, run twice as fast as me, and keep my juices flowing. It didn't hurt she was loaded and could pay for stuff I sometimes needed but could never afford.

For the time being, I took Olivia Powers at her word. What that meant was I assumed some blonde had gone overboard. I had to think that because out of this entire bag of mixed nuts, none of 'em was Clara Louise. If Olivia was lying and Clara, dead or alive, was still aboard: hiding, locked in a closet, sewn in a sack, dangling overboard on a rope—forget Captain Moody's crew or the Sip o' Sea's stewards, Jane would of found her by now.

Here's the kicker. Did she really jump? Or was she pushed? If she wasn't physically pushed, and Olivia said she wasn't, did she get pushed some other way? People were suggestible as

hell. Take Flo Zawadzki back at "home sweet 'n sour home."
Every week like clockwork, she'd send off a check to some
shark she'd heard over the radio. We could go hungry or
without heat, but seems Jesus needed the dough.

The kind of girl our jumper appeared to be also seemed
to have a weak mind. A weak mind could be persuaded to do
any damn thing at all. It didn't take a world war to tell me
that, but a world war showed me every single day how true
it was.

I saw men—even a few women—coaxed into acts that
should of damned their souls, or acts that scared 'em enough
to loosen their bowels, yet still do them willingly if they
were pushed hard enough.

Was that why Clara jumped? If she did.

I can't remember how long we waited around watching
the search at sea. All I know is someone ate all the shrimp, I
helped get rid of the champagne, most of us seemed to run
out of things to say, a few of us drank ourselves blotto, and
Walter Dew had gotten up his usual game of poker.

Not Toby Tyrrell but the other jockey, Tommy Feather,
was playing. So was the big singer in the tight red dress, the
German director, the guy who owned a factory somewhere,
King, the once upon a time leading man, the male half of the
writing team of Morton and Kline, and Joker himself.

We still couldn't leave the area. The Sip o' Sea was staying
right where she was until the Coast Guard got to her. Moody
told one of the crew, and he told Mrs. Willingford who told
us, that the closest station was in some place called Kill Devil
Hills. Vergil Sapster, our captain of industry, said, "All's balls!
What in doodah are the Kill Devil Hills?

Seems they were on some place called a barrier island
which made up something called the Outer Banks.

Kill Devil Hills. Wouldn't you just know it? When things
happened around me, one of those loopy names came with
it. Blood Root Valley aka Dead Man's Creek. Harvey the

Pookah. A guy called Carroll. A dame called Maudie Rivers.

Point was, the Sip o' Sea, and all aboard the Sip o' Sea, were waiting for the Coast Guard to show up. And who knew how long that'd take? Or what they would do or could do to us?

On top of that, Moody said the Coast Guard wouldn't be letting us go until they'd done every damn thing they could think of to find Clara Louise, dead or alive.

Watching Joker's reaction to that bit of news was a real treat. Kenneth had to stride off on long Rathbone legs to fetch a Rexall of varied pills.

As for us and all those boats that'd responded to our SOS, big and little, with or without sails, hell's bells, with that many searching, crossing back and forth in front and behind us, not one of us fished up a sock.

Walter Dew, whiskey glass in one hand and a roast beef sandwich in the other, got up from his hand of cards to go out on deck and yell down at one of the smaller boats, the one that could hear us since it was closest. "Anything? Anything at all?"

The young guy in the boat below us shook his head and yelled back, "I'll keep looking. There's still a chance."

"A fat one," said Irma Morton.

Her husband and partner smiled. It was a tiny smile, one not meant to be seen, but I saw it. Morton and Kline were one hell of a ghoulish team.

Holly said, "Poor Clara."

Mrs. Willingford put her arm around Holly's shoulders. "Did you like her, darling?"

Holly was startled. She stared at Lois. "Like her? What was to like? She was silly and pushy and gushy and such a liar. All those people she knew. Like hell she did. Besides, she was after, she was after what…"

Mrs. Willingford'd caught Holly's drift before I did. "She was after what you were after?"

I had to hand it to Holly. Clara Louise might of been, as Holly said, a liar, but Holly herself didn't lie. She said, "You bet. Like she was ever gonna get it, not with that movie maker, the one who looks like King Kong's brother. What's his name?"

"Otto Gerlinger."

"Right. Him. Not with Otto around expecting things."

I said, "Expecting things?"

"You know. She came aboard with him. She was his 'guest'."

That was news to me. I filed it away for later.

"But jeez, you guys, she was a living person only a little while ago and now she's not."

I said, "Now she's probably not."

"Oh, Sam. How could she still be alive after all this?"

I had answers for that. But they didn't seem too tasteful. Not just then. Maybe later. Maybe not. So I shrugged. "Good question. How could she be?"

We didn't get fed again until what a friend of mine, a certain Irishman back in Stapleton, would say was the "gloaming." Mickey'd say it soft and he'd say it with a lilt. He'd say it like that even if you were looking down the barrel of his gun and his finger was itching.

The rest of us would call it twilight.

The sun was down over one or the other of the Carolinas and the Coast Guard still hadn't showed up. How far out to sea were we?

Once they did, though, they wouldn't be leaving until their commander was satisfied that wherever the body of Clara Louise was, it wasn't on the Sip o' Sea and if it wasn't, it also wasn't where they could do much about it. Someone said they might find her washed up on a beach someday and they might not. Someone else said there'd be an investigation.

No one liked that part. Not even King the movie star. In the late 30s and early 40s, he famously said he was sick of the press in his face wherever he went, that he couldn't take a piss without it appearing in every magazine on every newsstand on every city block everywhere. Poor sap. Now he'd of had to been naked and dancing down Broadway to get someone to take a snap.

"Investigation?" said Joker. He didn't look good saying it.

"Routine," said Captain Moody. "Suicide's a crime."

"So's homicide," I said, but I said it only to Jane.

Walter Dew, who hadn't said a thing up until then about Clara Louise, must of heard me. He said, "Not if there's no body. No body, no crime."

"Usually," said Mrs. Morton-Kline, aka Irma Morton.

King Barton said, "Personally, I think someone who kills herself in front of a number of other people is selfish. Did she ever think once of what her act might mean to the rest of us?"

"What I think," said Mr. Kline-Morton, aka Carson Kline, "is that the government has no right to meddle in a person's private affairs. If a person wants to end it all, who's to tell them they can't?"

What Vergil Sapster said next proved the world's smallest industrialist or magnate or robber baron or whatever he was, was also a god-fearing religious man. He threw down his napkin, sucked in enough air to pop his buttons, and said: "I'd like to hear you tell your minster that, buddy!"

Irma Morton was slipping an oyster down her throat. "Send for him, sonny. I'll give him an earful he can't quote in his pulpit."

Sapster turned a tasty shade of ham as Kline turned to Morton. "You know, Pinky, there might be some mileage in all this."

Morton stared at him. "You mean like a story?"

"You bet like a story. We'll talk about it later."

From the look on Joker's face, the pills he'd taken were

wasted. He slammed his fist down on the table. The silverware jumped. The oysters jumped. We all jumped. He said, "Shut your mouths. I'm trying to think about being investigated."

None of us shut our mouths. But we did get it down to a din.

Most of our noise was directed at Olivia Powers. I thought that was reasonable. Olivia saw Clara jump.

"Did she just run for the stern and leap over?" said Irma Morton. Her hubby was taking notes on a pad he had on his knee under the dining table.

The Willingford's jockey, Toby Tyrrell, said, "Or did you see her standing there on the railing, thinking about jumping?"

"If you saw her standing there and thinking about it," said Carson Kline, looking up long enough to speak, "why didn't you stop her?"

"Good grief. That's right." said Charlie Dick, America's clown, who had come *this* close to raising his voice. "Am I to understand you did nothing but watch while some poor suicidal kid teetered on a ship's whatever it is... fence!"

Olivia was hit with the same questions I'd hit her with, but my bat was rubber. Now she was getting hit with the real deal. It was cruel but I got it. They were scared. Death in any form scared them. Me, I'd seen so much if it, all it did was make me sick. And sad.

I was just opening my mouth to stop them when suddenly a new voice spoke up.

"I saw her too."

Who said that? We all turned to look at Sandrine Brunetti.

I'd showed up for exactly one third of an evening of entertainment in the Grand Salon. That was last night, the first night out. Sandrine Brunetti was singing. I could tell Brunetti was pretty good at what she did. I knew right away I never wanted to hear anything like it again.

Sandrine Brunetti, opera singer, had turned the color of the painful dress I first saw her in. She repeated herself. "I zaw her."

"You saw what, lady?" Vergil Sapster was trying to stay calm but his voice was sliced thin as he was.

"I saw her, za girl who vent into za sea. I vasn't as close as Miss Powers vas, I vas inside and I happened to be looking out za vindow, but I saw her too. I didn't expect her to really... I mean, it vas over zo fast."

Otto Gerlinger was just about to pour himself the last of the dinner wine watched closely by King the washed up movie star. (Who came up with this guest list? Not Mrs. Willingford, I'd make book on that.) Otto said, "So what made you think she wasn't up to something, Frau Brunetti?"

This was a question I wanted to hear the answer to, so I leaned forward. Given my choice, I wouldn't get closer to Otto than in the same room but only if it was a very big room. As for that accent, I didn't want to get too close to that either. For years German accents were all the rage. As Yanks, we heard that guttural noise on radios, in the movies, all through our news broadcasts, plus all the Heil Hitlers and the heel clicking. My war was on the other side of the world, but there wasn't anywhere a person could get away from the Germans. By now, there were only a handful of Teutonic types left I wanted to hear a peep out of: Marlene Dietrich, Peter Lorre and Billy Wilder came to mind first.

Billy Wilder, now there was a director.

But as I said, I wanted to hear Sandrine Brunetti's answer enough to put up with Gerlinger.

He said, "I repeat, Frau Brunetti, what did you think the young woman was doing out there?"

King seized his moment as well as the last of the wine. "Say, that's right, Brunetti. What else could she be up to?"

Hit from all sides, Sandrine Brunetti had no time to answer one lob before another came bounding in.

Me, I'd stopped leaning forward in my chair and was now leaning back. Things'd gotten loud enough to hear from the wheelhouse. I was slipping Jane caviar on crackers—might as well; I wasn't going to eat the stuff—and watching Miss Powers.

Now the opera singer was taking the heat, Olivia Powers'd gone back to her poker face.

Sitting beside me, Holly was watching Sandrine Brunetti as she'd watched Olivia Powers. Hand under the table, she squeezed my knee. I knew what she wanted. She wanted me to make it all go away. If anyone knew about a pile-up, Holly did.

If it was still Olivia they were going for, I would of. But it wasn't. Besides, a lot of their questions were my questions. It's what I did for a living; I asked questions. Seemed to me, there were a lot of them hanging around. Were Olivia and Sandrine the only two who saw Clara jump? No one else but Olivia and Sandrine admitted it, but that didn't mean no one else was there. Sandrine had just proved that.

Even stranger for a suicide, if Olivia saw her jump and Sandrine Brunetti saw her jump, what a hell of a time to jump. If Clara Louise was desperate enough to want to die, why didn't she wait until she was alone? Why not do it in the dark? Dark was a good choice. People were in beds, some were even in their own bed. Maybe she knew it didn't matter. Maybe she knew the boat couldn't get back in time to save her. She had to know the captain would try, especially if people were watching. So maybe she knew she couldn't be helped no matter how hard Captain Moody turned the ship's wheel.

Then I recalled a few of her choicer lines. If Clara Louise knew anything except how to hold a fork and how to work most men, I'd eat my hat. I liked my hat, but not enough to eat it.

So maybe, when she jumped, she didn't know it was

curtains for her. I've always loved that phrase. Especially after practically living at the 48th Street Theater while *Harvey* was playing. Anyway, maybe she thought she could bob about out there until someone threw her a line.

So maybe it was a cry for help like so many suicide attempts.

Olivia Powers said she didn't know Clara Louise well. Holly didn't know Clara Louise well. The Willingfords didn't know Clara Louise at all. Even Otto Gerlinger didn't know Clara Louise. He'd been the one to ask her aboard, but he'd only just met her.

Clara Louise was driving me screwy.

If she knew she was really killing herself, you'd think a serious suicide would like a little privacy.

7

Mrs. Willingford rose straight up from her seat.

"That's it. I've had quite enough. You will all kindly leave Miss Powers and Miss Brunetti alone or I will have you locked in your staterooms—permanently."

They all shut up on the spot, and that went double for King who, until then, obviously thought he was being filmed.

I gave Mrs. Willingford a look I didn't get back. I was used to that. She was my girl. But only from time to time.

"What I want to know," said Joker, who heard her or didn't hear her, hard to tell, "is why *my* boat? I invite someone along out of the goodness of my—"

"Joker, darling?"

"Yes, Lois?"

"Tell the truth. Did you even know someone named Clara Louise was aboard?"

"No I did not. Which means that guests have brought their own guests even when expressly asked not to."

Otto piped up at that. "Now hold on just a minute here. Did I not clearly hear you say we were free to bring—"

Joker ignored him. "But that's not the damn point. The damn point is now with this girl jumping off my boat we're going to have to go through seven kinds of hell before we get to Hialeah."

Mrs. Willingford reached across the table to pat Joker Willingford's crumpled hand. "Not 'we', darling. You."

"What the hell do you mean by that?"

"I mean that Captain Moody and Kenneth will stick to

you like gum on a shoe."

That's when the Coast Guard showed up, bullhorn blaring and three strong spot lights strafing the ship and the sea and a tableful of startled faces.

Guys in uniforms never did things by halves. Just because most of us were rich and famous and the rest of us wished we were, cut no ice with them.

Or maybe they didn't know which was which yet and until then we were all fair game.

Me, I got up, I folded my napkin like Mrs. Otelie Coleman had once showed me, and then I wandered off to my big starboard side stateroom with its big bolted down bed, Jane bringing up the rear.

I think it was the starboard side. It could of been the port side. I was happy enough to know the words.

No one wished me fare thee well. Not even Mrs. Willingford who was buttering up an irate Mr. Willingford. Or Holly, who was still trying to vamp a suddenly impervious Cap'n Moody. I did get an up-from-under glance out of Olivia Powers, and that was nice.

I figured if anyone needed either one of us, they'd clang.

Once my shoes were off, my pillows plumped, and Jane asleep with her head on my chest, I did what Hercule Poirot always did. I took my little gray cells out for a spin.

My little gray cells didn't speak French and weren't as precise as the little Belgian's were, but they'd do. Especially since, as I've said, there was no case here. Except why a girl with a brain the size of a peanut would want to throw herself off a luxury yacht in broad daylight with, so far as she knew, one witness? And that witness, female.

I thought back to boarding this boat, to the day and a night and half a second day I'd spent on it before Olivia Powers, Hollywood star and New York City acting student, screamed out that Clara Louise, no Hollywood star but at least an acting student, had jumped overboard.

Did I notice Clara Louise before the big event? Sure I did. She was hard to miss. Clara was pretty in a Joan Blondell kind of way. Like an overblown rose. A few years down the road her petals would fall, and fall hard, but for those short thirty six hours Clara laughed. Clara didn't get up until noon. Clara batted her eyes. Clara pursed her lips. Whenever I'd seen her, she'd been smoking like Betty Davis smoked, those short sharp puffs, and chatting away about one fabulous thing or another she'd seen or done in New York or London or Paris or Hollywood.

I'd dropped a few names in my time, but for Clara Louise, dropping names was like those bent over peasants casting seeds out of huge sacks in a French painting. A man who'd spent as much time as I had in the Willingford's Park Avenue apartment had seen his share of French paintings full of seed casters.

No one was immune from Clara Louise. Clara would corner anyone. She'd talked to me, twice. It wasn't easy getting away but with my Staten Island charm, I did it. Her lone exception was Jane. She didn't talk to Jane. As I said, Jane didn't like Clara and I guess Clara Louise took it personally.

The rest of us got baby talk. Clara Louise could talk baby talk like nobody's business.

Lying on my bed, the Coastguard infested Sip o' Sea going nowhere, I asked myself: would I say Clara was a girl with the blues? Was she some poor kid hiding heartbreak? Or some dark secret? An addiction? A crime? A fatal disease? A bad review? Would I think: here's a girl if someone doesn't watch her was going to kill herself?

Not on your Nellie. What I would say was: here's a girl someone was itching to gag.

One of my favorite writers once wrote: "The race is not always to the swift or the battle to the strong—but that's the way to bet." I figured Ring Lardner would of come to the same conclusion as me. A kid as dumb as Clara might well choose something as dumb as suicide for no better reason than hurt feelings or a sudden urge. Or she might choose to jump off a ship at sea because someone else thought it was a damn good idea and forced her to think so too.

Just before I fell asleep Clara Louise had fallen as far from my mind as she'd fallen from the Sip o' Sea. From high jumps to race tracks, from slacks and a shirt to salmon pink and dark gray silks, I was riding Fleeting Fancy, hunched high over her neck, her mane in my face, and we were coming up fast on the outside, sure to take the Travers by daylight.

How long later, I couldn't say, but Jane woke me by using my stomach to propel her leap off the bed.

There's not much to do on a yacht, even less when the Coast Guard has charge of it.

Jane and I wandered the corridors, took a few turns maybe she'd taken before, but I hadn't. We went down a few stairs I didn't know were there, up a few ladders, through a few hatchways. I could tell she knew all about 'em. If I were a betting man, and I was, I'd bet Jane knew the Sip o' Sea from stem to stern. I'd even bet she knew it better than anyone else on board.

The ship smelled different the farther down we went. Oilier. Stuffier. Private. It got darker. No more big sea view windows. We'd passed the portholes, smaller portholes than the ones in the stateroom baths, portholes that didn't open. Any deeper and there'd be no portholes at all.

A door opened into the corridor right next to us. I stepped aside before it hit me.

"Oh!" said the redheaded steward. Or maybe she was a stewardess? Either way, her name was Merle.

I felt like a trespasser. This wasn't my place. It wasn't even Jane's place. It was Merle's place. It was the private reserve of the Sip o' Sea's staff, the only place they could go to get away from people like me, a guest.

She said, "Are you lost?"

Her voice, muted when she spoke to her "superiors," was still muted. The voice that came out of the cabin behind the door was loud. It was a voice that didn't sound like he thought me or anyone else was superior.

"Who you talking to, Merlie?"

"The man with the dog. Hello, doggie."

Jane hummed, picked up a white paw and held it there. Was Merle supposed to shake it? When she didn't, Jane dropped her paw, stopped her humming, and looked like the Jane I knew best: suspicious.

"Tell him and his dog to beat it. Don't we get any peace anywhere?"

I knew that voice. I'd heard it when it wasn't loud. As yet another good looking steward, Clyde had drawn the worst hand of guests he could of: Charlie Dick, Otto Gerlinger and Vergil Sapster.

Jane and I beat it.

When I'd left, Mrs. and Mr. Willingford's guests were all in the dining salon. Now they were all in the Grand Salon hanging around the grand bar. Leonard, the Sip o' Sea's bartender—another of Mrs. Willingford's handsome young men—was mixing and shaking and pouring and smiling as fast as he could.

I figured the Coast Guard was everywhere else.

Jane and I weren't two feet into the Grand Salon when I heard Joker calling. He and Mrs. Willingford and Kenneth were seated in one of the booths.

"Over here, young man. Come and sit down."

When Joker gave an order, people took it. I know I did. And so did Jane.

Joker lowered his voice. It wasn't low but it was low enough. "You're a guest, I know that. But as a Private Eye, you ever deal with this kind of crap before?'

"What kind of crap?"

"The kind the cops dish out. What am I in for here? As the owner of this boat, am I liable for anything? I didn't invite that girl. I didn't know her. I won't stand for…"

Happily for me, Lois broke in. "No need to stand, dearest. Captain Moody has already radioed ahead to our Florida lawyers. He's radioed our New York City lawyers. There'll be swarms of them ready to attend to your every legal need."

That made Joker smile. It made me smile. I swear it made Jane smile.

Mrs. Willingford's sleek blonde head turned towards the silvery white mane of balloon faced Walter Dew. Walter still hadn't said a thing to or about Clara Louise, not in my hearing anyway. She didn't say, she yelled so all could hear, "Should the Sip o' Sea be required, therefore detained, in the nearest port, wherever that might be, well… that's all arranged as well. There's a plane standing by to take us all to Hialeah."

She got a lot of smiles for that one.

"Assuming they let us all go."

A lot of smiles fell off a lot of faces.

Kenneth was fishing out two large green and blue striped pills, filling a glass with soda water, feeding soda water and pills to Joker. Whatever they were, Joker took them with suitable ill grace.

The Grand Salon's bar phone rang. Kenneth got up and answered it. He didn't hand the receiver over to Joker. He just listened and nodded his head.

Joker's smile was lost with the others "What if they detain *me*, Lois? Like Truman says: the buck stops here."

Mrs. Willingford smile was stuck on. "Our horse, dear old pot, is safe in her train car and on her way from Kentucky to the Florida track. She and Walter's team could be already there. In three days she's running in the Old Rosebud Stakes. Isn't that why we're going to Florida? But where's her trainer?" In high drama Mrs. Willingford pointed a finger at Walter Dew. "He's here. And where's the jockey who's going to do us proud?" She pointed at Toby Tyrrell. "He's here too."

Tyrrell turned pink. But he would. He was still too young to control his color.

She didn't point at herself but she might as well have. "And where, darling, am I?"

Joker hadn't lost his voice. "You're wherever I am."

"I shouldn't be. I should be with Fleeting Fancy."

Joker turned red. He was too rich to bother controlling his color. "Why?"

"Must I answer? Really, sweetest? Never mind. I will anyway. Because I'm the closest to a friend she has."

Looking down at Jane, I understood completely. Looking over at Joker, I saw he understood too.

Kenneth, like a man on stilts, came stilting towards me. Jane gave him a polite growl.

"It seems you're wanted on the bridge."

I would be. Someone snitched I was a Private Eye. Who could that be since who knew? It wouldn't be Holly or Mrs. Willingford. I was betting it was Joker. Anything to pass the buck.

8

The captain of the Coast Guard cutter—which was almost as big as the Sip o' Sea but not as white or as sleek—wasn't a captain, he was a commander. He would be. During the war, the Coast Guard was an official part of the Navy. The war might be over, but the Coast Guard wasn't. Standing off our port side, or maybe our starboard side—as I'd said, for me, it was enough to know the two names—the cutter was cluttered with uniformed crew and guns.

Before stalking off back to Joker, Kenneth ushered me into the presence of a Commander Jackson, a pushy guy with dandruff on his epaulets who was taking up Captain Moody's private domain. He looked like Van Johnson, maybe a few years older, maybe not. I was guessing he didn't have the talent. After the case Jane and I'd spent running around Broadway shows, with Mrs. Willingford making a special appearance at one of 'em, I could spot talent. It was something you saw in the eyes. This guy's eyes were shifty. He chewed his bottom lip. He was trying to grow a moustache. On him, a moustache looked like Joan Crawford's left eyebrow.

Jane found it fascinating. I kept my hand on her collar in case she tried for it.

There were medals on his chest. I recognized a couple of 'em. I had a few myself in a Prince Hamlet cigar box on my mantle. Some of them were the same medals.

The cigar box lived next to the paperbacks I'd read, a couple of hardbacks too, but only the picks of the litter.

I saluted. A war does that to veterans. We salute anything with medals, moustaches, and epaulets. All that dies hard. I was counting on it dying soon. If not, I'd have to kill it, but for now it was still alive and healthy.

Commander Jackson was reading a pad covered in penciled notes. This gave him a good reason to ignore me, and he took it.

Fighting my instincts, I sat down. My hand on her collar, Jane had no real choice but to fight hers and sit beside me.

"What's that?" said Commander Jackson when he finally bothered to look up and speak.

"That's a dog."

"She in the war? Funny kind of dog."

"Funny kind of day."

"I get 'em all the time."

"Actresses jumping off boats?"

"Trouble on the high seas."

"Damn. Is this a high sea!"

"Not quite. It has been. It could be again."

"What's that mean?"

"I take it you're not a sea-going man."

"You got that right."

"Fought on land then?"

"I did. On horseback."

That got him. His mouth made an involuntary pop. Nothing could of pleased me more. He said, "Horse?"

"Horseback. I was with the 26th Cavalry Regiment."

"We had a cavalry regiment?"

"We did. Guys on horses beat the Japs to Morong in Bataan."

Taking this in, I saw it changed him towards me. But it didn't make him like me. That was OK. I didn't like him.

He said, "Wind's rising. Storm coming tonight."

"There is?"

"Yep. I'm told you're a Private Investigator."

"Not now, I'm not. How bad is this storm?"

His turn to say, "What's that mean? Could be worse.

Could be better."

My mind full of South Pacific waves like green walls filled with surprised fish, I said, "That means I'm a guest here just like all the other guests."

"Nothing undercover?"

"Not so's you'd notice."

"What does that mean?"

"Means what you want it to mean."

"You do this for a living?"

"Do what?"

"Crack wise."

"Only when they feed me."

Commander Jackson had had enough of me. I'd had enough of me. I'd had enough of him. I went all limp, figured it was the fastest way to get back to the bar.

"It looks like suicide to me," he said, twirling his pencil, "Does it look like suicide to you?"

"I dunno. What does suicide look like?"

If the commander of a large Coast Guard cutter didn't want to reach across the table and smack me silly, I didn't know why.

"It looks like what this Clara Louise girl did today."

"If you say so."

"Goddammit, you. I've talked to everyone. Not one of 'em thinks it was anything else."

"Then why are you talking to me?"

"Believe me. I wouldn't if I didn't have to be thorough. Do you think she jumped?"

"I have no idea. I didn't see a thing."

"So you saw nothing occur you'd call out of the ordinary since you set sail?"

"Define ordinary."

"I repeat, did you— "

"No. Last night, before dinner, the girl in question, Clara Louise, said she didn't feel well. So far as I know she didn't eat a thing in her stateroom. This morning, she wasn't up until noon."

"She got up that late?"

"This morning she did. I wouldn't know about other mornings."

"Sounds to me as if she might have had something on her mind. Do you think anything else besides suicide could have happened?"

"It doesn't seem likely."

Commander Jackson sighed with relief and scribbled that down on his pad.

"On the other hand," I said, "she didn't seem the type to kill herself."

"What's that supposed to mean?"

"Exactly what it sounded like."

"Go away."

Walter's card game was bigger when Jane and I got back to the Grand Salon. The only people not playing were Olivia Powers and Holly. Olivia and Holly were sitting together by a window, quietly talking about something. Whatever it was, I'd get it out of Holly at some point.

But Mrs. Willingford was playing and Mrs. Willingford was winning.

Howard, steward to the Kline-Morton duo and to Sandrine, was hot-footing it back and forth to the bar where Leonard was mixing up a whirlwind of colorful cocktails.

If Gene looked like Montgomery Clift, Howard looked like a young Henry Fonda.

Right then it occurred to me if I told years by the winners of the Kentucky Derby, and I did, I saw people as the actors and actresses I'd seen in movies. I never saw 'em as Agatha Christie's Miss Marple did, people with traits like the people who lived in her small English village. Nope, not Sam Russo. I saw 'em as maybe one of those people who cast parts in movies did. Someone who'd snap his fingers, saying, "Get me a Henry Fonda type."

If anybody wanted one of those, they could of found it in Howard. Until he opened his mouth. He didn't have that drawly twang Fonda had. I'd say he talked more like Jean Arthur did. That cracked little voice coming out of Jean's mouth was enough for anyone to listen to, and listen to. Like in *The Talk of the Town*. When they showed that movie again while Holly was healing, we went to see it three nights in a row. But Jean Arthur coming out of Howard's Henry Fonda mouth was like Holly would of said of a few of her more interesting friends: "He'd never pass, not that one."

Holly was a male who was a "girl" who liked men. Howard was a boy who liked men. I was a male who liked women a lot better than most men. Seems like it was all even in the end.

King Barton's steward was a perky fellow named Nicolas. Nicolas needed a haircut. His dark brown locks covered his ears and the back of his shirt collar. If the others resembled movie stars, Nicolas looked like he could of too but hadn't got round to choosing which one yet. Leaning over, placing a drink carefully between King Barton and Otelie Coleman, he smiled at them both. Only Otelie was polite enough to smile back. I was staring at Otelie—Trinidad born and bred, round and smooth and efficient as a ball bearing, Otelie was playing poker with the guests?—when King moved his arm, clipped the drink Nicolas was placing just so on a Sip o' Sea coaster, and knocked it over. The cocktail missed Otelie and it missed King, but it soaked Nicolas' pants.

King was on his feet damn fast for a guy I could tell needed some exercise.

"Damn you! Do you know how much this watch cost me? You could have ruined my watch! I should make you pay for it!"

"I'm sorry, sir, it was an accident."

"You're not paid to have accidents!"

"No sir, I'm not."

"So what are you going to do?"

King's performance was what I'd heard someone say about an English actor's debut on Broadway. A real "carpet-chewer." It got everyone's attention but mine. My attention was on Nicolas, the only one here who'd gotten so much as a drop on him. I wondered if he had to pay for those pants. I wondered if anyone was going to notice that Nicolas, the steward, was humiliated. I thought of Gene, my own steward. Would I just stand around and let a clown like King make his grand scene in the Grand Salon?

I said, "Mr. Barton?"

I said it loudly. I had to be heard over King.

He lifted his once great movie star head in order to snarl at me. "What?"

I dropped my reply into the quiet around the table like I'd drop an egg into boiling water. "Your watch cost fifteen bucks. I know. I have one just like it at home in a Prince Hamlet cigar box."

King sat down, at the same time pulling his cuff over his watch.

Jane and I were still standing.

I said, "Nicolas?"

"Yes, sir."

"You should change your pants. Anyone needs anything while you're gone, I'll get it for 'em."

Nicolas smiled at me. It was the best moment so far on the Sip o' Sea. Except for one or two with Mrs. Willingford. And any time I had with Jane.

Speaking of Mrs. Willingford, the way she was smiling—I think I was in like Flynn there.

9

An hour or so later, Jackson and his cutter had chugged off back to where it'd chugged from, Captain Moody was snug in his wheelhouse, the crew was manning their stations, the Sip o' Sea was once again slipping along through the waves, and so far as I knew, everyone was in their own bunk.

I knew I was and so was Mrs. Willingford. In my bunk, that is, which in the Sip o' Sea's case could of slept four. I hadn't mentioned the storm already bouncing us around with worse to come. I figured the less said the better. I also figured since no one but Commander Jackson spoke of it, speaking of it was his way of trying to rattle me. It'd worked. I got rattled.

Until, that is, Mrs. Willingford'd walked in my door, as usual without knocking, slipped off her clothes, climbed into my bed and things went from there.

A half hour later, I was up on one elbow looking down at her face. No Fu Manchu collar, no huge hat, no garter belt, no silk stockings, no red lipstick, nothing but Lois with her hair loosened, floating around her head like Venus on the Half Shell... she never looked more beautiful.

I traced the curve of her breast with one finger. I said, "I never believed I could get this lucky."

"Don't fool yourself, Russo. It's not luck. It's skill."

"Skill?"

"Maybe you don't know where or with who, but you know I've been around. If I was stuck on a desert island, I'd choose you to be stuck with."

It was as close as she'd ever come to saying she cared. If

I said something, I knew I'd mess it up. So instead of saying a word, I did that thing she liked, something I liked as much as she did.

When I stopped doing it, she sighed and said, "See what I mean, Mr. Russo? You're a natural born wonder." Then she kissed me. If I had my way, that kiss could have gone on forever.

Later when I'd caught my breath and put my heart back where it usually lived, we were lying back, smoking and making small talk—mostly what we were really doing was working up to talking about Clara Louise—when came a tapping on my stateroom door.

Now what? Much more of girls jumping ship, and I was thinking of sleeping in a hammock in the engine room.

If it were up to Jane, she'd of answered it immediately. As it was, she stood on our side of the door staring from the doorknob to me back to the doorknob.

I looked at Mrs. Willingford and she looked at me. It was one thing to sleep with another man's wife, it was another to do it on his own boat, and even another to get caught doing it.

"Open the door, Sam," she said.

"Not unless you hide in the closet."

"Oh for pete's sake, why?"

"Have some respect."

"I do. More than you know. Which is why I know it's not Joker."

"Maybe you're right, but how do you know it's not someone who'll use this to hurt him? Your boat is crawling with types who'd do pretty much anything for an angle on you and Joker Willingford and all that Willingford money which all of 'em could use, some more than others."

I had her there and she knew it.

So there we were, her not hiding and me not opening the door and Jane not leaving it.

"Hell's bells, Sammy—open this damn door! I know you're in there. I can hear Jane humming."

Holly.

I opened the door and in flew Holly, green chiffon and green feathers swirling.

For the love of Mike, but Holly made a great looking dame.

Back in '48, just before I wound up in Saratoga Springs chasing the killer of not one but three jockeys, I'd seen a movie called *Blonde Ice*. Coming up for air on a hot night on the empty streets of Stapleton, I remember swearing I'd never get hitched. The gal in *Blonde Ice* taught me you could get killed that way.

And yet, there'd been times with Holly, times when we'd watch a movie together, sharing popcorn, or laughing over her Ouija board in my one room or in her one room, or we'd take Jane for a run down by a Stapleton pier with the glitter of Manhattan calling to us across the Upper Bay, times I'd forget her birth certificate called her "Baby" Shauer and that the box marked "sex" was ticked male, in those times I could see how a man might get to thinking about settling down.

And then I'd catch myself and laugh. Even if my friend Holly were built right in all the right places, Sam Russo wasn't the marrying kind. It just wasn't in me.

My Holly said, "I knew I'd find you all here. Hello there, Lois. You look swell."

"Evening, Holly. So do you."

"I do, don't I? And Jane! Oooh, snookums, you're my sweetie weetie doggywog, aren't you?"

Listening, I was getting the heebie jeebies. She had Clara Louise down pat.

Jane loved it.

Propped up in bed, I was drinking a whiskey cocktail while Mrs. Willingford was sipping a vodka and peach sour on the rocks—a drink of her own devising; I'd told her if marrying rich didn't turn out the berries, she'd never starve, she was a shoo-in for some high class joint's high class bartender—we were both waiting for Holly to stop playing with Jane and get to the point of her late night visit. She hadn't come to see Jane. That was a dead cert.

Her warmth warming mine, Mrs. W and I made one hell of a partnership. We both watched and waited and smoked and sipped from delicate cocktail glasses. Jane never would, but Holly was bound to wear herself out at some point.

It took close to five minutes.

Holly flopped on my bed and lay there, panting. Jane jumped up beside her and lay there, not panting.

"Alright. You two win. I was hoping you'd draw it out of me."

"I'm the patient kind," said Mrs. Willingford. "In my line of work, you have to be."

I said, "Draw what out?"

"Everything! You two canoodling in here, you don't know what they're all saying and doing out there. But I do."

"So spill."

"It's like one of your books, Sammy. One of those dime murder mysteries you've always got your nose in. The detective's got a whole clutter of suspects gathered in the drawing room or somewhere like that where they're all trying to pretend they're calm as clams, but all the while one of them is as scared as a Chihuahua."

"Suspects?" said Mrs. Willingford. "Commander Jackson has declared the loss of Clara Louise a suicide."

"Ah," said Holly, "but is it?" She turned to me, her scent as heady as Lamarr. "Do you think so, Sammy? You don't think so. I can tell you don't think so. Or at least you're not sure. I'm certainly not sure. Why would she jump? She couldn't be certain she'd die. She could have been rescued. She could have gotten hurt, but lived, and then what? Disfigured? Crippled? Who would do that? How perfectly silly. Besides,

I'd only just been talking to her."

That made me sit up.

"Aha! I've got your attention now."

"You do. All of it."

"OK, so it was like this. Me and that Olivia and Clara Louise, we all noticed Captain Moody at the same time which was about five minutes after coming aboard. They noticed you too, Sam, but they got it you're already taken."

Mrs. Willingford laughed. I loved that laugh. It was one of the things about Mrs. Willingford made me feel easy. No stranglehold. It's also what drove me crazy about Mrs. Willingford. What if *I* wanted to grab on? Also, what did it mean?

Making herself comfortable by squeezing between Mrs. Willingford and Jane and me—the bed was that big—Holly said, "That's what I told them. I said you were an item but best not to talk about it. They got that part real easy. So there we were. Of course we began with the usual silly business, spats and territory and such, but that's girls for you. We got over all that soon enough and then, well then we shared our crush on Captain Eigil Moody. Doncha just love that name: Eigil? So only this lunchtime I was in the Grand Salon with almost everyone else, but not Olivia Powers. I have no idea where Olivia was but Clara Louise was finally out of bed and she and I were talking up a storm about Captain Moody. You know: what we'd do with him and where we'd do it—are you blushing, Sammy?"

"No."

"Few would, but I believe you. Anyway, as I was saying, only this lunchtime Clara was full of beans about being on this big rich yacht and going to Hialeah racetrack with all these important people—that's what she called 'em: important people—and how she was sure at least one of 'em would help with her career. I also saw her maybe two minutes before she jumped off the ship. I'd ordered a Strawberry Daiquiri and one of the stewards brought it to me. Clara laughed when she saw it, said it looked icky-boo. Honestly, who says icky-boo? And then I went back inside and she stayed on that stern deck. What I'm saying, is: someone like Clara Louise would not jump off this boat."

I thought about opening my mouth, but Holly plowed right on.

"And that's what we were all talking about tonight. We were talking about how she didn't feel well last night which didn't seem like her. Of course no one really knew her but she was one bouncy kid, and everyone knew that. No one, and I mean no one, thinks she jumped. Everyone, and I mean everyone, thinks she was pushed. And they all think Olivia pushed her."

"With the opera singer watching?"

"They think the fat lady's lying."

"Why would she lie?"

"Attention? Covering for Olivia? You're the detective. That's for you to find out."

"Swell."

"Why?" said Mrs. Willingford.

"Why what?"

"Why would Olivia push Clara off the Sip o' Sea?"

"Oh that. That's easy. So many reasons. Captain Moody. Some other guy they both wanted. A lover's spat. They could be dykes, ever thought of that? Or maybe it was some part they were hoping for. Or a dare. Or a bet. Anyway, it doesn't help that Olivia's hiding or something, because she sure isn't around defending herself."

I said, "Excuse me?"

"You heard me. Olivia Powers has gone missing."

Before I could say it, Mrs. Willingford said it. "Fuck."

10

The whole time Holly'd been talking, I'd listened. But there was more than just Holly to hear. I'd tried hard, but I couldn't miss it. The Sip o' Sea had started to heave from side to side, then front to back. My hand inched its way towards the headboard. When she began pitching as well as rocking, I was doing what I did best, clinging. And while clinging made the mistake of looking out the window. The wind outside was rising with one of those high keening sounds… like an incoming mortar, or one of Mickey Cates' banshees.

What I saw out there made me almost swallow my tongue. A herd of stampeding white-maned waves were leaping over the railing. Other than that, it was pitch dark. If there were stars in the sky they'd been blown away by the wind.

I said, "Shit."

Without a word of her own, Mrs. Willingford picked up my phone, dialed one number only and waited. The wait lasted maybe a second. But not for me. For me, it was a grim forever. She said, "Uhuh. Uhuh. OK. When? How bad? OK. You'll try and run round it? Fine. Do whatever you have to do. I'll tell Joker."

It was close to the worst one-sided conversation I'd ever heard.

As Mrs. Willingford snatched up her wrap and swept towards the door, I said the only thing I could think of to say. "Run round what?"

"Tropical storm," she said, "coming up from the south. Not a big one, but far from small."

"Tropical storm!" said Holly, snatching up her feathery

green wrap. "You want me, I'll be under my covers."

Jane stood her ground. With me. If she hadn't, I'd be under my bed.

The next few hours were ten times worse than the entire last two days. Maybe not for Clara Louise, but for Sam Russo it was a case of black and blue funk.

I couldn't sleep. No one could. To a man and a woman, the Willingford guests were huddled together in the Grand Salon. It made sense. Fear loves company.

Clutching Jane, I fought off the screaming mimis by working: where was Olivia Powers? What really happened to Clara Louise? What if it wasn't a suicide but a murder? If we had a murder on the Sip o' Sea and if Olivia saw it, did we have another murder on the Sip o' Sea? Someone making sure the witness didn't remember what she'd so far forgotten?

And if we did, how was a gumshoe supposed to work it in a not-big but a not-small tropical storm? Didn't tropical storms turn into hurricanes? Already I couldn't see out my big window. It was awash with the wet slap of the sea. Had Bogart ever—hold on, why was I asking? Of course he had. *Key Largo*. A storm. Edward G. Robinson. Bacall. This terrific second lead dame called Claire Trevor who acted Bacall off the screen.

Talk about life imitating art. Talk about murder following a guy around. Talk about scared.

Fuck that. I went on the prowl again. It wasn't easy, but I did it. Once again Jane insisted on coming along. I would of gotten lost if she hadn't.

Another actress missing: as I said, another suicide or another murder? No time to wait out a storm. I had to look for Olivia Powers and I had to do it now.

The Sip o' Sea picked that moment to fall off the top of a wave the size of the Flat Iron Building. It was like an express elevator cable snapped, or I was back in the middle of the Pacific, or we were on that suspension bridge in faraway

Washington State that bucked like a bronco before it broke in two or three or however many pieces, the one they called Galloping Gertie. From inside her stateroom, I heard Holly yell like a man. As for me, Sam Russo, I stuffed my fist in my mouth so I didn't yell like a girl.

It was one hell of a long time before my stomach climbed down out of my neck.

First place to check once I could swallow again, was the girl's stateroom. She'd locked her door. So I pounded on it. Nothing. I yelled. Nothing. If she was in there, she wasn't accepting company. Or maybe, with the noise from the storm, she didn't hear me. I yelled a couple more times. If she was in there, she either didn't want to see me or she'd taken a little something to sleep off poor Clara Louise. If she was in there, that's the explanation I wanted.

If she wasn't in there, where was she?

My gun, a snubnosed Colt .38, wasn't in my pocket. My lock picks weren't in a pocket either. I'd left 'em in my own stateroom, a long messy way away.

Good thing it wasn't yet lock picking time but looking all over the boat time.

While I pounded, Jane trotted back and forth, yodeling. I'd seen her do a lot of interesting things since we'd become pals, but I'd never seen her do what she did then. She sat down on her haunches, held up her head and practically crowed. Much more of that and she'd strain her throat. I had enough on my conscience. I pulled her away. There were still a lot of other doors to try.

We both skidded across the companionway when the Sip o' Sea heeled over far enough to slam us up against a bulkhead. I got thrown from one side to the other, bruising my hips and shoulders. Jane did better being in better shape than I was. But it shut her up.

Searching for Olivia Powers meant I was practically crawling in the corridors, groping for doorknobs. I got smacked in the kisser by a suitcase making a leap across a stateroom. I hugged a lot of bulkheads, did a lot of sliding on polished floors, almost broke my nose on the side of a pink ceramic tub.

Jane went everywhere I went, sniffing what I couldn't smell. If we opened one stateroom door, we opened 'em all. Aside from Olivia, all the other guests were trusting, or careless. The doors weren't locked. Except for the door that once opened and closed for Clara Louise. That one'd been searched by Commander Jackson's men and left locked.

Jane wanted in, but I was looking for Olivia Powers, not Clara Louise.

We found nothing.

I shouldn't say that. We found one hell of a lot of stuff. We learned if something could be packed, it would be packed. No telling what people thought they needed on an ocean voyage.

Three of 'em thought they needed a knife. Three of 'em thought they needed a gun.

They weren't the same three.

Two thought they needed dope. One of those had one of the knives. The other had one of the guns.

And one had a war medal. It wasn't English and it wasn't one handed out by Uncle Sam. It wasn't military, not exactly. It was for "services rendered."

Time to go deeper into the secrets of the Sip o' Sea, to leave the part I knew behind.

No matter how we pitched and yawed, Jane and I forced ourselves away from the staterooms and the dining room and the Grand Salon. We went up ladders and down, along narrow passageways that only grew narrower, up a gangway, down a gangway, out a hatch, back in another.

"What a maze, eh Jane?"

Jane uncurled her tail. She hummed. She licked my hand. Jane was comforting me. No hiding a thing from Jane...

unless it was Olivia Powers.

We found ourselves far forward. It wasn't the private steward's corridor this time. I didn't feel so much an intruder. No Merle whimpering, no Clyde yelling, and no Olivia Powers, dead or alive.

We tried a lot of doors here too. Most of the time what was behind 'em didn't mean a thing. Not to me anyway. But the last door we opened—no knock, no warning, just a big confident effort at one that was bigger than the doors to the private cabins—and there I was again, in another fine mess made by Sam Russo and his faithful sidekick.

Turned out the room—cabin, salon, whatever they called it—behind that door wasn't meant for my kind. It was strictly for the crew, deck hands and such.

The tables and chairs were decent enough, the light bright enough, but no carpet and no portholes.

There were two surprised faces staring at us.

I could pick out one of 'em, knew his name, but not the other, knew they were resting before going back to save us all from the storm. I could also tell neither of 'em was the Powers dame.

These two'd been weathering the storm chatting, smoking, doing their best not to spill their evening cocoa— and here was Sam Russo and his mutt walking right in on them. Like he had the right to. Like they had no space of their own.

I never felt more an intruder either side of a door.

With a weak wave from me, Jane and I beat it back up to the Grand Salon. Next time I searched for a missing actress, I was taking a professional guide.

The Sip o' Sea was still getting hit with wind and waves. They were lesser wind and waves, but they were waves and wind. I had a look round. If I thought I'd been scared, it wasn't a patch on Charlie Dick or the opera singer. I'd never seen a single hair out of place on Sabrina's perfect tiara'd head. Now she looked like she was plugged into a socket. Charlie Dick would of been out with his head over a rail if he wasn't afraid the wind would blow the rail off the ship. Speaking of hair, the movie director and sideshow attraction, was babbling with fear in his native German, finally and fluently, at the same time smoking one cigarette lit off another.

King, the fading movie star, was lucky. He'd drunk himself into a stupor. Someone had rolled him up in a rug and shoved the rug behind the bolted down bar.

Dew, the trainer, and the two jocks, Feather and Tyrrell rode it out like they'd ride out some English race, one that was a mad scramble of horses and riders jumping over high wide bushes with wider ponds on the other side, half the time landing on a steep downward slope where one or two or more were sure to pitch head over ass. There they were, with all that pitching and yawing, lounging around on couches, discussing the meet at Hialeah, the now five year old Fleeting Fancy's chances in the Old Rosebud Stakes, how Your Host was doing in his races, how they'd do in theirs.

I hung on to a brass rail near the bar King was resting behind, and tried to listen. Your Host was one of the reasons I was on this expensive tub.

Your Host was a nervous wreck and as headstrong as Jane. There was wild talk he'd race in Florida. I wanted to see that. I wanted to see it enough to get on a boat.

Who wouldn't?

Your Host was foaled with his right eye and right ear set an inch or so higher than his left eye and ear, a crooked neck, low withers and light flanks. People were saying his neck was twisted thanks to some foolish thing he'd done as a yearling or maybe because something was wrong with his spine, but I'd heard his groom said he was as smart as they come. Your Host never did anything foolish. The groom said he held his head sideways like that so he could see out of those Barney Google eyes. When he was two, he got so sick the Hollywood mogul who owned him was sure he'd be dead by the morning. But the colt was not only lucky in his vet—as lucky as Jane'd been in her vet the night up in Saratoga Springs she was stabbed over and over with a steak knife—he was stubborn.

Your Host lived. He even thrived, winning some of the biggest stakes races going for two-year-olds. Now he was three and he'd taken the Santa Anita Derby, they'd stopped calling him "The Freak" and were now calling him "The Magnificent Cripple."

Not only me, but Mrs. Willingford along with me, we were sure he'd walk away with the Kentucky Derby. Fact was, he showed up in style. Shipped in all the way from Hollywood, the sign on his personal railroad car read: "1950 Kentucky Derby Winner." And then there was his jock to consider, the great Johnny Longden.

Middleground won. I wasn't watching Middleground. Middleground didn't even factor. I'd figured if it wasn't Your Host, it'd be a terrific colt called Hill Prince.

Your Host wasn't even in the money. What happened was, it turned out that the Magnificent Cripple was like Mrs. Willingford, he was a sprinter. As a sprinter, he was some horse. Aside from the Derby, he'd been winning all season since. If things went as rumored, way before now he'd of left California where he'd been mopping up the shorter stakes, and showing up in Hialeah just where I was supposed to be showing up.

That is, so long as a couple of pesky actresses didn't stop me.

Damn, but I'd of liked to of ridden out a tropical storm like Walter Dew and Toby Tyrrell and Tommy Feather did. I tried looking like I *was* riding it out like they were. I didn't pull it off but I didn't make a punk of myself either.

As for Mr. & Mrs. Morton & Kline, the movie writing duo, old as they were, they were made of sterner stuff, chips off my old pal Jimmy Stewart's block. They didn't like it, but they took it, seated together in the Grand Salon, not moving for anything, not even when their couch bucked and almost pitched 'em off. Talk about grips. I hadn't seen anything like it since I was a kid trying to pry this big pink starfish off a Stapleton piling.

When they weren't gripping something, they were writing. Here was me thinking I was dedicated. Years of doing Lino Morelli's work for him so I'd learn the ropes, grabbing in return all the time he gave me on the Stapleton police shooting range, taking dirty little cases to pay the rent on my crummy little one room dump, reading every detective novel ever written, watching all the crime movies, taking a course in lock picking in Bayonne, New Jersey, from the best lock picker I'd ever met. I worked hard, but watching those two bracing themselves against anything not moving as they took notes, I had to wonder.

Sandrine Brunetti had stuffed herself into a huge arm chair. Pillows either side of her, a blanket tucked everywhere she could tuck it. Every once in awhile, she'd jolt into my line of sight, and every time she did, she was a different color.

I'd seen women perspire, even sweat a bit. None of them as much as a man, but Sandrine was coming close. Hair out to here, her make-up was sagging with sweat.

Vergil Sapster, industrial magnate, was industriously making noise. People react to things they can't control in so many damned ways. Sapster was a talker. No one was listening, but that didn't stop him. I caught a line now and then. His wife back in Ohio, his kids, his cars, his New York City mistress and how much she was costing him, the confounded government, a tax inspector on his back had it in for him personally, the state of his horse breeding operation, how much it was costing him to send his best mares to the Willingford stallion.

The guy was boring when he wasn't talking. Talking, he

needed a padded cell. Not so much for him, but for us.

I did catch his line of work, though. He made nails. Name a nail, any kind of nail, it was made by the Sapster Nail Company of Dayton, Ohio. Sapster Nails, according to Vergil, held America together. I didn't doubt it. Vergil Sapster was born to make nails.

11

A little past one in the morning, all went quiet. The deck steadied. The bulkheads became vertical. And that was that. Our storm was over. We'd weathered it.

The Willingford guests'd toddled off to their bunks. Me, I was sunk deep in a comfy couch, drinking, Jane at my side, when two stewards in casual dress arrived to clean up the debris.

One of 'em was Howard. The other was Gene. I watched 'em for about a minute. Gene was usually as light on his feet as Fred Astaire. Did he look a little less nimble? Stewards didn't get to roll themselves into rugs or stuff themselves into big fat chairs. The way the ship'd been bucking and pitching, he'd probably done just what I'd done, got slammed into something while caring for his superiors.

Slumped on one of those big fat chairs, exhausted from my labors—even Jane looked a little the worse for wear—I was thinking about the three young actresses who'd come aboard this boat. I was thinking that two of them were gone. I was thinking about all that hope and all those dreams as vanished as Hitchcock's old lady had vanished. I was thinking that Miss Olivia Powers' stateroom was locked. Was she behind that door? Was she drugged? Had she taken something to get through a night after seeing someone die?

Worst question of all. If she was in her stateroom, was she alive?

I thought about the Sip o' Sea's guests. Each one of 'em thinking thoughts I'd never know, chewing on pain I'd never feel, living lives of hopes and dreams and lies.

If Miss Powers wasn't alive, was one of them her killer?

One of strangest movies I ever saw was *Dark Passage*. Bogie was in it. If Bogie was in something, I saw it.

The movie was one switcharoo after another. Bogie on the run for not committing I forget how many murders and getting his face worked on by a back alley plastic surgeon, and Bacall, the one woman who believed in him—there's always one—but on second thought maybe the movie wasn't so strange. Maybe it was just people acting like people always do. Lying and cheating and stealing and double-crossing, men and women hurting each other, killing each other, setting each other up, blaming the other guy, making dumb mistakes, believing what they wanted to believe, not believing what you'd think they could see right in front of their kisser, people not who you thought they were.

I guess I should be glad people were like that, or that they would be like that if they thought they could get away with it, or if they had the energy to bother. I ought to be grateful that they've always been like that. If they weren't, there wouldn't be a use for people like me. Or Bogie.

I must of dozed off for a bit. When I opened my eyes, the Grand Salon was clean and empty except for me and Jane. There was a clock behind the bar shaped like Versailles. France, not Kentucky. 5 A.M. on a Tuesday, our third day at sea. The only one not tucked up in bed aside from us was whoever was steering the Sip o' Sea. We were cruising. I couldn't see land, not a tree or a rock or a hummock or a hill. For all I knew, we could be off the coast of Georgia. Or Florida.

Hell, we could be off the coast of Cuba.

If I had to bet on what I was looking at the last time I'd seen land, what I'd been looking at could of still been some part of New Jersey.

Jane was yawning, a big wide effort full of white Egyptian

teeth and pink Egyptian tongue. Time for us to get tucked up too. That idea sent me straight off to the stateroom of Mrs. Willingford in the hopes that things were about to turn cozy and warm. Mrs. Willingford had a bed bigger than a boxing ring.

Jane clicked along behind me, her tail too tired to keep itself as tightly wound as usual.

The second I saw her face, the idea I'd nursed about Mrs. W. was snuffed out like someone in the ring with Heavyweight Ezzard Mack. She looked like the fifth man on Mount Rushmore.

She said, "It's you, Sam. I've never known anyone like you. Get in here."

I got in, Jane faster than me, also faster to jump on the bed, while I was still saying, "OK, I'll bite. What's that crack mean?"

"I mean murder follows you around."

"Wrong. I'm a Private Eye. I follow murder around. When I have to. If I don't have to, I get stuck following cheating husbands and wives around. Small potato stuff."

"Uhuh. Right. And what case are you following around now?"

I caught her drift but I wasn't going with it.

She said: "And what case were you on when Holly went missing?"

"Holly's my friend. You think I'd do nothing?"

"Or when that giant washed up under a Stapleton pier?"

"Low blow. Lino stuck me with the giant killer."

If that wasn't true, I didn't know what was. The case Jane and I'd spent running up and down Broadway for, getting slapped in the kisser by the Great White Way, wasn't supposed to be a case at all. It was supposed to be me identifying a corpse, nothing else. That it became a full blown double—counting me: almost triple—murder case was all Lino Morelli's fault.

And, except for my meager Stapleton Police Department expenses, no one paid me one thin dime.

But I did become pals with Jimmy Stewart and Josephine Hull. Lino never knew what he was missing. Lucky for them, Jimmy and Josephine also missed Lino.

Hell if I knew how, but while I was halfway across the world fighting in a world war on the island of Luzon, a cowardly kid I'd grown up with in the Kiddie House of Horrors—aka the Staten Island Home for Children—finagled his way into becoming a detective with the Staten Island Police. Lino Morelli was two years older than me, maybe three inches taller, but he was millions of brain cells dumber—which is why I was always getting called in to solve his cases. Any time of the day or night, there'd be a knock on the door of 4-A, Home Sweet Home, and whaddaya know, it was always my old pal Lino mooching around yet again for help. I got no pay, no credit, and no thanks, but I did get what I couldn't buy anywhere else—experience.

At 5:13 in the morning, Mrs. Willingford was fully made up, perfectly coiffed, and mixing another one of her lethal cocktails. Handing me something she could of made in a laboratory, she said, "You don't see it, but I see it."

"You see a lot of things. You see things I'll never see or care to see. But I'll tell you what I do care about and I'll tell you for free."

"Shoot."

"I care that I got on this damn boat of yours with three actresses plus a bunch of other mugs. I care that all three of 'em go to the same acting school and that one is a movie star and going to cause a lot of fuss for Joker if something's wrong. I care we still got all the mugs, but two of the actresses are gone. The movie star actress says she saw the other actress leap off the boat. Now that Hollywood actress is maybe gone, maybe disappeared. Her door is locked. She didn't answer when I came calling. I care about that. The opera singer said she also saw what happened. I care about that too."

"I also care about that, Sam."

"I'll bet you do. Joker's sick with liability."

Every once in awhile Mrs. Willingford really got my goat. Every once in awhile I got hers. I got it now.

She slapped me.

I've been slapped by a dame before. I've been slapped by Mrs. Willingford before. But this time she put some real effort into it.

Half asleep, Jane didn't lift an eyetooth.

When my eyes rolled back into their sockets and my brain stopped loop-de-looping, I said, "I deserved that."

She said, "Don't mention it."

Still half asleep, Jane hummed.

I knocked back a slug of her early morning pick-me-up. After I'd picked myself back up, I told her about the knives, the dope, the guns, and Olivia Power's locked door and how I thought maybe we ought to unlock it, even if all we found was a girl in shock. Which would be just dandy with me. Last thing I wanted to find was no girl, or worse, a girl in trouble.

I also told her about my lumps and bumps and bruises but all I got for that was Mrs. Willingford looking at her watch. 6:09 A.M.

"Joker'll be up. He's old. He barely sleeps. Come on. He needs to know what the hell is going on."

"You said it. What do we know?"

"More than my husband does. Someone will be serving him breakfast. Joker won't be happy about it, he never is, but we've got to get to the bacon before he does. Jane? You like bacon?"

Two years with Jane and I knew she could speak if she wanted to. But who'd want to speak to the likes of us if they were born the likes of her?

No need for her to speak. She wasn't Jewish, she was

Egyptian. Of course she liked pig.

She woke up.

Walking the short distance from Mrs. Willingford's stateroom to Mr. Willingford's stateroom gave me time to think. Not much time, but it was enough.

I didn't know if Clara was dead. Olivia said she saw her jump and if she did, Clara Louise had to be dead. But now one of the witnesses to the daylight leap was missing. Besides Olivia, no one but Brunetti said they'd seen Clara jump. No one, including Brunetti, said they knew much about her. The girl'd been invited along by Otto Gerlinger who'd been invited by Joker. It was one of Joker's "bring a friend" invites. Aside from me getting asked by Mrs. Willingford, so far as I knew the German film director was the only one who took him up on it. Otto said all he knew about Clara Louise was she was exactly what he wanted for one of the roles in his haunted movie palace flicker, the one he'd told Joker Bette Davis said she might do.

One minute the Willingford guests were all over Olivia and Sandrine about Clara Louise and what they saw and what they did, the next minute Commander Jackson and his Coast Guard shows up, and the minute after that Clara Louise is declared an official suicide and then along comes a tropical storm to blow us all to hell and back. And in the middle of one damn thing after another, Olivia Powers was gone.

Was Sandrine Brunetti next? Was Holly? Jesus, what about Holly! Or were two actresses enough for anyone?

I had to give it to 'em. The Willingfords were providing their guests with one lollapalooza of a boat ride. After this, Fleeting Fancy and Hialeah and Your Host might turn out a snooze. Not for me of course. I loved the ponies. And maybe not for Toby Tyrrell who was riding the Willingford mare. Or for Walter Dew who was training her.

But I'd lay down good money that maybe half of these folks would like to go home now please.

12

Mrs. Willingford knew her hubby. As we walked in, he had a forkful of bacon poised in front of his open mouth. He either still had all his teeth or he had a great dentist. I was guessing the latter.

"Merle!"

Merle, who wasn't Joker Willingford's steward, flinched. Then froze in place next to Joker's enameled tray. Like me, Joker was eating breakfast in his stateroom.

"So sorry, madam. Kenneth asked me to serve Mr. Willingford this morning. I had no idea he wasn't allowed bacon. When he asked, I couldn't say— "

Joker was gripping the arms of his chair. "Not allowed!"

Mrs. Willingford ignored him. "Couldn't say no? You bet your life you could say no. I say it to him every damn day. You want to keep this job, you'll want to keep Mr. Willingford breathing. Joker, give that piece of pig to Jane."

Joker threw his bacon at Jane who caught it between her teeth as carefully as nitroglycerin but ate it like it was a slice of bacon—in one deep inhale.

Kenneth walked in, followed by Mrs. Coleman. And Merle ran out.

Mrs. Willingford glared at Kenneth but Kenneth, to my deep admiration, seemed not to notice. Otelie served us Eggs Benedict and coffee. Joker was served unbuttered toast, some sort of mush, and weak tea, Kenneth quietly sweeping Joker's deliberate crumbs off the table with a small shovel shaped silver thing and a silver handled brush.

I thought about the hour. Mrs. Coleman had to be up

before the sun to feed this bunch. Then there were the lunches she came up with, and finally her wallop of a five course dinner. What did she do with the rest of her time? Probably wrote poetry. There was something poetic about her face, about the way she watched the Willingfords, about the way she dealt with the Willingford's assortment of "guests." Or maybe I meant saintly.

As for Kenneth, I didn't get him at all.

I lit a cigarette. Joker said, "Put that out. A man can't have bacon, he doesn't need smoke either." I stubbed it out in a saucer.

"Tell him, Sam," said Lois.

I looked at Kenneth and Otelie.

"You can speak in front of Mrs. Coleman and Kenneth."

"Tell me what?" said Joker, staring at Jane. Jane was staring at Joker. Where there was one slice of bacon, there was bound to be another. There wasn't.

I told Mrs. Willingford's rich hubby the latest news.

I didn't think Joker could look more sour than he'd done getting his bacon taken away, but he could. Two guests gone now. Counting staff and crew, how many of us were left? What if more went missing? We could be stuck in an Agatha Christie book, the one she wrote about a lot of strangers invited by some other mysterious stranger to a mysterious island where they all died, one by one, and not only did no one get caught for any of the murders, not even the host survived.

Maybe it didn't occur to Mr. or Mrs. Willingford, but it occurred to me—what if the Sip o' Sea was on its way to becoming a modern Mary Celeste?

The spooky tale of the Mary Celeste was one of Paul Jarrett's favorite bedtime treats back at the Good Old Home for Tormented Tots.

I had two "best friends" at the Zawadzki's House of Hell. One was Lino Morelli who was never much of a friend but was better than nothing, and the other was Paul Jarrett, the kid who made us laugh so hard half of us got sick.

He was also the kid grown into a man who shot me three times point blank, but that was a story already survived… no need to survive it again.

One night when the moon wasn't around, Jarrett gathered all us kids together after our light bulb went out and told us about a ship found in full sail headed for some huge European rock. On board was plenty of food, the crew's things were neatly stacked away, including their valuables like watches and rings, and the ship sailed true—but every man jack who worked her was gone, vanished into thin air. Poof! Just like that. Not one of 'em was ever found and no one ever knew what happened aboard the ghostly Mary Celeste.

And then, when all our little faces were agape with horror, Paul yelled: "Huzzah!" and more than one of us shit our little pants.

I think I've said I don't like boats.

"Fix it," said Joker. He said it to me.

"Fix it?"

"That's what you do, isn't it? Among other things."

I never thought I'd see the day, but the left corner of Mrs. Willingford's perfect blood-red mouth twitched. Was that guilt? Was it surprise? Was she trying not to laugh? Did the corner of my mouth twitch?

"Yep. That's what I do."

"Then do it. Make all this go away. I'll pay you triple what you usually get, with a fat bonus if you get it done before we reach Miami."

A case! Another case. Bonus or no bonus, it was money enough for months on my room—but by Miami? Even Bogie would be hard pressed.

Sure Jaysus, as Mickey Cates would say, a few more cases and I might start thinking of myself as a real Private Eye.

Mrs. Willingford and I made it to Olivia Power's locked door at 7:02 A.M. I didn't need my set of lock picks. I didn't need to pick a lock. I was carrying keys to every stateroom, every cabinet, locker, closet, door and hatch on the Sip o' Sea. They were neatly labeled, hung on a huge brass ring, and all together weighed enough to anchor a lifeboat.

I let us in, Jane first since she insisted.

The bed wasn't made up, but the covers were pulled up and over the pillows. Someone had tried to sleep. The storm probably ruined that idea. No guns and no knives, but there was a big box on one of the couches.

Mrs. Willingford saw it at the same moment I saw it which meant she got to it before I did.

The box was full of old movie magazines and old newspaper clippings. Mrs. Willingford began taking them out, one *Photoplay* or *Motion Picture Magazine* or *Silver Screen* at a time. King Barton's mug was on the cover of every magazine. The clippings were reviews from newspapers in cities across the U.S., faded but readable and cut out perfectly, not a slip up anywhere. Every single one of the reviews was about a King Barton movie.

He'd been pretty good looking in an oily sort of way. He wasn't that good looking anymore.

I looked at Mrs. Willingford and she looked at me. King Barton's career was long gone and undistinguished. Why would someone like Miss Powers, someone Hollywood already loved, as well as someone Holly said was a seriously good actress, save King Barton crap?

I also found a letter Olivia'd been writing. Unmoved by a tropical storm, it was in plain sight on her desk, stamp and envelope ready but unaddressed.

Something about reading other people's mail bothered me. It started a long way back, that much I knew. And it sure wasn't delicacy of feeling. I didn't see myself as all that delicate. I saw it more as a kind of guilt.

It didn't bother my old friend Lino Morelli. A born cop, Lino was always looking for ways to get the goods on other people. Things they wrote gave him power more times than you'd think. It was Lino who found a journal of one of the older girls at the Home. He spent over a week sneaking it in and out of where she hid it so he could read it to me and Paul and a few of the other boys. We snickered over Millie's journal. I think her name was Millie. I'm pretty sure of it. Millie wrote about her dreams, what she was going to be one day, who she'd marry—me, as it turned out—goofy things like that.

We'd punch each other's arms. A guy like one of us good lookin' heroes get hitched to someone as dopey looking as Millie? Sure. That'd be the day "Joltin' Joe" DiMaggio missed a high fly pop-up.

The night Millie caught Lino and the rest of us snickering dolts with her journal was the last time any of us ever saw her. She ran away. I don't know if she got very far. I don't even know if she got anywhere at all considering who was running the Staten Island Home for Children. None of us ever knew much of anything about her except the sad and sappy stuff in her journal. And we didn't ask.

She was thirteen the day she might of run off.

So maybe Millie was why I didn't like this part of being a Private Eye. But like it or not, it came with the job.

I read Olivia's unsent letter.

> *Dear E,*
> *I know you said not to write, that someone might see the letter and it could get you in trouble, but I just can't help myself. You mean so much to me. It all means so much to me. And I want what you want. I*

want it terribly. But for now I'm stuck on this boat with a lot of jerks. I really couldn't say no. Someday I'll tell you why. Besides, I need a break from all my pain and your difficulty at the studio. Not to mention the calls I keep getting from my own studio. You should see the scripts they send me.

I feel sick about us. The last time I saw you, you were sneaking out of a hotel room when you thought I was asleep. I wasn't asleep. I was lying next to you wondering what was going to happen next. The truth is, and I know it just as well as you do, that nothing is going to happen next. Not for us. Except maybe a few more out-of-the-way midtown hotels. You've got a wife and an important job. You're a real artist and I'm only a fool who signed that long contract. I'm not even a blonde. But I'm going to make a great Eve, you said so, and I believe you. I'll make you proud, at least on the stage, even if I have to die doing it.

That's where it ended. Until it got read by one of the jerks also stuck on this boat.

I opened the desk drawer. There were at least half a dozen other letters in it, stamped, sealed and addressed.

"E" was some foreign sounding bozo named Elia Kazan back in New York City.

That's when Mrs. Willingford, who never shrieked, shrieked. It made me slam the drawer on my fingers.

Jane'd gotten Olivia's closet door open. Inside was one hell of a pathetic mess. It didn't seem to bother my Egyptian dog but Mrs. Willingford spent a moment or two gagging at the sight. I gotta admit. It wasn't pretty.

Meanwhile, Jane tugged at a dead white leg with a dead white foot at the end of it.

The rest of the body was still in the closet.

13

It was Olivia Powers, all right. Dead as they come. Stuffed into her closet with her nightie pulled up past her breasts. Nice breasts. Mrs. Willingford was just about to kneel down and cover her for modesty's sake.

I said, "Don't."

Mrs. Willingford turned into her version of a detective right before my eyes. She left the nightie alone.

I turned into mine. No more fooling around.

"Right, Sam. Clues."

I opened the closet door as wide as I could. The side of the poor girl's head, shoved far towards the back, was a mess of blood. Her dark hair was matted with it. Down on my knees, not wanting to, but having to push suitcases and shoes aside, I tried lifting her well-tended hand to look for defensive wounds. Nothing doing. She was as stiff as a steel girder.

I said, "She was bludgeoned to death. Three blows. Two hard, One very hard. About twelve hours ago, give or take a few hours either way. That makes it sometime before or during yesterday's storm." I pushed aside a lock of matted hair. Olivia's scalp came with it. Under the rolled back skin the sleek white bone of her skull had a hole as big as a gun butt in it. The biggest and hardest blow had exposed her brain.

"It was done with something very hard and round. Not as big as a baseball bat and not as small as poker. Maybe made of metal. Maybe some sort of rod? Is there something like that around here anywhere?"

I heard Mrs. Willingford searching.

"Nothing, Sam. And we don't have curtain rods on the boat. Or pokers. Or baseball bats."

I said, "My best guess was she was napping when she first got hit, maybe trying to hide from the storm, but that blow must of woken her up. Bit of a struggle then, s'why she's out of bed, but hit like that, as hard as that and as woozy as she must have been, she didn't stand much of a chance."

I straightened up, walked over to the bed and threw back the blanket that covered the pillows and went halfway up the headboard. Blood all over the sheets, top and bottom. All over her pillows. Two sprays of blood on the bottom of the headboard. One spray looked like a Japanese fan. The other looked more like a spider's web with wings.

"See that?"

Mrs. Willingford nodded. Yes she saw it.

"And this pattern? I've seen something like this before, one of Morelli's messes in the better part of town. It was a guy in his own house and done with one of his own golf clubs, an overhead swing with a nine iron. And with force. You saw her head."

Mrs. Willingford nodded again. She'd seen the head.

"Whatever the weapon was, it wasn't a golf club, no edges sharp or otherwise."

I looked around. The staterooms weren't all exactly the same but they shared a lot of the same things. None of those things were useful for smashing someone's head in with. This was a boat. Boat's rock. They get tossed around in storms like the storm we'd just gone through. So the sort of stuff you'd find on land you wouldn't find on a boat: big ashtrays, lamps with heavy bases, statues, vases.

I said, "The killer brought his own weapon. I'm guessing a solid pipe. It started with Olivia in bed. It ended in the closet where she was trying to get away. She was dying, almost already dead when she was hit a third time. No need for that last blow yet it was the hardest of all. That says a lot about the killer. So then she was shoved farther in and had the door shut on her. He, or she, fussed with the bed, covered up the blood. Why, I dunno. All anyone had to do was look in the closet."

"Why bother?" said Mrs. Willingford in a tone I'd come to expect of her: saddened for and by her fellow mortal, but ready for anything. "The deed was done. The door was locked."

I was peering at the floor. All I saw were two small drops of blood. They led into the bathroom. I said, "Maybe to buy time in case Olivia's steward came round for some reason?"

Olivia's stateroom wasn't near mine. She didn't share the same good looking steward I shared with Toby Tyrrell and Tommy Feather.

Mrs. Willingford touched the pillow, drew back her hand. "That wouldn't work. When the steward came round, she'd have a key. When she saw the bed, she'd make it. She'd see the blood."

"She? Oh right, the little redhead feeding Joker bacon. I forget her name."

"You ever get rich, Sam, one of the first rules is don't forget the names of those who serve you. They have ways of getting back, ways you'd don't want to know about."

"I'll remember that."

"You do that. Merle."

"Merle?"

"Merle is the name of Olivia's steward. Merle also takes care of Holly and…"

"I remember now. She takes care of Clara Louise."

"She did. Now, I guess she doesn't. Gene takes care of you, Toby and Tommy. Nicolas has King Barton and Walter Dew. Howard has Carson and Irma as well as Sandrine."

"And Clyde got stuck with Charlie and Otto and Vergil. You couldn't pay me enough."

"I'll relieve Clyde of one of those and give him to Merle."

"She'll be thrilled. Maybe whoever killed Olivia Powers either couldn't get her back into bed or didn't have the time. So the body got left in the closet. Closing the closet door, messing with the bed, and using a pipe the way this pipe was used all adds up to an amateur. A pro would do a nice clean quick job and beat it. I know one thing for sure. Whoever it was, they couldn't be seen leaving Olivia's stateroom in bloody clothes carrying a bloody pipe."

I walked into the bathroom. Leave it to Jane. She was already there sniffing a hand towel on the floor. Soon as she saw me, she yodeled, one of her best and loudest. She was telling me something. Something important. What was she telling me?

I never wished I spoke her language more than I did at that moment. I'd bet Mrs. Willingford's watch she wished it too.

I said, "They opened the porthole and threw the weapon into the sea. No one will ever find it. They threw out anything small enough with blood on it, anything they wanted rid of. Then they fastened the porthole again, wiped off any fingerprints with the hand towel, and left."

When we were on a case, and at times in bed together, I'd get that look from Mrs. Willingford, the one I was getting now. I finally knew what it meant. It meant she thought I was pretty swell.

I wish I felt the same.

One girl kills herself. She was gone forever, taken by the sea. The girl who sees her do it is killed right under my nose.

I'd been through a war. In war, when dreadful things happened, you put 'em out of your mind just to keep going. No war now. Now I went to movies about people getting shot, sapped, killed. They showed the body but they never showed the blood. You couldn't smell a movie, or look into the dim eyes that once were bright.

I didn't get used to war and I wasn't getting used to this.

So who was in charge over such things? Maritime law? Or some town along the coast? Which town? The one closest to where we were when Olivia died? Or the one closest to where we were now? Where were we when Olivia was killed? Where the hell was the coast? We'd done a lot of sailing since we got rid of Commander Jackson. Was it back to Captain Moody calling the Coast Guard again? Or was Eigil in charge here?

Probably not.

I had a feeling, for the time being, it was me. It was my case and I was on triple wages.

Jane was all over that stateroom. If there was another clue, something the killer left behind, or didn't notice they should take away, or something left for us to find meant to lead us astray, anything at all like any of those things, she'd find it. She didn't find it. What she did do though, struck me as odd. But Jane being Jane, there'd be a reason for it, a good one.

She was humming in front of the door. She wanted out. And she wanted us out with her.

"Lois. Move! Go check on Holly. If she's OK, put a guard on her. If she's not OK, find me fast. I'll be talking to Joker and our captain. Oh, and check on the fat dame too, the one who sings."

"You got it, Sam." Before she left, Mrs. Willingford kissed me. It was the kind of kiss that watered my eyes.

I said I'd be talking to Joker and Captain Moody and I would. But Jane was hell bent on her need coming first. Who could resist Jane? I followed her and wound up doing what I should of done already if Commander Jackson and a tropical storm and all those other staterooms and ladders and levels and ship's crew quarters hadn't gotten in the way.

Jane led me directly to the stateroom of Clara Louise.

Commander Jackson and his men'd already searched it. Looking for a suicide note, for a clue to her state of mind, for anything to settle the matter as soon as possible. It was as locked as Olivia's had been. But I had all those keys.

Searching for things was a big part of being a Private Eye. Going through people's private belongings, dead people, missing people, people suspected of making people missing or dead. I was getting better at it. Jane was always good at it, but not in the same way. Like Jack Spratt and his wife, we made a good team.

Talk about slobs. Clara Louise made the bum back in Room 4-C look tidy. OK, so I exaggerate. But not by much. The Coast Guard search couldn't of helped, but Clara Louise did the rest. Poor Merle. She was either paid off or got her life threatened. Either way, it was a sure bet Clara's steward never set foot inside this stateroom. Not to do any cleaning anyway.

Didn't matter. There wasn't a thing in Clara's stateroom that said she was suicidal. No notes from a lover or a husband telling her he'd found someone else. No forms from a bank stating she was about to lose whatever she owned. No blackmail for any of the usual things people want to hide: bad deeds, embarrassing connections, sordid habits, sexual escapades. No doctor's letter saying she had a month to live. Nothing but a couple of the usual letters signed Mom and the name and number of the Hudson River dock the Sip o' Sea was sailing from. It was signed: Otto. He'd added: "PS, it'll be hi-ya-lay-ya all the way to Hialeah."

My gorge rose. I shoved it back down by concentrating on horses: horses running, horses grazing, horses I'd won money on.

It was going to be hard but I needed to ask Otto, the desperate director, about his selection of a female companion. Was it really because he wanted to cast her in his latest?

No value in dragging her along for people he was trying to impress. From the brief taste I'd already got, whatever the "It" was that Clara Bow used to have, this Clara didn't have an ounce of it and never would.

The only thing left was fucking her. Which explained both of them. He got laid, a hard image to keep down. It made me question his species. She got a boat ride with a few people it might be good to impress. Otherwise, I doubt they'd ever of exchanged a word much less exchange bodily… forget it. No need to follow that thought.

Clothes were strewn about over everything, bobby pins were scattered on a vanity, powder spilled, enough make-up for the entire cast of *Gentlemen Prefer Blondes*, none of the trash made the toss into the waste paper basket, the bathroom would need a day's scrub by Merle, but there weren't a lot of empty booze bottles in the drawers or under the bed. There was no gun, no knife, no piano wire, no pipe, no vial of undetectable poison.

There was a screenplay on the night table. It wasn't Otto's ghost story. It was something with the catchy title of *Sunny of Sweetheart Farm*.

I read a few pages. If Clara was in it, she wasn't the lead. The lead was a nine year old kid with a pet goat. I couldn't tell how old the goat was. The kid and the goat were getting evicted from their farm along with the rest of the farm animals. Clara wouldn't be playing the kid's mom either. Or her dad. Both of them'd been run over by a tractor. The farm belonged to the kid's granddad who couldn't pay the back taxes… the best I could make out, any money went into feeding the old fart's bartender. I flipped through the thing. On page 78 I found notes. If Clara was in it, she was playing the mouthy girl in the feed store.

I threw the script back on her night table. If they ever got round to making that clunker, I wouldn't be seeing it, not even if Bogie played the goat.

Around about then, I opened the drawer in her bedside table. There was a bottle of tablets in plain view. I'd seen tablets like these tablets before. When Holly was hurt, and hurt bad, she was given tablets for her pain like Clara Louise's tablets. There was no doctor's name on the bottle. Clara's name wasn't on it either.

In the back of the drawer, pushed back far enough to miss a fast look, there was a small leatherette purse filled with a white powder. The powder could be this or that, but I was betting it was cocaine.

Clara Louise was a snowbird.

She said she was ill. Maybe she really was. She had uppers and she had downers. I still felt I was missing something. But what? What was here I'd missed? Or maybe I should ask myself what wasn't here I'd missed?

What I couldn't miss was Jane. She'd hopped up on the bed briefly used by Clara Louise to sleep in but who was now asleep in the deep. Jane was sitting there staring at me. Once I stopped looking through the mess and looked at her, she began talking.

How many times have I sworn I'd learn Egyptian? Too many to count. Had I learned? Nope. But if I had, I think Jane was telling me exactly what happened in this stateroom and what happened in Olivia's stateroom and what happened when Clara Louise jumped. She probably even knew why all of it happened.

But with all her humming and yodels and her black nose pointing here and there, I was none the wiser.

I was glad I couldn't read her mind. It meant I didn't have to know what my own dog thought of me.

In any case, there was no time to work out what Jane was trying to tell me. I had a report to make to Joker. It was his boat and his mess.

I'd never pitied Joker Willingford before, not even when I saw what he had for breakfast. I did now.

Closing and relocking the drowned girl's stateroom door, I did have one thought. Suicides, especially suicides with time to think about it, tidy up a bit, they get their affairs in order, they leave a note.

Clara Louise left her room like any harebrained pill popping dolly would leave it, like she'd be back any minute to make it even messier.

14

Joker Willingford sat in the wheelhouse, leaning forward on his cane, jaw grizzled, lips slack, neck sagging, but eyes and teeth as alert as Mickey Rooney's, listening to what I told him about Olivia Powers like he was listening to an episode of *Dick Tracy*. Captain Moody listened like he was hearing a guilty verdict in a federal courtroom.

In her own version of a ship captain's hat, Mrs. Willingford'd commandeered the wheel of the Sip o' Sea, Jane at her side.

Before I was done speaking, Joker whipped his head round, fast for a man his age. "Captain Moody!"

"Yes, sir."

"Are we still hugging the shore?"

"Yessir."

"Then get us the hell away from land right the hell now."

"Yessir."

"And step on it. We have to get out of here before something else happens. God forbid."

Away from shore? Away from shore was farther out into the open sea. There wasn't anything out there but eventually various bits of maybe Europe and maybe not, but wherever it was, it was one hell of a long way off.

The captain took the wheel from Mrs. Willingford, who stepped away with more good grace than I'd seen out of her in ages. That didn't feel good. It meant things were serious.

So now we were headed straight out into the Atlantic Ocean. When we'd begun this sticky conversation, I couldn't see land. I couldn't see it even more now.

Two minutes later, Joker said, "How much farther,

Captain Moody?"

Our captain glanced over at some dial or gauge or whatever it was and said, "We'll be in international waters in a few more miles."

Words to chill my heart.

We hadn't notified the Coast Guard of a second death on the ship (or, to be picky, one off and one on), we hadn't told anyone aboard but those of us who already knew: me, Mrs. Willingford, Jane, Joker Willingford, and Captain Eigil Moody. No one but those same people, plus Holly, plus Toby Tyrrell (who'd landed his mount on the Willingford filly, now grown into a mare, thanks to me and my Saratoga case), and—hopefully—minus the culprit, knew I investigated crime for a living so that made things easy for me. If I wanted things easy. Thinking about it, I didn't know what I wanted.

So far, all we'd done up in the captain's wheelhouse besides make a run for it, was have a heated discussion. Correction: after I'd said my piece, all they'd done was have a heated discussion. Jane's sharp red ears cocked this way and that way through it all.

Unless we reported the death of Miss Powers to somebody, Eigil could lose his captain's license. I could probably lose my private detective's license. The Willingford's could—I don't know, face a fine? Worse?

After a lifetime of doing the heavy lifting for Police Detective Lino Morelli, I knew a thing or two about the police and the law, which was not always the same thing though they got close now and then.

I knew not reporting a crime was a crime. Covering up, or at least not reporting a murder, was a bigger crime.

But that was only how it went on land. On water, I was at sea.

The decision, made by Mr. Willingford and seconded by Mrs. Willingford, was based on a few simple lies. Lie one: we didn't yet know Olivia Powers was down in her blood splattered stateroom crammed into her closet with her head pulped. Lie two: people knew she was missing, but with her door locked—and Mrs. Willingford's instructions to Merle the female steward to leave Olivia and her stateroom alone—the story was we'd assumed she was in shock and needed some peace and quiet after the horror of watching Clara Louise leap overboard. Lie three: we'd discover her when the time was right.

After that, I was sure my list of lies would grow much longer.

How long we'd allow Olivia to "recover" before finding her dead body, was still undecided. For Joker, things were decided by how much he had to spend on them, but for now, when the "time was right" seemed to depend on me. Could I solve the case and save the day and make it all better? In other words, could Sam Russo, Stapleton's finest, and so far as I knew only, Private Eye, basically get all innocent parties out of one hell of a jam as soon as possible?

I'd asked myself that same question more than once. Could I? Could Jane? I bet she already had. I bet she'd made me search Clara Louise's stateroom for a damn good reason. Trouble was, though I could ask her and she'd tell me, I wouldn't understand her answer.

One thing though, with Jane at my side, I wasn't alone.

Meanwhile it couldn't hurt for the Sip o' Sea to be in international waters which I'd just learned were called the High Seas. I'd always wondered about that. The High Seas. You learn something new every day.

Somewhere in all this, Joker leaned forward to pat my hand. His was dry and warm and bony. Mine was still and clammy. "Solve the case, Sam, and then we'll report it to the Miami authorities. They can get stuck with the cleanup duties." His Mickey Rooney eyes got suddenly brighter. "Or—we could just throw the body overboard out here!"

Mrs. Willingford turned away from whatever she was

doing to fix him with that hard blue stare. Jane turned too.

Joker squirmed. Who wouldn't?

"Or not. Probably not. Someone might see us."

In the end, why did Captain Moody agree to our lies? Because Joker was rich enough to make Eigil Moody rich enough to own his own boat and Joker's accountant would barely notice the dip in the Willingford bank balance. Also because, as our captain himself said, "The law is so convoluted about what happens at sea, you wouldn't believe how often *nothing* happens."

And why did I agree? Mainly because, short of jumping ship miles out into the ocean where I couldn't touch bottom without drowning to get there, I couldn't do a damn thing about it. No one was letting me near the ship-to-shore radio. I wasn't sure I'd call the cops if they did. Or the Coast Guard. What good would calling them do? I'd met Commander Jackson. If he was anything like the rest of 'em, best to clean up our own mess.

All I could really do was find the killer, a killer who in my opinion killed not once but twice. Not that I'd make book on that.

But I couldn't truthfully say I bought the suicide anymore, not with one of the witnesses murdered. On the other hand, two murders on one boat in one day? I'd say: not on your nelly, but I'd be blowing bubbles if I did. We had a sweet little problem here. And a lot of people who could of done it... whatever *it* really was.

I looked at my watch, a birthday present from Mrs. Willingford. It didn't cost fifteen bucks like I'd said to King Barton. His did, but mine cost a hundred bucks if it cost a dime. I couldn't remember how often I'd thought of pawning it, but so far, so good.

Every year, my birthday was whatever date they ran the Kentucky Derby on... and why not, since I had no idea when I'd slid into this world? If the Zawadzkis knew—and

I'm pretty sure they did since it was the first day God spoke to Mister—they never told me. My mom was a kid, a fifteen year old kid dumped off at the Staten Island Home for Children to get rid of the baby in her belly. Instead, Mister got rid of my mom. He sent her to his god to make her clean. He didn't send me because I wasn't dirty yet. I was just a baby they didn't name who got raised by the older kids.

Since I didn't have a father or a mother or even a name, I named myself. After giving myself a name any kid would think was neat, I must of been six, maybe seven, I decided I needed a birthday. What better birthday than Kentucky Derby Day? I chose the year Man o' War should of won the Derby: 1920. That year the Derby was run on the 8th of May.

This year that day was May 6th. But I never said May this or May that. I said it was the year of Citation or of Whirlaway or of Black Gold or of Zev or of Regret or of Old Rosebud.

This was the year of Middleground and Mrs. Willingford's Swiss gift said it was 8:54 in the morning of our third day at sea. By now most of the remaining Willingford guests would be heartily grazing at the breakfast buffet. None of 'em would notice if we were safely moored or lost at sea. Not one of them knew beans about ships.

I'd thought about where to start. Thinking, I came up with the opera singer and second witness to the "suicide" of Clara Louise, Miss Sandrine Brunetti.

I'd told Mrs. Willingford to guard her. That meant the crew member washing windows wasn't just washing windows.

I doubt Miss Sandretti, being Miss Sandretti, noticed him. If I were her, I wouldn't.

Pouring most of the available maple syrup on half the available waffles, Sandrine looked in fine shape. No one had bashed her head in and there'd be no leaping overboard for Miss Brunetti. First she'd have to climb up and onto the railing. Oliver Hardy would stand a better chance of making it.

Jane and I waited until she carried her haul over to a table like one you'd find in the Stork Club. We watched her sit down and dig in. Before making my move, I checked out the rest of the guests. Not one of 'em seemed as interested in our opera singer as I was.

She was lifting her second forkful of dripping waffle to her mouth when I sat down in a spare chair. Jane hopped onto a window seat and watched the both of us from there.

It took Miss Brunetti four long satisfied bites before she let me know she knew I was politely waiting. I didn't care. There was time. Besides, I was dreaming about getting one of the lifeboats or launches into the water and rowing me and Jane back home. It wasn't a complete wash of an idea. I'd never even rowed a dingy, but I'd seen it done in movies. Hell, if Gene Tierney could row a boat, Sam Russo could row a boat. I just had to do it for a lot longer. We had to be more than twelve miles out now, maybe sailing along on the Gulf Stream for all I knew. But I was still in good shape after riding my horse Magpie around Luzon for three years as we got shot at by Japs. I'd looked at the weather and water conditions. After our minor hurricane, the sea was calm. I could make it. Jane would talk me through it. All I needed was to wait until no one was looking. Good thing I packed so little and—

"Mr. Russo?"

I almost fell out of my chair. Forgot what the hell I was doing since what I was really doing was rowing like hell for dry land.

"Is zere zum reason you are zitting at my table?"

It took a second, but I remembered my answer. "I'd like you and me to have a little talk."

I'd noticed most of the Willingford guests didn't like talking to Sandrine. Some of 'em liked hearing her sing,

Joker Willingford for instance, and Walter Dew, Joker's horse trainer, but none of 'em were too fond of hearing her talk. I'd also decided her accent wasn't French. Or German. It wasn't even Kosher. Whatever the heck it was, I got her complete attention with my last remark.

"Oh? Und vhat vould you like to talk about?"

"Clara Louise, the girl who jumped off this boat."

Others might shoo me away, but not Sandrine. "Vat about her?"

"Where were you when she jumped?"

Sandrine pointed at a window, one that looked out on the deck at the back of the boat. "Right zere. I vas getting myzelf a cup of tea und lemon, zat's vere za tea und za coffee table vas at za time, und vile I vas pouring I looked up und zere she vas, at za railing."

"Before she climbed up and over?"

"Oh yes."

"Where was the other girl, the actress Olivia Powers?"

"I didn't zee her at first. She vas behind vone of zos big vite air vents, za vones zat look like tubas. But ven za blonde girl started to climb, she moved toward her."

"Miss Brunetti?"

In response, I got a dimpled smile. If she'd put her finger in one of her dimples and turned it round and round, I wouldn't be surprised. Sickened but not surprised.

"Could you cut the crap?"

"Vhat!"

"The accent. You're driving me nuts with it. It really stinks."

"How dare— ?"

"Where are you from? Tulsa? Cleveland? Slowpoke, Colorado?"

"I, you, I vas born in— "

"Stop. I'm begging you. I won't tell anyone. A girl died, a young girl killed herself and you saw her do it."

Sandrine had stopped eating. She'd almost stopped breathing. She sat staring at me and whatever I saw in her eyes, I couldn't describe. My best guess? Relief.

"You're a singer. You sing just swell. But I can't do a thing for your career. So help me out here. How close did Miss Powers get?"

"I wasn't really looking at her, Sam. May I call you Sam?"

"People often do."

"You are a very good looking man, Sam."

"Thank you."

"You're more than welcome." Along with that remark, she leaned in which made me lean in. That close, she smelled like olive oil and gardenias. And then she winked. I drank her tomato juice to settle my nerves. "I was looking at the other one. But Miss Powers wasn't too near. Not near enough to stop her if that's what you mean."

"Did Clara Louise look around?"

"Well, I only just caught the last moment or two. But no, not once while I was there. I only saw her from the back as she climbed right up, stood on the railing... "

"Stood on the railing?"

"Remarkable balance. I even thought so at the time. Almost balletic. Especially with those shoes."

"Shoes?"

"Low heels, but very stylish. Black with open toes. I also thought that's not what I would wear for a swim. I wouldn't wear a gray wool skirt and a thick wool sweater in a nice shade of gray to match the skirt either. It was very tasteful, the whole ensemble, but strictly meant for the open air, not the open sea. Then she dove."

"Not jumped? She dove?"

"She dove. A lovely dive. Graceful. One that took her as far out as I suppose she could go. But who wouldn't dive? The ship's propellers were right under her. I can understand wanting to die badly enough, not that I have ever wanted to, you have no idea how many people would grieve, and I do have a following, Sam."

"I don't doubt it."

"But I can't imagine wanting to get chopped into pieces."

She had a point there.

"And what did Olivia do?"

"She screamed. And right away you came dashing down the ladder from somewhere. You and your chewed up dog." Sandrine glanced at Jane who hadn't taken her eyes off Sandrine. "What kind of a dog is that? And oh my goodness, I've so wanted to ask, whatever happened to her?"

"It wasn't a propeller. Did you see anyone else?"

"Not a soul. Just Miss Powers and you and your dog. Not until Charlie Dick showed up, huffing and puffing. Did a lion or a tiger get her? Or was she bull whipped, the poor thing?"

"You could say that. I'll be back."

Sandrine lit up. It cracked her make-up. "You will? How divine. I'll be waiting."

"Thank you, Miss Brunetti."

"You're welcome, Sam. And it was Bozeman, Montana. I'm a rancher's daughter."

"That explains why you're here, doesn't it?"

"You bet. My daddy's got a horse running. Awful glad he's not in the same race as Fleeting Fancy."

"Good luck then."

"Oh, za horse, it vill vin."

I smiled, she smiled, and off I went, thinking about the white powder Sandrine kept in a small enameled box on her nightstand. With a tiny golden spoon nearby.

The exact same white powder I'd found in the stateroom of Clara Louise.

15

The last time I'd seen Jane, we were both headed for Gerlinger's table. Otto was being silently served by his steward, the unlucky Clyde. The movie director who'd fallen out of a tree, the German ape who'd claimed he'd spent the war in Hollywood, the knuckle dragger who didn't know much about the actress he'd brought along on the Willingford's sail to Florida and didn't much care, that was the specimen I needed to talk to now.

What I'd gotten from him so far was that Clara Louise was along for his personal ride. And that was the whole of it. But he had to be my next best bet since everyone else said they knew less. Except, maybe, for Holly. But all Holly knew was that Clara had a shine for our dashing Captain Eigil Moody. Just like Holly did. Just like Olivia Powers had.

On the Sip o' Sea, no one really knew Clara Louise. Aside from Charlie Dick, the last person I'd of thought would care about Clara Louise, no one gave a flying fig. If she'd been suicidal, my guess was stuff like that didn't help her.

On the way over to Gerlinger's table, Jane took a right hand turn when I took a left. I wasn't concerned. Mrs. Willingford was just walking in from wherever she'd gone after our dawn in the Sip o' Sea wheelhouse. I figured Jane had business with Lois.

I still called her Mrs. Willingford. I'd probably always call her Mrs. Willingford unless Joker died and she married again. And she would. The new hubby'd be some other rich old fart and then I'd call her Mrs. Some Other Rich Old Fart—no surprise if it turned out to be a Mrs. Getty or a

Mrs. Rockefeller—but Jane probably called her Lois and always would.

As alone but not as lonely as Sandrine Brunetti, Otto did not look up from his food. Otto wasn't putting away as much as Sandrine but he placed by a nose.

Asking a man questions who wouldn't look at you wasn't as easy as asking a man questions who would, but it had its good points. I didn't have to watch his eyes or his mouth for nervous tics. I didn't have to watch him chew. All I had to do was study the rough black hair that grew on his head and down the back of his neck as he scooped in a selection of everything on offer.

He had half a dozen cowlicks Brylcreemed to his bullet shaped head, then vigorously brushed in a useless effort to make them lie down. They looked as pointless and uncooperative as his career must look back in L.A.

I'd asked Mrs. Willingford why the choice of guests. She said, "It's Joker's money and Joker's yacht. I don't tell him what to do with either of them. All I do is insist he stays alive. I like him. I want him around."

Otto said, "I didn't know her. She was just another stage actress wanted to be in the movies. What a big surprise, eh? I thought: was könnte ich verlieren? She might do for some small role. Sehr klein."

I said, "Like keeping you company on a boat ride to Hialeah? And then Auf Wiedersehen?"

He said, "Gut gesagt. Exactly like that."

No pretense. No guilt. No conscience.

"Why her?"

He shrugged shoulders that sloped like something you'd ski down. "There I was, in New York City making love to a rich man who spent money on Broadway shows in case he might also spend money on a moving picture. This girl, this Clara Louise, she too was in New York City going to the Greek man's acting school just where I was wooing Mr.

Willingford's dollars. Kismet."

Kismet. A word like kismet coming out of Otto's mouth caught me a little off balance. But I steadied quickly enough. "So she let you buy her dinner and… "

"No. No dinner. I saw her after I saw Mr. Willingford. The girl, she was acting—not a big part, she did not stand out—but Mr. Willingford had told me about his boat and the sail he was making. I'd asked him if he would allow me to come along so I might speak to him about my movie. What a good surprise when he said yes, I could even bring a guest. It would amuse him, he said. I did not ask him why."

"You can see where he got his name."

"Excuse me?

"Forget it."

"When he had gone, I stayed for a bit, I watched the acting."

"You mean the actresses?"

"Yes, that is what I mean. That's when the girl somehow fell against me. I helped her up. I used my best line. I said, 'Hello good looking'. She said, 'How true'. These days, I have not been so lucky but I could tell right away I could get lucky with this girl. She was not my type… "

I couldn't stop it. A vision of his type popped into my head. I crammed it back in its box.

He shook his head. It only made him look more like a gorilla.

"I do not fool myself. Women do not hang on me, not even if I can get them into the movies. But I am a man and a man needs the woman from time to time. So with this one, I said I was going on a nice boat ride which was leaving early the next day, a Sunday. At this she smiled at me, such a sunny smile, so I opened up like, maybe you'd say: like a daisy. I told her what Mr. Joker Willingford told me about the boat and who would be on it and where we were going. She listened to all that I said, and then began the oooh, I love the ocean and the boats and how much fun we could have, and how it would be just a boat ride and I would owe her nothing. I did not know her at all, yet I heard myself asking if she would come along, be my guest. I told her I was allowed to invite a guest. She looked at me with such a shine in her eyes and I felt I had given her something of great value, which to tell the truth, felt odd because I admit that at this moment I have nothing of great value to give."

He'd raised his fork and shook it.

"But I will. I will make another movie and it will be a good movie."

I suddenly felt like I was watching Scarlett O'Hara. In any case, I couldn't think of a thing to say to that, especially since I knew who he'd made his last film for, so I said, "Sure."

Otto tried out a smile. I don't know if it hurt him, but it hurt me. "She said no time for dinner, she had to get ready for an ocean voyage. She said we could meet at the ship and then off we would sail. I was very pleased. But I will tell you a truth. If I had known how she could talk and what she would say I would have thought twice, three times, before asking her along. I got her into my stateroom as soon we entered the ship. I was thinking what a delight, to be making love before lunch, until yak yak yak. I have never been with an American girl from the south, but Himmel hilf mir, she never shut her mouth. It got very tiresome very fast. And then we did not even do the thing. She said we must wait until night."

"So you're not in mourning?"

"Mourning? I do not remember what she looked like. Sometimes this way, sometimes that. Excuse me. Steward! Steward Clyde! Would you bring me more maple syrup? You are saying it is gone? What, then, is left for the waffles? Honey? I do not like honey."

Watching Clyde run and fetch, noting the look on his face, I hung in there. "Are you surprised she jumped off the boat?"

Otto Gerlinger looked up from his food. It was the first time since we'd begun our little chat. I expected to see those recessed eyes you usually see on an apelike face with six cowlicks scraped across its bean and glued there with hair cream. But what I saw were big green eyes with thick black lashes, the kind of eyes fawns have. Or cows.

He blinked at me. "Surprised? I almost made a mess in my pants. That girl had the brain of a Wurzelgemüse. She was the last person on earth I thought would kill herself. If she'd *been* killed, I could understand that, oh yes. Before we had even passed your Grand Lady with the Lamp, I admit I'd thought of it myself more than once. You know the quotation: won't someone rid me of this meddlesome priest? I was not displeased when she did not show up in the bed for sleeping. Aside from the talking, I was too tired to mount her. The female steward came to tell me the girl wasn't feeling well."

With that, I was dismissed. And then I wasn't. Otto called me back, and back I went. You never know what people will all of a sudden remember. Like maybe that a giddy southern actress had seen what I'd seen. A medal for "service rendered" from the wrong country.

He said, "You know who you look like?"

"I'm guessing I look like me."

"You look like the actor with the hole in his chin. I am forgetting, what is his name? I know! Mitchum. You look like Robert Mitchum. Have you ever thought of getting into pictures?"

"Not once."

Then he waved me away for sure and went back to inhaling the Willingford bounty

Now for the King of Nails.

Vergil Sapster had taken a place at Walter Dew's table, easing himself between Toby Tyrell and Tommy Feather. What this meant was that Clyde was serving their table as well as my guy Gene was.

Seated between two trim finely muscled jockeys made Vergil look shorter, thinner, flimsier. It made him sound louder. It wasn't his best choice of setting.

It was more than hard to like Vergil Sapster. It was impossible.

But what if the Ohio nail maker knew something? What if Walter or even Toby or Tommy knew something? No sense not asking. No sense not trying to figure out who was lying and who wasn't.

Besides, there was one thing I'd learned and learned well. Anyone could be a killer. Movies dressed the bad guys up in scars and great haircuts. Movies let 'em chew toothpicks or crack wise. More than one movie made 'em appealing. But Cagney couldn't star in all the appealing ones, so most movies had to settle for watchable.

Off the big screen, out here where I lived with things that stank and things that bit and things that bled and nothing faded in or faded out or came to The End, truth was a killer with no distinguishing features.

Vergil had a lot to say about Clara Louise, a lot to say about doxies killing themselves when people were trying to have a good time, a lot to say about goodbye and good riddance and oh boohoo.

Virgil's heart was obviously as small and hard as the rest of him.

He also had a lot to say about Joker's damn boat and him being a schmuck for coming along and missing the Yankees and Dimaggio. "How much longer we gonna get to see Dimaggio? A year? Two years? What if this is his last ever year? What if he's gone before I get back from fucking Florida? What if I'm missing some of the best games of his career? What if he has another one of those hitting streaks? I could be missing the best of Joe!"

Vergil was a guy with a lot to say. By the time he finished saying it, not only Toby, Tommy and Walt but most definitely me wished Vergil Sapster would do what Clara Louise did: take a flying leap off the rear end of the Sip o' Sea.

But he did say one thing that made me wonder. He said he saw Clara Louise the morning she jumped. Hours before, so he'd figured it didn't count as witnessing anything.

"What a dame does, how important is that?"

I said, "Rather hammer a dame than a nail."

Big mistake. I got a laugh from the jocks.

Vergil's bow mouth stopped and his pointed jaw clenched. Normally what a relief that was. But this was not normally. I backpedaled.

"Let me rephrase that, Verge. Nails. Can't live without 'em. So you saw her. Doing what?"

I still got punished. He gave me another minute of silence. No one was laughing anymore. What Walt and Toby and Tyrell were doing was leaning forward, elbows on the table, cooling coffee cups up to their mouths, waiting as eagerly as I was for him to say more about the "dame."

"All right. Then I'll tell ya, buddy, because I'm the kind of man who helps when he's asked to. I just happened to be passing her stateroom, right? And her door opened. Well, most folks look in open doors. It's natural, right? We all do it."

This time I was quick out of the gate. "Of course. Who doesn't?"

"So what do you think I saw?"

Toby couldn't help himself. "What? What did you see?"

Vergil answered Toby but he stared at me. "I saw her coming out in more clothes than she usually wore and they were different clothes and what do you think she was carrying?"

All four of us shook our heads. How the hell would we know what she was carrying? A cake with a bunch of lit candles? Roller skates? The Liberty Bell?

"She was carrying a canvas duffel bag. You know, like for a soldier or a sailor or a marine? Not that big, though. Maybe half that size. There was something in it."

I was now leaning as far forward as the Willingford's trainer, their jockey, and the other jockey who was maybe just hitching a ride, one he regretted. I said, "You know what that something was?"

"You're askin' me, buddy? The bag was closed. But I knew there was something in it because it looked like there was something in it."

Fine. Now what did I know? I knew that silly giddy gushy Clara Louise didn't seem the type to own a canvas duffel bag. I knew everyone thought she'd slept in that morning, but everyone was wrong.

"Did she see you?"

"If she did, I didn't get a morning kiss."

"Where did she go with it?"

"I should know? I don't follow dames around, buddy. Besides I was hungry. I'd been on my way to breakfast and I was still on my way to breakfast."

With that, the skinny little man stood up which didn't get him far, and walked away. Watching him go, I thought about the gun I'd found in his shaving kit.

Walt said, "They say nice guys finish last. I'd buy a win ticket on that one."

Time to go looking for Jane. I found Mrs. Willingford who was also looking for Jane.

I said, "When's the last time you saw her?"

"Just before you took breakfast tea with Otto and the boys. She was headed down to the staterooms."

"Let's go see her. I need her advice."

Mrs. Willingford didn't bat an eyelash at that.

An hour later, halfway through looking everywhere, my

heart was racing. Five minutes past halfway through looking, if I was going to have a heart attack, I was having it on the Sip o' Sea.

At some point, Mrs. Willingford gripped my hand. Hers was as clammy as mine. She looked at me with eyes that were terrified. I knew I was looking back with those same eyes.

Like Olivia Powers, Jane was gone.

16

I knew it. I felt it. My dog'd had her head bashed in like that poor unhappy kid Olivia Powers, or she'd been thrown overboard and was now as far down under the cold green waters as Clara Louise.

So where was Sam Russo? Sam Russo was soaked in a half pint of expensive hootch and sprawled all over Holly's bed in Holly's stateroom. I didn't know where Mrs. Willingford'd taken herself off to, and for once since I met her, I didn't much care. Russo was more than feeling sorry for himself. He was as lost as Jane was and where he'd gone didn't feel like it had a way back.

How many times have I blabbed on about doubting myself? A better question would go like this: when in hell did I ever believe in myself? Me, a Private Investigator? A sleuth? A war veteran? A kid who'd survived growing up in Missus and Mister Zawadzki's Chamber of Childhood Horrors? The kid who thought he'd survived playing tag on his mother's unmarked dead-of-the-night-dug shallow grave?

Sam Russo was a grown man who went to the movies more than a grown man should, a guy who believed that the people he saw up on the silver screen were real, a guy who could barely afford a cheap one room walk-up in a cheap one horse town five miles across the water from the big city, the real city, the greatest city, one he could take a ferry to, but couldn't live in. Sam Russo was a guy who couldn't even keep a dog alive.

If someone'd killed Jane, if they'd gotten close enough to throw her overboard, it was because she was ten times the detective I was. If she was dead it was because she'd found the killer while I was sitting around white-clothed tables with napkins shaped like swans and rosebuds in silver bud vases asking the wrong people the wrong questions.

If Jane was dead, I didn't want to be Sam Russo anymore.

I was lifting up the bottle, getting all set to swallow the rest of it when Holly knocked it out of my hands.

"Hey!"

"You're lucky it was me and not Lois. She'd have loosened a few of your teeth."

"Leave me alone."

"Leave yourself alone."

"I'm serious, Holly. I'm finished."

"You think I'm not serious? As for finished, you're not done until Jane says you are."

"She's gone."

"Says who?"

"Me and Mrs. W, we've looked everywhere."

"If you'd looked everywhere, you'd have found her. Even if she was dead, you'd have found her."

"You're forgetting where we are. Sitting on a lot of sea."

"I haven't forgotten where we are. Stop sniveling, stop drinking, and get the hell up. You're wasting precious time. Lois told me about Olivia— "

"She told you?"

"Of course. Lois and I are like this." Holly crossed her eyes. "You're searching the engine room."

"G'way. We already searched the engine room."

"Not like this, you didn't."

I was kicked off the bed and into the bathroom. Holly was a woman, but there was still a man in there somewhere. She could kick.

Giving my teeth a quick brush, I thought about it.

The Sip o' Sea's engine room was not only huge, it was

a complex mess. There was a great big green enamel engine
with great big black pistons pumping away down there.
There were pipes and hoses running along the metal decks,
the metal bulkheads, the metal ceiling. There were wires and
gauges and railings and walkways and an assortment of what
I was sure were handles and hinges. There were things I'd
never seen before and wasn't all that eager to see again. I had
no idea what they did. There were compartments for every
spare part or obscure tool a ship like the Willingford yacht
could ever require. And there was noise. Up above, the Sip
o' Sea was as quiet as a small town library, but down below
it was as loud as a New York City midtown deli. And that
meant it made one hell of a racket.

Holly was right. First time round Mrs. Willingford and
I'd run through the ship's engine room like it was a warehouse
stacked with every kind of nail, brad, tack and spike Sapster
ever made. You couldn't look at 'em all.

I wasn't exactly sober and I sure wasn't clean, but Holly'd
made sure I was going through that engine room again, and
this time like locusts through the Good Earth of China.

Mrs. Willingford was sober, clean, and back in one of her
sneaking around outfits, the kind I'd come to love. And fear.
Wise choice since an engine room was more than a match
for what she usually wore slinking around the Sip o' Sea.

I was in the same clothes I'd been in since whenever I'd
put them on. They didn't murmur money then and they
weren't smelling like money now.

Down we went, two rungs at a time.

Was the guy working the place the same guy when we
first came through? I guessed he was since he was doing what
that guy'd been doin' in a ship's engine room. Which meant
sweet fuck all to me. He wore the same dark blue coveralls
smeared with the same dark brown grease, had the same
long sideburns, the same thick curly hair, and the same black

mustache. I didn't know and I didn't care. I was opening every locker, climbing behind every pipe, all the while yelling my head off. If Jane was down here, I'd find her.

The ship's engineer looked like William Bendix. Burly, bent nosed, and with a jaw like an entire ham, he had no time for me, but for Mrs. Joker Willingford, he opened whatever she asked him to open, climbed into whatever she asked him to climb into or behind or between.

I caught his name. Alki Kormos.

Alki Kormos wasn't as small as Toby Tyrrell or Tommy Feather. He wasn't as thin as Vergil Sapster or as big as Sandrine. No one was as hairy as Otto Gerlinger, not even Jane. And he sure wasn't as affable as his double, Bendix, but Alki fit everywhere he had to.

Alki showed us the deck plates. The deck down here was steel and the steel was bumpy. The metallic nodules meant a better grip if something spilled or if water got in. How water could get in was an idea I put out of my mind as soon as he mentioned it.

Jane wasn't under a deck plate. She wasn't behind a pipe. She wasn't in a tool locker.

While Alki climbed, I called. Jane was an Egyptian. She didn't bark, she hummed or she yodeled. She could be close, she could be humming like crazy, and I maybe couldn't hear her with the engine roaring away like it was.

But she could make noise. There were those toe nails. Maybe she could scratch and I could hear that. So I called her name until I was hoarse. I called until Alki just stopped and shook his big head. There was nowhere else to look.

And when that happened, I sat down hard on a rung of the engine room ladder and I cried. I cried in front of Mrs. Willingford and I cried in front of some lug who looked like Bill Bendix.

Mrs. Willingford had turned her face away, but before she did, I saw she was crying too.

Holly and I ate lunch together. We weren't in her stateroom or in mine. We ate it in the dining room with everyone else but the Willingfords.

Lunch was a forkful of Lobster Newburg I fought to keep down. Holly's was two forkfuls. We sat across our white linen covered table and stared at each other over our single white candle and single white rose.

Gene moved around me with the quiet grace of an English butler. He was feeling better. He'd stopped limping. He murmured his questions, nodded at my short replies, didn't clink the china or clank the silverware. Merle served Holly. Holly's Merle wasn't as composed as my Gene. She'd been hired to care for three young women. One was dead. One was locked in her stateroom.

Merle'd tidied Olivia's stateroom, put away her clothes, made her bed. She must know about the pills. It crossed my dulled mind—did Merle wonder if Olivia'd taken just enough of those pills? Or did she wonder if she'd taken too many?

Merle was down to one young woman, my friend Holly.

The girl who lived in the room next to mine back in Stapleton sat as silent as an old movie. Dressed by Lois, her hair grown long enough to curve round her face, her makeup perfect, she held her lovely head upright and still.

Her brown eyes glittered with unshed tears.

I was a man. I wasn't supposed to cry. It helped I already had down in the engine room.

Life without Jane? I couldn't bear it. Jane was my dog. I was Jane's person. Holly couldn't bear it either. Jane was her friend.

I felt the grief changing me. Staring at Holly, born a woman in a man's body, someone who'd sold herself in Tompkinsville Park to pay the rent, I felt the change flow like blood flowed through veins. I was looking at a girl who'd been snatched off the street by monsters, a girl beaten so badly what was left was like a bloody sack filled with shattered bones. But here she was now, sailing on a rich man's yacht: alive, vital, resilient—but close to broken by the death of a dog. Just a dog.

I met Jane when her man was murdered. She'd sat for hours over her jockey's dead body. To get her away took a lot of time and a lot of human cunning. We disliked each other on sight. Jane was a one-man dog and I wasn't that man. I was a no-dog man. But we got stuck with each other anyway, and that got her stabbed, not just once but eleven times. That she didn't die wasn't my doing. It was thanks to a friend of mine, a real friend, a guy who was a great vet. Because she got stuck with me, she was shot twice. Or was it three times? Three times was me. Fuck. I was beginning to forget things.

Somebody said looking at her was like looking at something mauled by 'gators.

Jane had stayed vital, resilient, unbroken. But now she was dead. Because she'd met me.

In the dining room of the Sip o' Sea, I went from grief straight to rage. I wasn't a hard guy. I wasn't a cynical guy. I wasn't a lot of things that made for a good cop and a better Private Eye. I was one of those powder puff guys that took Mrs. Willingford five minutes, maybe less, to spot. Lucky for me, most people weren't Mrs. Willingford. Most people buy a guy's act—like I bought Bogart's.

I wasn't that guy anymore.

Someone killed a poor kid called Olivia. Maybe the same someone killed Clara Louise. And then killed Jane—because Jane would know the killer from smell alone.

Sam Russo was finding that someone and when he did—

"There's that guy who's following me around," said Holly. "See him? He's pretending to fix a light or something."

I looked. "Don't mind him. He's just keeping an eye on you."

"Keeping an eye... oh, you mean!" Holly covered her mouth. "You mean I might get killed too?"

"Never pays to be sloppy. Three actresses on board. Only one left and that one's my friend. He's a Willingford guy. If I'm not around, don't let him lose sight of you."

And then I had an idea.

I stood up so abruptly the rose in our vase flew at Holly who ducked. The slender crystal vase itself was launched off our table and smashed on the hardwood deck.

Gene appeared from nowhere to clean it up and disappeared back into nowhere.

Holly'd caught the rose. "Thank you, Sam."

I gave her what was left of my smiles. "You know I love you."

"Yes," she said, "I know."

17

The first time I searched Olivia Powers' stateroom, I did it with Jane and Mrs. Willingford. The second time it was just me and Holly since Holly's idea of staying safe was sticking with me.

I tried, but I couldn't argue her out of it.

Olivia was still in the closet. Holly took one look, gagged on the rank and rotten air touched with that sweet tinge dead bodies give off like cheap perfume, and went off to search the bathroom.

She was back in a minute or two to slather a gob of Vaseline under my nose. Her nose was already clogged with the stuff, a pale yellow moustache of it. On her it looked good.

She said, "Gee, what a sad loss. She was awfully good. All I wanted was to be half as good as her. She was also a sweet kid. Wait 'til the press hears." Then she was back off to the bathroom again, opening the porthole.

"You think the killer could have gotten through here, Sam? In? Out? In *and* out?"

I had the same porthole. All the staterooms did. I didn't look up but I did answer.

"Only if the bad guy was Tom Thumb."

I went to work. This time I'd pull up the carpets if I had to, cut open the mattress, strip the wallpaper.

What I finally found, I found in a suitcase. The suitcase was in Olivia's closet along with Olivia. I had to move her body to get to it.

You know a guy like my good old boyhood friend Lino Morelli, you get to meet more than a few dead bodies. In my own cases, I'd met a few more. Once life left someone, it wasn't fooling around, it left. What remained was a carcass. Rotting meat and maggots.

It was like that oddball writer dame Gertrude Stein said about roses. A body is a body is a body is a body.

Who knew? Maybe somewhere down the road, Miss Powers' death might get investigated by some actual authorities. She might even get decently buried. But I had to get to a suitcase, one I hadn't searched that was stuck under her fish-cold legs.

I almost fell on my back pulling. When it came, it came with a rush. Holly would of laughed if there was anything funny about it.

Inside I found the script of a play. It wasn't the same script I'd found in Clara Louise's stateroom. It wasn't even close. There wasn't a goat in it.

I was flipping pages when Holly plopped down beside me. "Say! That's Mr. Kazan's new play. Gosh, I wonder if he knows Olivia took a copy? He's real strict about that."

"Have you read it?"

"Sure. At the school, we all did. It's some play. We all wanted the lead. But Mr. Kazan chose Olivia."

Then she was up and off again, still searching.

Not everything I'd ever read cost a dime and not all of it was a murder mystery. The Christmas before this last one, Holly gave me a brand new book as big as the Manhattan telephone directory called *Raintree County*. The guy who wrote it killed himself right after it came out. Why he'd do that beat the hell out of me. He had a wife, some kids, the book was selling. Some people don't know when they have it good.

Because it was a gift from Holly, I read every word. I liked it.

This Christmas she gave me two books: *The Day of the Locust* and *Miss Lonelyhearts*. I liked those two more. I liked 'em enough to let 'em take up some of my precious mantel space.

The guy who wrote the locust book and the lonely book smashed himself up in a car and took his wife with him.

What was it with writers?

I'd also seen *Harvey* on Broadway. I'd seen as much of *Harvey* as the actors had.

Point being, for a guy who never spent a day in a real school with someone who knew how to teach, or what to teach, I knew a thing or two about good writing and a thing or two about what went into a play. I guess it came from reading. No one taught me to read. I did that. Even when books were hard to come by at the Poor Orphan's Drop-off, I found 'em at the Stapleton library. I was one of those kids who lived in a book… if I wasn't hanging by my fingertips off Mister's shed with Lino and Paul listening to Mister's radio.

That was why I knew the script about the goat wasn't going to see a curtain rise or fall unless its writer owned the theater—but the script in Olivia's suitcase was.

I looked at the title page. *Dead on the Rocks*. It was written by some dame I'd never heard of, but the guy Holly'd just mentioned, Mr. Kazan, was the same guy Olivia'd been writing that letter to.

I'd say, lead part or no lead part, he was making Olivia Power's life miserable.

A few of her lines remained in my head.

The last time I saw you… you thought I was asleep. I wasn't asleep.

Elia Kazan must be some humdinger of an acting teacher.

The play wasn't my kind of thing, but right out of the gate I was hooked. The lead was a young woman which right there was unusual. Eve wasn't a wife or a girlfriend or a prostitute or someone's mad sister. There was no lonely guy in a cheap suit spitting out short sharp lines, no gats, guts or girls-for-rent. It was set in the depths of the Depression and Eve was not only struggling to save her father's crummy little pre-war business, she was out to catch his killer. A kid collecting rocks had found the old man on the beach at Far Rockaway, shot once right behind his left ear.

That part wasn't shown on the stage, it was just talked about a lot.

From almost the first scene, I got that the whole play was one long gritty gripe about social injustice.

So maybe it didn't sound like a fun night out but right away the girl on the page was in your face. Eve was someone. Stanwyck would knock her out of the ballpark. There was also a new kid I'd caught in a movie called *Crossfire*. Gloria Grahame had something worth watching. She could play the part.

Could Olivia Powers? Who'd ever know? She never got the chance.

Under the script I found a little leather bound journal. That went right into my pocket for later.

I found something else. Olivia, the serious movie star, was a reader. Not the same stuff I'd read, but a reader. I'd missed it the first time, how I couldn't say, but the book by the side of her bed was called *Hollywood King*. The dust jacket had a terrific photo of Barton on it. I flipped through. It was a lightweight biography of King Barton which stood to reason since he was a lightweight actor. Holding her place was half a matchbook, the half without the matches. I looked at the page number. She'd gotten about two thirds through.

I looked over at her couch. Yep. There it was, the box full of old newspaper clippings and old movie magazines, the ones with King Barton's kisser all over their covers.

The number of things I'd call odd on the Sip o' Sea were beginning to get past my math skills.

The matchbook marking her place had come from the Carnegie Bar.

Jane and I once spent a day at the Carnegie Bar with two guys supposed to be studying acting across the street at the American Academy of Dramatic Arts under Carnegie Hall. My pals Jason and Don were studying the art of sitting on barstools for as long as possible without falling off.

Jane got me back to our hotel.

That was when we were looking for who the giant was washed up under a pier in downtown Stapleton, a giant missing one entire hand and wearing half a pair of torn black tights.

Thinking about Jane made me feel like the title of the script under a dead girl's dead legs—dead on the rocks.

I left the script where it was, but I took Olivia' journal, the King Barton biography and the bookmark.

I didn't know why, I just did.

Holly tried hard, turned the place upside down. But she didn't find anything.

One of the things she didn't find got me to thinking. It got me to thinking hard.

18

The world I knew, places like Stapleton, Manhattan, Saratoga Springs, Monmouth Park, Bayonne, Belmont Park, my one room on the fourth floor over a Rexall drugstore, even the Gothic brick pile I grew up in, were starting to fade like memories I couldn't remember.

My home was a ship and a lot of blue water.

How long before we ran out of food? Before the fresh water was gone? Before we became another Mary Celeste?

I was in my own stateroom reading Olivia's journal aloud to Holly. Holly was listening. She was also washing her hair in my sink instead of hers.

Olivia Powers wrote in a small neat hand. She was tidy, she was controlled, she was unhappy.

I learned what she thought of Hollywood (so far, not much), what getting accepted into the Actors Studio meant to her (a lot), that her fellow female students weren't happy she'd walked in and was right away given the part of Eve over serious, long suffering kids who'd die to be the star of two movies, much less get chosen by Elia for his next production. One of 'em, she wrote, was "... so angry it was like a fever."

Olivia Powers had been young, talented, and determined to be the best she could be. Thinking of her now, dead in a closet, her body uncared for and unreported, made me almost as ill as thinking about Jane.

That great married lover and towering genius Elia Kazan—what did I know, maybe he was a genius—was *this* close to also casting her as Eve in the movie he was planning if the play went well. Starring in his movie could make her more than a light weight. It could make her a serious contender, a new Ingrid Bergman.

Holly plopped down on the couch beside me, drying her hair. "Poor dear Olivia. I was in most of her classes. When that play came along, we all wanted the part of Eve. But Olivia got it. I mean she deserved it. Of us all, she really was the bee's knees."

"But who was sick about it?"

"Hell if I know. Everyone scared me. They'd all gone to acting schools or dancing schools or some sort of school, most for years. I have to admit, Sammy, I feel like a fraud when I'm there with them all. And anyway, some people are always jealous of someone else's talent, or plain old good fortune. You should have seen the working girls at Tompkinsville Park. Talk about snitty when a fatcat john showed up and chose only one. Cat fight? No kiddin'."

Olivia's journal mentioned Holly.

"Oooh. What does she say? No, don't tell me. I'll be sad. No, please, tell me. No don't."

I read the passage.

"Today Elia chose my understudy. She's not as new here as I am, but she's new enough. Holly Shauer is simply charming. And so much promise. Marlon is very impressed and when Marlon is impressed, we all sit up. Over time, I hope Holly and I become friends. I sense a kindred spirit."

I looked up. Holly had crumpled into herself, silently weeping. "Poor Olivia. Poor darling Olivia."

I sat and held her. I rubbed her damp hair with the Sip o' Sea's fat monogrammed towel. No one I ever knew had a softer heart than my friend Holly.

The last two pages of Olivia's journal explained why she was "stuck on a boat with a load of jerks."

Just like Clara Louise, Miss Olivia Powers wasn't invited by the Willingfords. Clara said yes to Otto Gerlinger's expectations. Olivia said yes to King Barton's.

"I'm telling King today," she'd written. "I'm telling the creep in front of everyone he killed my mother."

Sam Russo, Private Eye, was more than surprised, he was dumbfounded. That twist never occurred to me. Not even when I saw them standing side by side... and I had seen them standing side by side plenty before Clara Louise did her high dive and turned the boat on its head.

It was Holly who spotted the letter in the King Barton book. It was an old letter, fragile and faded, dated November 17, 1939. That was the year the heavy favorite, Johnstown, won the Kentucky Derby. He also won the Belmont Stakes but that summer the track had come up muddy in the Preakness over at Pimlico. Johnston didn't like an off track so Challedon took that one. But Johnston was the better horse.

Holly whipped the letter out of the book before I could read more than the date.

"It's not a letter, Sam," she said, reading the whole thing like she'd swallow an oyster.

"What is it then?"

"It's a suicide note."

"What?"

"It's a suicide note."

"Will you fucking give me that piece of paper?"

"No need to be rude, Mr. Russo."

"Will you fucking please fucking give it to me?"

"That's much better. Here."

I tore it. Not badly, but enough to make me give Holly one of my Mitchum looks.

I read the letter. Out loud.

November 17, 1939

King,

You said you loved me. You lied. You never loved me. We exchanged vows. I meant my vows, but you didn't mean yours. They were just words to you. You said you'd come back. You didn't come back. You said you'd tell the world the baby was yours. You never told anyone. You said you'd support me and our little girl. We never saw a penny and you had so many pennies. When the drinking got bad and I needed help, I swallowed my pride and I came to you. You said you'd get me help. You lied. I should have expected that. It was a long time since I'd been seventeen and thought you had wings. But I didn't expect it. I was a fool. They took our little girl from me. No one ever told me where they took her to. They just showed up one day with some papers that called me an unfit mother and they took my Olivia. She cried. She kicked them. She called for her mommy. She didn't call for her daddy because she didn't know her daddy's name. They took her anyway. They said it was for her own good. I don't have anything left. If you get this letter, you won't care. I hear you're drinking now too. I saw your last picture. I'll be kinder to you than you've been to me and not say anything more about it. I hope your drinking kills you like you killed me.

Love, Gracie Powers Barton

Holly and I stared at each other. She spoke first. "Olivia was the daughter of King Barton. How awful for her."

I said, "Yes to all that."

"Guess you'll be talking to King Barton."

"Guess I will."

"Can I be there?"

"Can you keep your yap shut?"

"I can do anything. You know that."

"I do."

"Good. I'll be right back. I need to choose the right ensemble and the right sunglasses. I need to fix my hair. And so, Sammy dear, do you."

19

The last time I saw Barton he was rolled up in a rug behind the Grand Salon bar. The tropical storm was pitching us all over the place but I don't suppose he noticed.

Then again, drunks are sneaky. Frank Fay got Barbara Stanwyck to marry him. How, I'll never know, but that's beside the point. He also managed to star in *Harvey* playing Elwood P. Dowd, a sweet harmless drunk. Frank Fay was a real life first class useless slub of a drunk.

Actors. You never knew who they really are.

Don't assume a thing, Russo. Olivia was killed during the storm. You know where she was at the time. She was in her own stateroom. You only think you know where King Barton was. He might not of been rolled up in his rug. As a matter of fact, you have no idea where any of the Willingford guests were—except Miss Powers.

I imagined Barton throwing Jane off the boat. Jane could do just about anything, but living through a fall into bottomless blue water probably wasn't one of them. I saw her gone in the tossing waves as easily as Clara Louise was gone.

I got rid of that image faster than Barton must of been to catch Jane off her guard... if he had.

But if King Barton killed my dog and if King Barton killed his own kid, the one he'd ignored all her life, what did that have to do with Clara? As I've already said, I had a lot of trouble with a suicide and a murder and a missing Basenji all on one boat in a matter of a couple of days.

What the hell was going on here?

King Barton was sober. He was groomed. He was sitting on one of the gleaming sun-soaked decks with all the deck chairs. He wasn't alone. Mr. & Mrs. Morton-Kline, the movie writing duo, were with him, one either side. They were sober too. It was one of those sobering days.

As far as I knew they knew, from here on in it was all plain sailing right down to Miami. Clara Louise was chalked up to a strange sad suicide. Olivia Powers was shocked and locked in her stateroom. Jane could be anywhere. We were far out to sea—but how far, how should they know?

Holly, in cuffed pink shorts, a short pink matching top, dangerous shoes, a white sailor's cap slanted to the left, and a pair of dark sunglasses with bright pink frames, flounced down on the closest deck chair. Where she got those long slender legs I never understood. They weren't a gift from Dr. Bloomberg.

Bringing up the rear, in rumpled gray slacks, a rumpled white open-necked shirt, and no hat, was me. I didn't have a grip on much, but my shoes did. I stood behind the chair Holly chose. I bet she could smell me. I bet they all could. I bet under the stink of old booze I smelled like pain.

King stared at Holly with red-rimmed hungry eyes. I stared at King. What my eyes looked like after a night of no sleep, discovering a dead body, crying over Jane, and a drink too many too early, I had no idea. And fuck if it mattered.

As for what Irma Morton and Carson Kline heard or saw, I'd get to them when I got to them. They wrote clever movies, funny movies, one-of-a-kind movies. I imagine they were well paid for their work. But if they had a sideline, one that had something to do with the circus currently going on aboard the Sip o' Sea, I'd weasel it out of 'em one way or another. Sam Russo was in no mood to take prisoners.

Right now it was all about King Barton.

I started off with a bang. Might as well get his undivided attention and get it immediately.

Leaning over to stub out a butt, I said, "For a man who never cared one way or another about his own daughter, why ask her along on a sail?"

King's eyes almost crossed. "Excuse me?"

"You also drove her mother to kill herself. Or didn't you get your wife's suicide note?"

King was trying to rise. Even sober, he was unsteady, but his voice worked well enough. Only thing wrong with it was the squeak. Sandrine Brunetti could probably identify the note. "How dare you speak to me like this! Who are you?"

"Sit the fuck down."

King sat down. People didn't usually do what I told them to. Maybe I was getting better at this PI job.

King slid his eyes around to see how Irma and Carson were doing; was I going over as big with them as I was with him? Catching the ear of two of Hollywood's hottest writers… what could be meatier to an actor off his feed? So, from his point of view, me showing up had to be about the worse thing on the Willingford yacht he'd so far sailed through.

I was going to make it worse. I was going to do it for Olivia and for Gracie Powers Barton. If I was also doing it for Jane, things were going to turn into Barton's own personal Snake Pit, courtesy of Sam Russo, alumni of the Zawadzki Turreted Tower for Tormented Tots.

Holly was watching with as much interest as Carson and Irma were. Those two had no idea who I was, but Holly was my biggest fan. She thought I'd saved her life a year or so back. I didn't. Mrs. Willingford did. And so did Joker Willingford since Joker paid the bills. But Mickey Cates, Sweet Davy Malloy and me, we avenged it with the help of the Irish mob.

If I could feel good, I'd feel good about that.

Back to King Barton. Barton was the smart guy who once turned down a role in a movie when he was enjoying his moment on top of the world, a role that the young Clark Gable accepted. Barton thought the movie stunk then and he still thought it stunk, especially with Gable in it—or so he announced to one and all our first night out on the Sip o' Sea.

Nicolas was fussing over King, setting down his plate just so, pouring him wine to the brim of a huge wine glass. After spilling King's drink without getting a drop on the king but soaking his own pants, Nicolas was taking no chances.

Gene was around to tend to me. I caught Gene's eye and he caught mine. Obvious we both thought Barton was a punk.

King Barton was trying to ignore us both and doing a bad job of it.

I yanked out the last chair, flipped it around and straddled it backward. Lighting another Lucky like Bogie would light a Lucky, one hand cupping the flame from the wind, I said, "Where were you during the storm?"

"What storm?"

Shit. He was good or he was no more than the drunk he looked like. I shifted gears. "Why'd you invite Olivia Powers on this trip?"

"Miss Powers? You mean the young actress? The one who saw the other one jump?"

"That's the one."

"Well, I, uh, well, you know how it is, a young woman like that."

"A young woman like what?"

"Good looking. Young. Good looking."

"And young. Are you saying you didn't know she was your daughter?"

This time King found his feet and his voice. "My what! My daughter? Where the hell did you get that idea? I don't have a daughter. I've never had a daughter. Or a son for that matter."

Holly said, low and throaty, "How do you know?"

King opened his mouth to answer, then shut it. We could all tell he was thinking. Or trying to.

Irma Morton, sixty if she was a day, blinked twenty year old eyes in a fifty year old face. "Carson," she said, "do you smell a subplot here?"

Carson Kline, a man I hadn't pinned down except to say he used his hands like a butterfly used its wings, said, "I was just going to ask you the same thing."

King Barton was digging deep, looking for what once made him a star. He looked at me, but he was speaking to anyone within shouting distance. "If I ever see or hear anything about daughters or sons or me killing anyone's mother again, Mr. Russo, I will use what remains of my personal resources to ensure the source of that slander will rue the day he, or she, was ever brought forth on this earth."

I had to give it to him. He timed it well. Before his last word faded, he strode away, his back perfectly straight, his head held high.

"Applause applause," said Holly.

Irma looked at Carson and Carson looked at Irma. Carson said, "Have we just heard our title?"

Irma said, "We have. We've sold the script already. All we have to do now is write it."

Holly looked at me and I looked at Holly. Did the cold blooded Mr. & Mrs. Morton-Kline have anything to do with any of this?

If so, how or what or why beat the hell out of me. Except to create a set of bizarre circumstances where they could both sit back and watch all the reactions and then write a movie about them.

A lot of trouble and a lot of risk for another movie. But artists were wild cards in a deck with too many cards. Wild enough to keep a gun under their pillow.

I'd found the third gun in their stateroom, but under whose pillow, Carson's or Irma's, only Irma or Carson could say.

A much more important question, one I'd keep asking until I knew was: what happened to Jane?

20

Jane was as close to a human being as anyone I knew.

The thing that set her apart, made her better than most if I was honest, was that she wasn't afraid. Jane was full of life. She didn't fear living and she didn't fear dying.

Jane wasn't a whiner.

Some people would say that was because she was just a dog. They'd say animals didn't think and they didn't feel. That they did what they did by instinct alone, like they were some sort of machine, and if they were good for anything, it was for what use they could be to us.

I'd heard that so often during the war when our horses were shot out from under us, I wanted to shoot the guys on our side.

Most people were fools. No wonder Jane had no time for them.

Sam Russo was afraid. But he was more afraid of dying than of death. It might last too long. It might hurt. Long lived pain humbled a man.

In the war where guys were buying it all around me, I'd be standing over a fresh corpse trying to imagine it was me down there on the bloody dirt of Luzon, curled up and broken. But all that happened was me looking at my own dead body while I lit a Lucky and smoked.

Death for the dead was just death. It was an ending, a final curtain with no curtain call.

It was the living who really bought it. The ones left behind.

Which is why I did all I could not to think about Jane

being dead—and what could be better than the radio star, funny man Charlie Dick. Charlie turned my stomach, made my hands itch and my nose twitch. If there was any man I'd ever wanted to throttle more than him I hadn't met that guy yet.

Leaving Holly to be trailed by Mrs. Willingford's man, I found Dick where I'd expect to find him, at the bar in the Grand Salon serving himself. Who knew where Leonard the bartender was. As for Clyde, Dick's steward, he was either cleaning Charlie's stateroom or taking a break in his bunk. If so, Merle was probably taking it with him.

King was a drunk, Dick was a drinker. Dick was drinking alone and waiting. People like Charlie Dick were always either waiting for an audience or playing to an audience. That's what other people were for… drums for him to bang on.

I saw he didn't know who I was, didn't remember my face, wouldn't know I wasn't going to laugh. As soon as I came into focus, his empty face filled up with dirty jokes. Old material, new material, it didn't matter. Here was someone to sell them to.

I took three minutes of the Charlie Dick Show.

"OK," I said, "time to wrap it up."

He didn't hear me.

"So the bald guy walks up to this door, he's got this old key, right? and he says— "

I shouted. "Dick!"

That made his left eye blink, twice, but it didn't stop him. I let him finish his joke.

He had one brown eye and one gray eye, both bloodshot. His nose was bent, not at the bottom like bent noses usually were, but at the top. His teeth were perfect. I don't know where he got 'em, but they didn't grow there themselves. He was wearing a tie on a ship. On the orange tie were black cats. There was a sunflower in his jacket lapel. If it squirted water, I was ready to duck.

I decided to punch him. Not hard, not somewhere that mattered. I chose, for what passed, I think, as his bicep. It didn't shut him up but it changed his tune.

"Say! Why'd you do that?"

"No knobs. Only way I could think to turn you off."

He got it. He liked it. I could see him working out how to use it. I got in quick before he did.

"Why'd you say you liked Clara Louise, a girl you didn't know?"

"Who?"

I expected that from Charlie Dick so I had a ready answer. "The young actress who jumped ship, the girl lost at sea."

He remembered her now. I saw it in his gray eye. Someone jumping off the rear end of a boat the great Comic was also on got stored in his brain somewhere. Not in the compartment marked "jokes" which must of been huge, but some small place reserved for other people.

He said, "She was a cute kid. Not all that smart, true. Actually a solid ditz and how she was going to make it in the business beats me, especially with that cracker accent, but she knew how to laugh. It's sad to see people like that go, someone who laughed on the outside but cried on the inside."

I took a second look at the guy. He still made me sick, but maybe I was being too harsh. So his feelings weren't deep enough for a minnow to swim in, but he did have some.

"You're saying you never met her before this boat ride?"

"If I did, I don't remember it."

I could believe that.

"What I remember is how she jumped. You ever watch people at big public swimming pools, the ones with those tall diving boards? That's how she went, like an exhibition diver."

Hard to credit, but Charlie Dick'd done it. He'd got me

more interested in what he had to say than in what I wanted
to hear.

"Hold on," I said. "You saw her jump?"

"I wish I didn't, but yeah, I did."

"This is the first time I'm hearing it."

"This is first time I'm saying it."

"Why wait?"

"You saw how it was. People say they've seen something
and everybody else jumps all over them."

He had a point. I'd seen how it was.

"But I saw her. She was out there standing at the back rail
in the sun. I usually like being with people but I was alone
at the time because of this tummy ache I had. Probably just
sea sickness which got a lot worse with that storm we went
through. Remind me next time someone asks me to take a
ride on a boat, even someone as rich as Joker Willingford,
remind me, say: Charlie you don't like boats. They make you
sick."

He had another point.

"Anyway, there I was trying to feel better when I saw her.
I saw the other one too, the one who's in shock and sticking
to her stateroom. That second one seemed to freeze when
Clara climbed up, but I didn't. I was trying to get down the
goddamned ladder as fast as I could under the circumstances.
But she was gone before I got close. What a diver though. I
watched the Olympics two years back. You see that on the
television? You ever watch television? I have a television
show. *Dizzy Days with Charlie Dick*."

"I know."

"You know! You ever watch it?"

"I was up in Saratoga watching the horse races."

"Hey! I like the ponies too. S'why I'm on this fucking
boat. Gonna bet on the horsies. If we ever get there. Anyhow,
Clara Louise looked like Vicki Draves doing that dive. You
know who Vicki Draves is?"

I nodded yes. Of course I knew who Vicki Draves was. Two years back, she'd won two gold medals for the U.S. in the '48 London Olympics.

"So I just stood at the railing like everybody else, you were there, I remember that, we were all looking back at our wake and she was gone. And I mean gone. So what was I gonna say that would make a difference? I don't know why she dove. I didn't know her and I didn't save her."

"You could tell me one thing."

"Shoot."

"What's the gun for?"

Charlie Dick did not bat an eye. Both brown and gray remained where they were, steady and calm. I did get a smile, large and guileless.

"I see you've been in my stateroom. What gives you the right I'm guessing is your relationship with Joker Willingford's wife. But if you must know, I'm Charlie Dick. Most people love me. But some don't. The ones that don't love me really got a bug up their butts."

Dick just scored a hat trick. Three good points in one conversation.

That's when Leonard the bartender showed up. Leonard didn't look all that hot. I knew that look. I was wearing it myself.

I'd guess he'd gone a few rounds with someone. He could of being doing anything. Almost everyone aboard could of been doing something else.

It wasn't the Queen Mary, but it was a big and complicated boat.

21

Most of the stuff that went on in my brain was done on the run and most of it consisted of hunches. This time I'd collected a lot of dots. I figured it was time to do some connecting.

The best place for that was in my own stateroom.

Gene was already there making the bed, cleaning my bathroom, tidying my things.

It wouldn't take him long. My things amounted to one small bag just so I'd have clean underwear and something snappy to wear on the day we went to Hialeah to watch Fleeting Fancy win the Old Rosebud Stakes. My bathroom was full of a toothbrush and my safety razor. Jane didn't bring a thing.

Me showing up startled the steward I shared with Toby Tyrrell and Tommy Feather.

"Sorry, Mr. Russo. I'll be out of your way in a minute."

I threw myself on a couch, one I couldn't see a window from.

I said, "It's Tuesday afternoon. I go to the movies on Tuesday afternoons. Also Mondays and Saturdays and any other day something's playing I haven't seen."

Gene smiled. "So do I."

"I could really use a movie."

"So could I."

"I'm missing *Sunset Boulevard*. I hear it's something to see."

Gene was fluffing up my pillows. "Soon as we make land, I'm looking for the nearest movie house."

"How about Bogart? You like Bogie?"

Gene stopped messing with pillows. "Do I like Bogart? If I was a girl, I'd pry him off Bacall with my teeth."

Gene straightened my oil painting. When he got done, it looked exactly the same to me.

He said, "Do you mind me saying you look quite a bit like Bob Mitchum?"

"Not if you don't mind me saying you look like Montgomery Clift."

"I've heard that. And you've heard about Mitchum."

"A few times."

Gene laughed. I laughed. My first laugh in I'd forgotten how long. It didn't last long, but it felt good doing it.

He said, "Better leave you alone. Plus, I have to do Tommy Feather's stateroom. I think he smokes something besides Camels in there, and it's not a peace pipe."

I liked that. I liked people who surprised me.

With Gene gone, I had one last simple thought before trying to do some difficult thinking: the Sip o' Sea was the Waldorf on water.

I got off the couch and lay back on my freshly made bed. I punched my pillow, kicked the covers onto the floor, moved my lightweight ashtray from one side to another—nothing worked.

I'd wondered if Bogie thought out his cases. Reading the guy behind him, Raymond Chandler, I knew Marlowe did some thinking, but mostly he got sapped a lot and the people who sapped him kind of gave the game away.

Hammett's Nick Charles would pour himself another cocktail, pour his dog Asta a cocktail (a mutt Jane wouldn't hum to for all the sand in Egypt), crack another joke, come to with Nora Charles dumping another ice bag on his head and then one on Asta's head (big ha ha). If he thought, I don't know when he did it.

Philo Vance floated across my mind. Maybe I stumbled

over Vance too young. Maybe he bored me because Philo was a dandy and a snob. Or maybe he bored me because for someone so smart, his cases weren't.

I gave up trying to work that one out right about the year Lawrin won the Derby with Eddie Arcaro in the irons.

Thinking about it, the only guy I knew doing a job like mine who'd sit and think out problems was Christie's Hercule Poirot... but Christie only told us he thought, she didn't tell us *what* he thought. She'd tell us he felt he was missing something, but not what he was missing. At some point Poirot would leap from his chair yelping *Mon dieu, but of course!* This meant he'd solved the case, but not how he'd done it or who it was.

What happened then was Hercule gathering his suspects together in one place, and they'd all show up, and while they waited, listening, like good little possible killers, he'd tell them who the real guilty party was.

Right up to the last second, the real guilty party'd sit there like someone watching a play that had nothing to do with them.

Believe you me, that part was hard to swallow. I always wondered why the guilty party wasn't already long gone. I know that'd be my plan.

But I always toughed it out because it was Christie and I had to know *who did it*.

So far, I hadn't been sapped so that was no good. I wasn't going to find my killer that way. Mrs. Willingford wasn't going to make me a magic ice bag. And Vance could go jump in a lake.

So I had to do what Poirot did and I had to do it soon.

I was on a ship. Whoever killed Olivia Powers was also on the ship, and he or she, like me and whoever didn't kill Olivia Powers, had nowhere to go but with the Sip o' Sea.

They had to come when I called 'em together. Then all I had to do was eliminate 'em one by one until I was left with the killer.

As soon as I knew who that was. Which I'd better know soon. The coast of Florida was on its way.

Problem was, I wasn't Hercule Poirot. My little gray cells must of numbered half of his.

Fuck it. I'd chosen this job. I was doing this job.

I was flat out in bed on a calm sea, smoking and dropping ash on my chest, thinking in a New York accent which made sense since I talked with a New York accent.

I had a process on the boil and it went like this.

Clara Louise was a dumb dolly who wasn't so dumb she couldn't get into a good acting school. She wasn't so dumb she didn't know how to casually bump into the usual useful horny bastard who got her a ride on the Sip o' Sea where she'd meet the kind of influential showbiz people she hoped to be part of. She wasn't too dumb to laugh and talk and flirt and make herself a presence among them. But then, when she'd gone to all that trouble and done a swell job of it, she got sick, spent the evening alone in her stateroom, came out for lunch the next day, and when that was over, she walked straight out the back doors onto the back deck, didn't look right, didn't look left, just hopped up on the railing, and threw herself off the boat. Correction: she dove off the boat, a dive that impressed all who saw it.

How many saw it? Three said they had. Were there more?

With that dive, we had what looked like her first dumb move. If she was seeking attention, she got it. But being dead, the attention wasn't much use to her. So let's say she really *was* that down in the mouth, that the cheery blonde ditz was all an act. She may have been a ditz but she wasn't cheery. In that case, even there she wasn't so dumb. She chose a time when we'd sailed far enough from shore to make swimming back impossible except for those loony tunes who greased up and swam back and forth across the English Channel. She chose the back end of the boat where getting rescued was the long shot of long shots. And when she went overboard, she didn't jump, she balanced on the rail, as Sandrine Brunetti said, like a ballerina in street shoes. Charlie Dick said she dove like Vicki Draves would of, like a double Olympic gold medalist.

She did it in broad daylight. She didn't look around to see if she had company or an audience or a rescuer. She didn't hesitate. She climbed up, balanced, dove, and was gone.

That's what a ditz called Clara Louise, a pretty blonde Southern girl on the make in New York City, did.

From there I connected a few more dots, strung together a few more remarks made by this one and that one, and then hooked some of my connections into a few more of my connections and some more after that. The dots, remarks, and connections felt good. They felt like I'd done some actual thinking. I might of been way off track, but at least I was on a goddamn track. First time I thought I'd found an answer or two since Olivia Powers screamed and I threw *The Man with the Golden Arm* straight up in the air.

Speaking of which, Algren's book was back on my desk. I guessed Gene put it there, but maybe not. Maybe Holly did.

So now I had some possible whats and some possible wheres, even a possible who. As for a why, I'd didn't have a clue.

Rolling over, I picked up the phone. Every stateroom had a telephone. On the ship, from a stateroom, you could only call the other staterooms or the wheelhouse or the galley or the bar, but that was fine with me. It was all I needed.

I dialed a two-digit number. When it was answered, I said, "You alone? OK. Can you come here? Half an hour? I'll be waiting."

Mrs. Willingford swept in, checked her lipstick in my mirror—perfect as usual—and uncoiled herself on a couch.

I had two of 'em. We all did.

She said, "Joker's getting nervous."

Joker's wife wasn't taking anything off, especially not the latest hat, one of many just small enough for a big boat. She wasn't taking off her jacket. Black bugle beads on a black jacket didn't say "ocean going" to me.

I'd learned not to question Mrs. Willingford's clothing choices and she'd learned not to question mine. I was wearing new underwear, and only the underwear. They were the usual boxers but not the usual white. These were pale gray with red and black playing cards scattered on them. There was an ace of hearts over the fly.

I kept my mouth shut about the bugle beads and she kept hers shut about my shorts.

We both kept our thoughts about Jane to ourselves.

"I don't blame him," I said. I was talking about Joker. "He got away with the possible suicide… "

"Possible?"

"Maybe jumping wasn't Clara's idea."

"Fuck, Sam. The ideas you get."

"Not all clunkers. As I was saying, he got away with Clara Louise, but a dead body isn't going to go over so well. Especially not this dead body with its head beaten in. And we can't keep quiet about it for too much longer, for so many reasons."

Mrs. Willingford stared at me. "Sam Russo. This mess isn't your mess. You didn't get me into it but you've got to get me out, me and Joker. You have no idea how hard I've worked to stop him having that poor girl thrown overboard."

"He's still working on that idea?"

"Obsessively. It's why I've stuck by his side and not yours… which is much more interesting if equally irritating. Everyone knows how many people came aboard this ship. They'll know if two fewer get off. Not even Joker's money can explain that one."

"I'm not sure that's true."

"Of course it's true."

"Let me put it this way. It doesn't have to be true."

Mrs. Willingford gave me that eye she was so good at giving. "Explain."

"Think about it. Few know the poor girl is dead. Those who do won't talk, and that goes double for her killer. All you and Joker have to do is dress up one of the stewards in her clothes, have him walk off the gang plank and disappear into Miami. Olivia was never a talker. King doesn't seem to care, daughter or not. Who'd notice?"

"The steward, Sam, she, or he'd, notice."

"That's where Joker's money comes in." Before Mrs. Willingford could say a thing, good or bad, I had a better idea. "Holly could do it. She could leave twice. Once as Olivia, the second time as Holly."

"You're not seriously suggesting… "

"Not really. Only thinking out loud."

I wasn't thinking out loud. I wasn't thinking at all. What I was doing was reeling from this great idea that'd suddenly hit me like a golden brick.

If Sam Russo, the kind of PI who tripped over the answer, hadn't all by himself just connected a last dot, I don't know what the hell else I could call it.

I said, "What if I can't figure this out by Miami?"

"Then you don't get that bonus."

OK. That got me talking. Time to share my connect-the-dots with my self-appointed sidekick.

I talked. Mrs. Willingford listened. Listening, she looked up, she looked down. I wasn't sure what any of it meant, but I didn't stop talking, not until I wore myself out. And then she looked at me.

I waited for the left hook.

It didn't come. It didn't come for so long I got jumpy. I said, "Well, that's about it."

Still looking at me, she licked her lips. Women. How do they do that without getting their tongue red?

We sat there long enough for Mrs. and Mr. Morton-Kline to stroll by my window, both too involved in whatever they were talking about to glance in at us.

I couldn't take any more silence. "So? What do you think? Was it the perfect crime?"

"By 'perfect crime' you mean getting away with it?"

"Right."

"They didn't get away with it.

"You mean— "

"I think you're on to something. I also think Jane knew what happened."

"Me too."

"I think because she knew what happened, who it happened to, and who made it happen, she had to go."

I said, "Right again."

"But I don't think she was thrown overboard."

"Same reason I think that?"

"Depends. Do you think it's because our killer couldn't take the risk of a dog swimming a lot longer than Clara Louise could swim."

"Yep. That's what I think."

"Also because they didn't know she doesn't bark?"

"Yep."

Not everybody noticed Jane. She was choosy who she hummed or yodeled with.

22

The last time I wasn't in the US of A, I was in the middle of a Bataan battlefield.

Now, me and the Sip o' Sea were beyond the territorial waters of the United States and I was still at war. A small and private war.

In an hour, Captain Moody would spin the ship's wheel and take us straight towards Florida. In two nights and a day we'd dock in Miami.

I had to move if I wanted that bonus.

Outside the Grand Salon the sea was as black as oil, the sky as black as the sea, the moon as dead white as the Sip o' Sea. In the depths of the night, I wasn't asleep. I was sitting at the bar, just me and a record player. I'd been drinking straight Kentucky bourbon made by Joker's Special Blend Distillery and listening to music. Leonard the bartender kept a shelf of record albums behind the bar. If he chose 'em, I had to give it to him... he had good taste.

I was half stinko and didn't much care. I didn't much care if it was Clara Louise's idea to kill herself or if someone else had thought of it for her. I didn't care that a young woman was viciously murdered and already decomposing in her stateroom closet. I sure didn't care that King Barton was her daddy who'd denied it barefaced for years, was still denying it, and driven some childlike fan bride to kill herself, a besotted young bride he'd long ago used and left with a kid to care for. And who could give a damn if the writing team of Morton and Kline would make a sack full of money off making a musical comedy out of such an uplifting story.

All I cared about was the idea of Jane being gone. I

didn't believe for a second my red and white talking dog got outdrawn or outwitted. I believed she was cornered, trapped. It was being on a boat. On a boat, there were places where something like that could happen to her, places even my Jane couldn't duck and dodge or bare her teeth out of.

So where was her body? In a box or a trunk or a locker or a bag... ?

My glass, almost to my mouth, stopped. What was Clara Louise doing with a duffel bag early on the morning she left us in an award-winning dive off the back of the Sip o' Sea?

That's what Vergil said he saw her carrying, said it didn't suit her, said what business was that of his?

Suit her? I'd seen her luggage. It was still in her stateroom. It was almost as cheap as mine was, but hid it better. I'd seen her clothes and her shoes and her cosmetics. None of these things were a patch on what Mrs. Willingford could afford. Even Holly had better stuff.

What I hadn't seen was a duffel bag.

Where was her duffel bag? What did Vergil see? Who was Clara Louise?

It didn't come easy, but I did some more of what I called thinking. Adding Clara's duffel bag to the connections I'd already made and, holy mackerel, what do you know—I made a few more.

I stopped drinking, stopped listening to Leonard's music, stopped feeling sorry for myself, put Jane away somewhere safe in my heart, and looked at my watch.

Dawn in about an hour.

I had one day and one night, a little over twenty four hours, to make Joker's bonus. Fuck Joker's bonus. I was past making extra money. Knowing what happened would be my bonus. Not the kind of proof a court of law needed—that wasn't my problem—but proof enough for me.

I got off my butt, fished out a flashlight from behind Leonard's bar, and went looking for what I hoped was there.

I was *this* close to believing it would be.

"Lois!"

"G'way."

I flung off her covers. Lying on her side, her body lit by the first of the morning light flooding in her window, Mrs. Willingford was breathtaking. I took a breath and shook her.

"Get up. I have something to show you."

"I said g'way."

I shook her harder.

"I said I have something to show you."

"Show me? What time is it?"

"It doesn't matter. Here, wear this." I'd found a robe, soft enough, warm enough and large enough to avoid her having to wear anything else.

Holly was waiting for us on the back deck. This far from land, this early in the day, a breeze took the sea spray off the tops of the white caps and threw it at us. We got chilled and we got wet. I'm sure they cared, but not me. I was there to show them something, to make them see what I saw: the first key puzzle piece that began to make sense of the mystery on the Sip o' Sea.

They didn't complain. I was being tolerated. Because of Jane. I was used to that, especially when it came from Mrs. Willingford. I ignored it. I always ignored it, especially when it came from Mrs. Willingford.

I pointed at the railing. It wasn't where Olivia Powers, Sandrine Brunetti and Charlie Dick said Clara Louise was poised when she made her fatal dive, but it was what I'd been looking for and what I'd found. It was where I'd of made it if all this was my doing.

Clara Louise dove off the back end of the Sip o' Sea. Where we were standing was maybe halfway along one side of the Sip o' Sea. Behind us was a door that led, as doors in boats as big as the Sip o' Sea did, into a passageway that led into other passageways with stairs and ladders going up and stairs and ladders going down.

Outside the door, it was all much simpler. A door into a passageway on one side of us, a side deck beneath us, a railing on the other side of us. Beyond the railing it was directly down into the ocean blue.

As I pointed, I said, "Look at that. Tell me what you see."

They both looked, Mrs. Willingford longer than Holly.

Holly said, "Sorry, Sam. What are we supposed to see?"

"You're not supposed to see anything. That's the point."

Mrs. Willingford was still looking. Still looking, she said, "What I see you have to be really paying attention to notice."

I said, "So what do you see?"

She straightened up to answer, snatching her robe closed before the sea breeze gave us an even better look. "Just before we sailed, I had the Sip o' Sea gone over from stem to stern. Her bottom was cleaned, her brass was polished, her teak was oiled, we had a radar system installed, her engine was serviced... basically whatever a boat like this boat needed, she got."

"And?"

"Either someone was sloppy or... "

"Or?"

"Someone marked the railing. A nice new mark. Dammit."

"Like something dug into the railing?"

"Precisely like something dug into the railing."

"And what, Mrs. W, would that something be?"

Mrs. Willingford looked again, and when she was finished looking, Holly looked.

Holly said, "Oh yes! I see it now. There's two little dents in the wood. You're right, Lois, something's gone through the varnish and hurt the wood."

I ran my fingers over the dents, felt them better than

I saw them. I'd never of seen them at all if I hadn't been looking and I wouldn't be looking if I hadn't decided to solve this damn case.

Looking at my two fellow sleuths, I said, "So what would make marks like these?"

Holly was once a poor kid growing up in a town called Tottenville at the southern tip of Staten Island. No one came from Tottenville. No one went to Tottenville. Her birth certificate read: "Baby" Shauer. There was no name listed as father.

A kid like "Baby Shauer" would grow his hair, polish his nails, come up with a convincing pair of tatas, call himself Holly, and run for it.

Once a working girl in the triangular park below my room in Stapleton, once on someone's menu to be killed for pleasure, now she was a student of serious acting at some serious new school on the Isle of Manhattan.

In other words, Tottenville's "Baby" knew beans about boats.

But Mrs. Willingford knew about racehorses and fine cars and Park Avenue penthouses and the best hotels in the most exotic foreign countries and haute couture hats and mixing cocktails and whorehouses, so a yacht was an open book.

"A hook. Some kind of small grappling hook."

I shook her hand: shamus to shamus.

We were back in the Grand Salon. It was too early for the Willingford guests but not too early for the Willingford stewards.

Gene headed our way with a silver coffee pot on an enameled tray. He served us coffee in cups that weren't silver but they might as well of been.

Watching him walk away, I said, "What else do they do besides kiss our butts?"

"They're well paid to kiss our butts, Russo. They clean staterooms, do laundry, shine shoes, set tables, serve meals, take the odd request— "

"Odd request?"

"Not that kind of odd."

"And the crew?"

"Do what a crew does. Keeps things shipshape and Bristol fashion."

"And every single one of them was checked out— "

"Under a microscope. After Holly… "

She didn't need to finish that sentence. All three of us knew what "after Holly" meant. "After Holly" meant anyone working in anything the Willingfords owned went through a wringer. Their house in the Hamptons, Beeswing Farm in Kentucky, their chateau somewhere in the south of France, the Sip o' Sea, whatever and wherever else—I knew a lot about the Willingfords but I didn't know it all.

Holly said, "Anyone going to explain the hook?"

I explained the hook.

Holly opened her mouth and she shut her mouth. The words she finally got out were, "Well, if that doesn't beat all."

Mrs. Willingford set her coffee cup down. "So now what?"

"Now we go through Clara's stateroom, and this time we find something."

Holly stood, straightened her skirt, watched an early rising Vergil Sapster making his way to the breakfast buffet. Her nose wrinkled. "There's that ugly little cluck. I'm sure I've seen him before. I mean before we met on this boat."

Mrs. Willingford had just noticed her robe. She'd be making a break for it any second now. But me, I was wondering when one of the Willingford guests was going to ask about Miss Olivia Powers. When was she coming out? Was she OK? How long did it take to get over witnessing someone she barely knew jump off a boat? Look at Sandrine. Was she locked in her stateroom?

The stewards must of talked. Merle must of said she hadn't brought her a single thing to eat or drink.

Someone was sure to ask the Willingfords to open her door, by force if necessary.

Mrs. Willingford saw her chance for clothes and took it, leaving me with Holly.

Holly said, "Hotcha! How could I forget someone who looks like him? I saw him talking to Mr. Willingford at the Actors Studio and then this other girl was vamping him, some girl Olivia and I had in most of our classes. Olivia was going to star in Mr. Kazan's next play. But right after Olivia, we all thought the best one of us girls was her, the one I'm talking about. And she was the one breathing all over that creep Sapster. But why? Beat the heck out of me. If a girl needs a sugar daddy, lots better than him around."

Holly tapped my hand.

"What the heck was her name? You'd think I'd remember. Right on the tip of my tongue."

I was staring at her. I'd begun staring at her right about the time she mentioned Sapster the Nail Tycoon.

"Holly."

"What?"

"Why didn't you tell me this before?"

"Tell you what?"

"What you just said."

"Didn't I? I thought I did. Anyway, who cares? The girl I'm talking about isn't Clara anyway. Damn it. Her name is almost there, I can almost say it."

23

First time I ever saw Mrs. Willingford must of been what it was like for a horse trainer going toe to toe with Boston.

Boston was a race horse. When he felt like it.

Bred by Aaron Burr's defense counsel—Burr was one of my heroes; he not only fought a duel with the slick and slimy Alexander Hamilton, he killed him—Burr's lawyer lost his unbroken two-year old colt in a card game.

The guy who won him named him after the game they'd been playing. If the game of "Boston" was popular once, you couldn't prove it by me.

This guy gave Boston to a trainer named John Belcher. It took Belcher exactly one day to find out the colt was unmanageable, untrainable, and intolerable. Belcher tried to get rid of him by passing him on to another trainer named White. White sent him back, saying, "The horse should either be castrated or shot, preferably the latter."

To stop Boston rolling on his riders, Belcher tied him down so stable lads could sit on his head and beat him with sticks.

It didn't work.

Who the hell knew how, but Belcher got Boston into a race. His jockey even got him running. The final wonder was that Boston was winning. But then he simply stopped dead and he "sulked." After that display, Belcher sent him out as a common hack on the streets of Richmond. For a season, Richmond watched Boston in traces buck and balk his way all over town.

I don't think too many paid for that ride.

In the end, I guess you could say man won and horse lost. Boston would race, but he bit horses who tried to pass him.

More than a hundred years back, Boston was a great horse.

Mrs. Willingford was Boston in human form. The both of 'em were temperamental, headstrong, fast, beautiful, tremendous, dangerous, and one-of-a-kind.

I don't know what made Boston what he was— intelligence probably; he knew a bum rap when he saw one, meaning getting stuck with humans—but I'd learned bits and pieces of what made Mrs. Willingford tick.

One summer night at my place when she was feeling almost soft—I mean soft inside, outside she always felt soft— she told me. Not all of it. I doubt if it was even close to all of it. But she told me some, and that some was as hair-raising as the time I heard her tell Edgar Hubbard, Manhattan's Queen of Quotes: "When I was four, my father beat my mother to death. I was under the kitchen table. I saw it all."

I still couldn't tell you the name of the state she was born in. Not the south, it wasn't in the south, but whichever state it was, it was hilly and woodsy and Lois came from the dirt poor part of the hilliest and back-woodsiest.

It was hard as hell to hear that before her father murdered her mother, he'd already pretty much killed the little kid Lois must of been, the little kid she still was with me every now and then. He beat her. He beat all his kids in a shack stuck way back in the hollow they called home.

Lois ran for it when she was twelve. She didn't tell me how she got out or what she had to do once she did, but I'd thought about it from time to time as I looked at the woman she'd made of herself. What I saw was someone who'd do whatever she had to do, a woman who *could* do anything she had to do.

In the backwoods, a girl was nothing, worth less than moonshine or silver fox skins, worth a lot less than a good hunting dog. But to Lois, she was Boston. Her father could work her, beat her, kill her mother, he could even let his own brother shame her, but he never tamed her. And he couldn't keep her.

I still didn't know a lot of things. Like how a twelve year old found her way out of those hills, where she first went to, how she kept herself alive.

If I knew her much longer, I was betting I'd find out more about all those things. I wasn't sure I wanted to find out.

That night, listening, I'd thought I had it bad. I'd thought growing up with a guy who was sure God wanted him to kill the little girls in his care if they weren't "right" was hard, that going without meals if Mister and his lovely wife Flo used the state food money on themselves was hard, or wearing the same clothes until they fell off my back and sleeping in a rotten turret under a picture of my savior, the one who never showed up to save us, especially not the ones chosen by Mister to give back to God, was hard. I thought all that was worse than anybody ever had.

My life was jam compared to the road Lois walked towards becoming Mrs. Willingford.

Was she some other Mrs. before that? A Mrs. to a Mr. who taught her to read and to write? Was there a Mr. before that one? Some guy in some town who taught her to eat off a plate with a fork.

I sure knew now why she could run like she did. I knew how she knew about Holly's world. The one thing I knew best was that the leap she'd taken somewhere along her way was beyond any I'd ever taken.

Holly would know that leap. If I ever came to it, I'd know it too. But would I jump?

Who the hell knew? Not me. Not yet.

What I did know was some of what Jane knew, but not all of it. I knew we were on the Sip o' Sea. I knew none of this started aboard the Willingford yacht. It began back in New York City before the yacht ever left its Hudson River dock. It started there and it was supposed to end in New York City with no one the wiser.

If I had anything to say about things, whoever wrote the cruel and complicated little script we'd all been playing our parts in, was in for a rewrite. With my ending.

Holly was under Clara Louise's bed. Mrs. Willingford had all of Clara's clothes laid out on top. I was in the closet.

We knew what we were looking for because I knew what we were looking for.

Someone aboard the Sip o' Sea murdered Olivia Powers. Olivia was gifted. Holly said so. Holly'd shared acting classes with Olivia, she'd seen her work. I'd never heard of Elia Kazan but a lot of other people had. He was a big cheese in New York City's theater world, a world I didn't know well, but I knew it. He was becoming a big cheese making Hollywood movies. I hadn't seen a single one of his movies, but after this was all over, I probably would. *Panic in the Streets* sounded right up my Stapleton alley.

The actors and actresses he trained were getting noticed.

Kazan had noticed Olivia Powers.

Someone aboard the Sip o' Sea killed Jane. Why? They did it because dogs weren't people. Dogs don't judge the world by words spoken or clothes worn or things owned or shared beliefs about how people ought to think. They knew it by its smell, the subtle movements it made, how it felt to be touched by a hand or called by a voice.

Jane was killed because she knew who beat Olivia Powers to death.

I wasn't Bogie. I wasn't Philip Marlowe. I didn't write their stuff. I wasn't a real cop. What I was, was barely a real Private Eye. I'd had a few cases all my own. I didn't mess 'em up, not too bad anyway. But I wasn't stupid. A giddy cracker actress going to the same high class acting school

Olivia and Holly got to go to, a kid who knew a brass ring called Otto Gerlinger when she saw it, and grabbed, that kid just happened to jump off the back end of the Willingford boat on the same day her classmate was killed.

Clara Louise didn't jump. She had to know if she jumped there was a good chance she'd get sucked into the Sip o' Sea's propeller. Not many who want to die want to suffer that kind of pain getting there. So she dove. She dove like Vicki Draves in the Olympic games.

And that was that. But what was that?

I'd made my connections. I knew what I knew. If Jane were still with me, we'd have the killer by now. We might even know why Clara Louise went overboard. But Jane was gone and I was on my own here.

Except for Mrs. Willingford. Holly was an extra pair of hands and eyes and ears, but Mrs. Willingford was my good right hand.

I had to find what I expected to find in Clara's stateroom, what I found the first time when it was just me and Jane poking around. But this time I expected to understand what we found.

We didn't find what Jane and I didn't find the first time. It should of been here but it wasn't. We did find what we found the first time, stuff that shouldn't be here but was.

Sam Russo, Private Investigator, was working it out. No one was more surprised than me. I cared about something again. I was getting somewhere with a real case. Best of all, I had a plan.

I needed to ask Sapster what he was doing at the Actors Studio. I also needed to get to Merle, Clara Louise's steward, so I could ask her one simple question.

24

I found Merle where I expected to find her. In the dining room. My question was as simple as her answer. Both were loaded.

"Did Clara Louise ever ask you to brush her hair?"

"No, never, sir."

"Thank you, Merle."

That's how simple it was.

The last time I'd seen little Vergil Sapster, he was headed off to stick his snout in all the breakfast he could inhale. I barely noticed him. Why would I? I wasn't a nail maker in his nail factory. I wasn't his wife. Or one of his kids. Or the banker who took care of his money. We meant nothing to each other. But now, when I needed to have a little word with Mr. Sapster, he was nowhere. Not at the clotted cream brunch, not in his stateroom, not on the aft deck practicing his golf swing, not in the Grand Salon yelling at Clyde, who drew the short stick for guests, not in the wheelhouse demanding to know why we were weren't in Miami yet.

I couldn't find him anywhere.

One possible suicide, one murder, Jane gone, and now Ohio's Nail King's disappeared?

With what I thought I knew, with the answers to some of my questions worked out, where the hell was Vergil Sapster? If something happened to him, what the hell was it?

I'd gone through this with Jane. I didn't want to go through it again. I didn't want to think about Jane.

I could feel myself getting angry. Sam Russo was not an

angry PI. Let me put that differently. Sam Russo, PI, did not bring his anger along on a case.

I stopped at the turning of one passageway into another, stood there catching my breath. The Sip o' Sea was rapidly turning into Agatha Christie's *Ten Little Indians*. That not only angered me, it scared me. It didn't scare me that I was going to die with everyone else. It scared me that I wouldn't solve the case before we got to Hialeah. Of course I wanted the bonus. Why wouldn't I want the bonus? One thing I was always short of was folding green. But that's not what angered and scared me. What angered and scared me was what always got to me, every case, big or small. It was that moment that always came, no matter how I tried to avoid it, the one that said: this is the case, Sam, the one that'll prove you're so far from being like Bogie, you're Jerry Lewis.

If I hated any comic more than Charlie Dick, it was Jerry Lewis.

Lewis squawking and mugging away in my head, I still managed one good solid thought: if the ship was a version of *Ten Little Indians*, the killer didn't have time before bumping into Florida to kill *everyone*.

Probably.

Another scene out of *Dark Passage* played itself out in my head, the one where this shady cut-rate doc told Bogie's on-the-run character, "There's no such thing as courage. There's only fear. The fear of getting hurt and the fear of dying. That's why human beings live so long."

Not on the Sip o' Sea, they didn't.

I found Mrs. Willingford. No one had shot her or knifed her or strangled her or thrown her overboard or poisoned her perfume.

She was in the wheelhouse with Joker Willingford and Captain Eigil Moody. As a kid, if I'd ever wanted to captain a ship, I was over it now. A captain watched out for pirates, he watched out for crooks pretending your boat was salvage, he watched out for bootleggers and dope runners, he watched out for whales and for icebergs and for the odd passenger jumping overboard.

I pushed Lois out on one of the small topside decks for some privacy.

One look at my face and she said, "Fuck a skunk, now what?"

Not what I'd say, but I wasn't raised in a "hollow."

"I can't find Vergil Sapster."

"What?"

"I can't find another of your guests, the one who makes nails. And yes, before you ask, I've looked high and low. He's a bit bigger than a dog. I looked in those places too."

Mrs. Willingford turned a color I'd never seen her wear before. It was a pale shade of unhealthy gray. "This is a nightmare. Please tell me this is a nightmare."

"It's a nightmare. You and Joker have a killer on your boat. Someone who kills whenever he, or she, needs to. Someone who's OK with bashing a girl's head in if it solves whatever their problem is. Someone who would kill a dog. And we're all stuck on a ship with nowhere to go if that killer ever decides we're a problem too."

"Is it you, Sam?"

"Is *what* me?"

"Before I met you, death and I weren't well acquainted. Pain and sorrow, sure. Nasty business, you bet. But murder? Never."

"Does this mean you'd like me to leave and never darken your door again?"

I'd never been more tired in my life. I'd never felt more sick at heart. Not even on the island of Luzon after Magpie, my Morgan mare, was shot out from under me and I lay next to her in the rain and the mud for two days and a night as she slowly cooled and turned cold. Not the time I paced in a pink hotel as my vet friend told me Jane was finished, she'd been stabbed too many times. Not even the first time I saw Holly in her narrow hospital bed, broken and blooded and so far as I knew, dying. Sitting by her, I knew she wouldn't make it. Someone had hurt her too much.

If Mrs. Willingford answered yes, I thought I might just do what Clara Louise did: jump. I didn't think I could swim to shore, wherever that was, but I didn't give a damn whether I could or not.

"Oh, for crying out loud, Sam. Can't you be serious?"

"I am being serious."

She looked me straight in the eye. I didn't blink. She didn't blink.

"No, I don't want you to leave."

"I'm glad. I'm not ready to die yet."

"You could though. And you know you could."

"I know I could what?"

"Leave. If you really wanted to. Anyone could. We all could. We have lifeboats. The crew could lower any one of them. You could row away. I could row away. There's a motor launch too. Don't think I haven't thought of it."

Don't think she hadn't thought of it? Hell, *I'd* thought of it. Back when I had a dog, me and Jane were rowing away in a lifeboat. And now I learned there was a motor launch somewhere?

And right then and there, I knew. I knew as well as I'd ever known anything.

As my Home Sweet Home's "Mister" used to say: Jumpin' Jehosephat!

The goddamn lifeboats.

Normally, I wouldn't, because normally she'd slap me, but I grabbed Mrs. Willingford's hand. "The lifeboats! Come on!"

She didn't slap me. Instead, with the same sudden bright look in her eyes, she ran faster than me.

25

Mrs. Willingford and I found Vergil Sapster. It took us four minutes. Three of the four minutes was used up getting from where we were, a small front deck overlooking a larger front deck to one of the two upper side decks where the covered lifeboats were kept. A few seconds got used up looking down at the blood on the decking near the lifeboat. It only took a few because there wasn't much blood. There'd been more, but that'd been wiped up. By the look of it, not a long careful job, no more than a quick swipe with a rag that was now, no doubt, left in the sea far behind us. But quick or careless, the rag did what it was meant to do. If we'd never come near the lifeboat, rain or the ocean would of wiped away all trace of the blood better than any swabby could ever do.

One minute was spent removing the lifeboat cover. Inside it was hot and it smelled god awful.

Vergil Sapster lay in the bottom of a lifeboat—Mrs. Willingford said it was portside—dead as a dead pipefish. He'd been stabbed. Just once but once was enough. It was done with something long and sharp and as thin as he was. It was done with precision, up from under a rib and straight into his heart. He was probably dead a minute or two after he felt the blade. Maybe less.

There were no defensive wounds. Vergil either hadn't seen it coming, or he was as weak as he looked.

Inside the lifeboat, the Nail King hadn't bled all that much. The dead don't bleed when the heart stops pumping, although they can seep a little.

Sapster's blood wasn't coagulated. He hadn't been there long. Plus, as I said, it was hot as an oven from baking under the sun.

Last I saw him was in the dining room, the first Willingford guest to shovel breakfast onto a plate. What time was it now? 12:38 P.M.

He was killed anytime between 8:30 A.M.—that was about when he'd finished eating—and maybe 11:30 A.M. His death had to of happened at least an hour ago considering the state of the blood as well as the state of his body. That left me three hours plus or minus a few minutes to account for.

There were a lot of people doing all kinds of things during those three hours.

I had this growing idea I only needed a few minutes of one person's time.

Even Lino Morelli would figure out Vergil Sapster wasn't in the lifeboat when it happened. Lino on his worst day would get that poor Vergil was standing next to the lifeboat.

The question was: why would he do that? The lifeboat decks were seldom if ever visited by anyone, even the crew. I'd lay down good money that he was asked to meet someone here. He was the usual unwitting sucker who got lured someplace chosen by someone who said they wanted to see him. If Vergil noticed no one else could see him there, I don't think he cared. What Vergil Sapster, the man who nailed America, thought he was doing and why he'd let himself be lured, I thought I knew. What the killer thought they were doing I was sure I knew—getting V. Sapster somewhere peaceful, quiet and unvisited so he could be dispatched quickly and silently. All that needed doing after that was tossing the small dead body of Ohio's Nail King into the lifeboat and making sure it was well covered again.

Whoever did that had to be strong enough to get a dead body up and into the boat. But not that strong. Sapster weighed about what a jockey weighed. Maybe less.

The big plus in this plan was the lifeboat. If Mrs. Willingford and I hadn't looked, Vergil Sapster could of spent months in the thing. Lifeboats weren't checked that often. Once we docked, everyone aboard would be long gone and unless the killer left prints or a calling card no one could prove a thing.

From one moment to the next, I stood stock still. I was having a revelation. It wasn't the kind of thing you're supposed to get in a "Come to Jesus" revival tent or a Eureka moment over a microscope. It was the kind us sleuths get when the penny drops.

Lifeboats weren't checked that often? Lifeboats were covered? Lifeboats were kept where few ever went?

Mrs. Willingford barely yelped when I grabbed the silken white sleeve of her silken white jacket. She didn't need dragging round to the starboard deck, the one where the second lifeboat was kept. Mrs. Willingford was with me every step of the way.

Here's where we found the kicker, the bonus, the biggest win on the longest long shot in a whole season of racing at every track in the U.S. of A.

Her legs trussed up, her belly sunken since she hadn't eaten a bite since we last saw her and way too hot, my dog Jane was in the starboard side lifeboat. She was lying as Sapster'd been lying—on the bottom. But unlike Sapster, she went in alive. Also unlike Sapster's lifeboat, there was a small puddle of rainwater down there with her. Water she could reach. Her tarp had leaked in the storm. That leak had saved my dog.

Jane was unconscious, but she was alive.

I knew it. I knew it all along. OK. So sometimes I didn't know it. But I knew it.

Mrs. Willingford and I hugged each other like lovers reunited—which is how I'd been feeling for some time, off and on, the lovers part I mean; I couldn't speak for how she felt—then we gathered up Jane and turned to hotfoot it down to my stateroom.

For now, Vergil Sapster was staying in his lifeboat, exactly where we'd found him. He was dead. What did he care if he cooked away in there until Jane was cared for? He'd be just dandy until the time came to haul him out.

Mrs. Willingford wrapped Jane up in her fine white silken jacket, hid her from sight.

One thing that couldn't happen now was someone seeing we'd found my dog. It'd be all over the Sip o' Sea in minutes. And that meant whoever thought she was taken care of would know they'd botched the job.

In no time, Jane, covered by a soft blanket, was lying between Mrs. Willingford and me.

I couldn't stop looking at her, watching her long and shallow breath go in and out. Her heart was beating too fast. Her tongue was as dry and cracked as old leather. Her eyes were caked. The skin of her nose and the pads of her feet were cold. How much longer before she'd died in that lifeboat even with her puddle?

Mrs. Willingford leaned over Jane to whisper in my ear, "I'll find Holly. She'll want to know."

"God, yes. Get Holly."

Holly got two feet into my stateroom, cried out, "Oh, my poor love!" And was right back out again.

Holly was back so fast, her leaving barely registered.

She had an eyedropper with her. And a big jug of water.

Of course. Why didn't I think of that?

The way I nursed Holly, Holly nursed Jane. She pushed me out of the way, snuggled into bed with her water and her eye dropper, and there she remained, cooing and rubbing Jane's paws and squeezing drops of water down her throat.

Mrs. Willingford, watching, nudged me. "Sam?"

"Hmmmm?"

"Why is Jane still unconscious?"

It was the same question I'd asked myself before Holly showed up.

"I don't know. I'd ask a doctor if I could ask a doctor."

Mrs. Willingford shook all over. I'd never seen her do that before. It made her breasts move about in the most alluring way. I mentally kicked myself.

She yelped, "Doctor! Of course we can ask a doctor. Joker doesn't go anywhere without some quack. Hold on. I'll be back."

And then, as ever, she was off like Superman's speeding bullet. A few minutes later, she crashed back in through my door as fast as Holly had and with her came Kenneth.

"This," she said, "is Doctor Kenneth Archer. Kenneth gets stuck doing all sorts of things for Joker whenever he gets stuck with Joker."

That explained why Joker's "steward" didn't look like a movie star. He wasn't a steward and he wasn't here just for this sail.

Kenneth ignored Holly's gape and my rude stare. He went right for his patient. He opened one dim eye and peered into it. He opened the other. He held Jane's paws in his hands. He opened her mouth and looked at her tongue. If Jane'd been herself, Doc Kenneth might of been opening his own mouth to yell when she bit him.

He said, "She's seriously dehydrated."

I was hovering. "Is that bad? Will she be OK? What do we do about it?"

"Slow rehydration. She probably feels very ill. She'll be ill for some time. She could have died. Mrs. Willingford told me where you found her. Much longer and she would have died. But she's got a chance."

I didn't think Dr. Archer would like a kiss so I let that urge pass.

Holly glanced at her eye dropper. So did the rest of us.

Kenneth said, "You've done well, young lady. But the dog could really use an intravenous drip. Unfortunately, we don't have one. Next time I get stuck on this ship, we will."

Mrs. Willingford shook her head. "You said it. Write a list. Whatever you need. I'll add it to the ship's supplies."

Kenneth caught himself before he smiled. "Good. Meanwhile, if the young lady with the eyedropper keeps doing what she's doing, it's fairly close to the constant feed of a drip. But she can't stop. She or someone else will have to keep doing it for quite some time."

Holly snuggled closer to Jane. "I'll stay with her as long as she needs me. I'll slip water into her, drop by drop for as long as I have to. But I'll be needing coffee."

Easy. All that took was me ringing for my steward. Gene was at my stateroom door as fast as I expected him to be, then gone, then back with a pot of fresh coffee even faster.

His face told me everything. He said, "I'm so glad you found your dog. Can I do anything else?"

Holly looked up and gave him one of her best grins, the one that always got me. "Tell Merle I'll be taking my lunch here."

"Of course. And you, Mr. Russo?"

"Don't worry about me. I'll find something when I need it."

He nodded. And then he was gone again.

I said, "I'll be in and out, Holly. You'll be relieved as often as possible."

"That goes for me too," said Mrs. Willingford, "It also goes for Doctor Archer."

Joker's doctor managed a thin smile. "It'll be a pleasant change. Don't say I said so."

Lois and I shook our heads. Of course not. Never. Secret was safe with us.

I had a sudden thought. "Doctor Archer?"

"Yes?"

"Don't mention Jane's been found, that she's alive."

"I wouldn't dream of it."

Fuck. Gene had seen Jane. I had to tell Gene. And fast.

Holly was dripping water into Jane, drop by drop. I knew she'd do it for hours, that she'd stay forever if she had to.

I caught up with Gene in the nick of time. No, he said, he'd keep his mouth shut. He said he hadn't seen a thing, not a thing.

I was off to visit our Captain Eigil Moody. We had a few things to talk about, a few papers to look at. I'd be commandeering the ship-to-shore telephone or whatever its boaty name was. I could be making two calls. I could be making a dozen calls. It all depended on the answers I got. I expected to learn some good stuff making calls.

As for Moody himself, I didn't care if Captain Eigil Moody was master of all he surveyed. What I cared about was how well he kept his records.

An hour later, I was finished with the meticulous Moody, who was now a concerned and nervous Moody thanks to me. But no time to deal with Moody's mistakes, I needed to check on Holly and Jane. Captain Moody's part in all this would come round when it came round.

Jane was still sleeping or unconscious or maybe something else I didn't want to think about. I could tell Merle had been and gone by Holly's enamel tray and empty dishes.

"Any change?"

"I haven't stopped with the water, not once. And I didn't let Merle in so she didn't see Jane. I've been doing what Dr. Kenneth did, looking at her eyes. I'm sure they're brighter. And her breathing isn't so shallow."

"That's good, right? That's good?"

"Dr. Kenneth's been by. He said it was."

I took over the eye dropper, gave Holly a chance to stretch and visit my bathroom.

I was feeling Jane's feet—were they cooler, less dry?—when came a light rap on my stateroom door. I looked at my Mrs. Willingford watch. 2:47 P.M. Time was pressing. Less than eighteen hours to Miami assuming the weather held. If I knew Joker, he was rattling with Doc Kenneth's pills and fretting about the dead body in one of his staterooms.

Wait'll he heard about his guest from Ohio.

Holly stood in the bathroom door, her mouth full of tooth paste. She said, "That steward of the opera singer and the Hollywood writers... "

"Howard, the one who looks like Henry Fonda?"

"Right. Him. I'm sorry but he saw Jane. He was here trying to feed you. He promised he'd keep his trap shut." She was back looking at Jane again, crooning to her.

Well, I could forget that secret. By now everyone had to know Jane'd been found alive.

Rap tap rapping at the door.

"That'll be another one of 'em."

I opened my door and there was Clyde, holding a tray just like the tray Holly had. Just like the tray I always got.

Clyde said, "Mr. Russo. Gene said he knew you said you'd find something to eat, but I checked. Howard said you haven't. You missed lunch but I saved some of the best of it for you."

"Thank you, Clyde. I'll take it. No need to bring it in."

Clyde was taller than me. That meant he could look over my shoulder. His face lit up like Broadway.

"I heard about your dog. She's looking good. That's wonderful. Will she be all right?"

"I hope so. Clyde, does everyone know about my dog getting found?"

"No. Yes. I don't know."

"Damn."

"I won't say a word."

"Forget it."

He walked away with grace. I could never do that. Maybe I did look a little like Mitchum but I didn't carry myself like Mitchum.

26

Walter had his usual poker game going at his usual table in the Grand Salon. On his right sat Carson Kline, draped in a baby blue jacket, a baby pink shirt, and pale yellow slacks. It was so Hollywood, I was embarrassed for him. On his left sat Irma Morton. Today's hairstyle was a wartime Betty Grable look, straight up on the back and sides, a froth of white curls pushed over the top of her head and halfway down her forehead. It must of taken Woolworth's entire bobby pin supply to keep it up like that. Across the table was Toby Tyrrell, ace jockey with most of the game's chips in front of him. Next to Toby was Otto Gerlinger. Otto was smoking a cigar. I could tell any second now someone was going to leap at him and throw it overboard. If I weren't so busy, that someone would be me, especially now I'd made a few calls about him.

But kicking Otto's ass would have to wait.

Sandrine Brunetti was wearing her usual wrong time, wrong place evening gown, but this time she kept her considerable cleavage to herself. Tommy Feather was sitting out the hand. Could be because he'd lost his stake. Could be because he was half Indian and losing stole his soul.

King Barton and Charlie Dick were holding down barstools keeping Leonard the bartender busy. Charlie was telling King the usual jokes. King wasn't listening. I had a feeling King hadn't listened to anyone else once in his whole life. Maybe he'd heard the word "cut" or the words "top billing," but that was about it.

I wondered if Walter Dew's regulars noticed they were

missing a short thin man who made nails for a better-than-good living. I wondered if they wondered when Olivia Powers would grow up and get over being shocked. I wondered if the stewards shared that none of 'em'd brought her so much as a soda cracker since Monday evening and this was Wednesday. I wondered if I sat in on a hand or two, I could stop thinking what I was supposed to do next.

Four of the Sip o' Sea's stewards were doing their jobs in the Grand Salon. The fifth, Merle, was somewhere on call for Holly. The sixth, Kenneth, wasn't a steward. He was a doctor stuck acting like a steward because Joker either couldn't tell the difference or didn't give a damn. I figured Mrs. Willingford wouldn't be telling anyone else about Vergil, but by now she'd already told her hubby. I figured Joker was stuffed to the gills with a drugstore of pills, enough to let Dr. Kenneth attend to Jane and Holly.

Clyde'd been stuck with Vergil. Maybe he knew it and maybe he didn't know it. That was one of those things I had to know.

Me, I knew a lot more than I had before about what was going on aboard the Sip o' Sea. I thought I might have a handle on why. I thought I might know how a lot of it worked. I was sure that there was at least one more death involved in all this. Best of all, I thought I knew who the killer was and I was pretty sure I knew why they killed.

Worst of all, I had no way to prove it.

If I couldn't prove it but I still went ahead and accused my first choice of being the guilty party, trotting out my reasons for thinking so, could they sue me? They couldn't sue the cops. I knew that much. Lino'd done more than his fair share of arresting a guy whose lawyer would have 'im out of the Stapleton pokey twice as fast as Lino got 'im in.

But could they sue a Private Eye who'd be saying what he had to say in front of witnesses?

I thought back over all the books I'd read, the movies I'd

seen. Bogie was always right. Marlowe and Poirot and that English Lord fellow with the silly name, Whimsy something or other, they were always right. As for Sherlock Holmes, he wasn't a detective, he was one of those whatchamacallits, some sort of new calculating machine.

Up in Saratoga Springs, I caught the bad guy, but never had to tell anyone except the world's nicest hotel bathroom attendant. And Mrs. Willingford. In my second big case, the one that starred mud, a big sloppy dog, and a bigger rabbit, the whole thing wound up embarrassing as hell—although I did nail the bad guy in a round-about sort of way. The cops got called, more than once, but not by me. In the case where Holly almost died, the illegal part, the solving part, *and* the mopping up part took place deep in the wooded heart of the Isle of Staten. The Staten Island cops never knew a thing about it. I could thank Mickey Cates and his good friends, the soft spoken, soft-hearted hard as nails Irish mob, for that.

In this case, it was happening on a private yacht sailing away on the high seas and there wasn't a cop to behave like a cop for nautical miles around.

I was alone here. I knew what I knew. Mrs. Willingford knew what I knew. Holly knew what I knew. And Jane knew what she knew. Not one of 'em would be talking about it. That was my job. I got to talk about it.

Fuck.

I sat down in the chair Vergil Sapster should of been sitting in and said, "Deal me in."

I caught Gene's attentive eye. He shook his head. I figured he meant I'd get cleaned out with this crowd. I waggled a finger at him. What I meant was I was always pretty much cleaned out. What difference would it make?

Toby said, "My luck's in today, shamus. Hope you're flush."

Carson Kline's eyes were off his cards and onto my face instantly. "Shamus? You're a Private Eye?"

"When the mood strikes me, yep."

"You hear that, Irma? Our plot thickens."

"I heard it, partner."

Did I hear a quickened breath? I'd bet my life I did.

As for the game on the table, I was out in three hands. Almost a record.

Back down to Holly and Jane. Nothing had changed. Holly was smoking my cigarettes and reading *The Man with the Golden Arm*. She looked up and smiled.

"She's swallowing now," she said. "Doc Ken said she's looking a lot better."

I smiled. Jane wasn't going to die. It might take her some time to be Jane again, but she wasn't going to die. Even with the chance her wannabe killer tried again, she wasn't going to die. I'd sworn an oath she wasn't.

Off to Joker Willingford's stateroom.

It was twice as big as mine or anyone else's except Mrs. Joker Willingford's stateroom. Kenneth was bending over Joker's bed tucking in his blankies.

Before I got through the door, Mrs. Willingford headed straight for me, took me by the upper arm, and frog marched me right back out.

"Kenneth had to sedate him."

"I'm not surprised."

"You know what he said? The first thing he said?"

"Why me, God?"

"Close. He wanted us to throw Vergil Sapster's body over the side with Olivia Powers' body. He wanted them sewed into the same gunny sack. That's his solution. If Kenneth hadn't knocked him out, he'd have found someone to do it."

"Kenneth heard all this? He knows this too?"

"You bet your ass he knows. Thank god it's Kenneth. Joker's judgment is going."

"And Kenneth's judgment?"

"Is immaculate. Usually he's at the farm in Kentucky. His dad owed everything to Joker. Plus Joker sent Kenneth to med school. Doctor Kenneth Archer is gold."

"I'm beginning to wonder if hubby's not right."

"About what?"

"Getting rid of the bodies."

"What!"

"Come with me. We have to talk."

"Where?"

"Anywhere where no one can overhear us. Somewhere you're sure of."

Mrs. Willingford gave that a minute of thought. "There's only two places on the Sip o' Sea where we might be seen but not heard."

"Yes?"

"The large deck where Clara Louise dove off. If we stay right at the very end, there's no way anyone can sneak up on us."

"And no walls with drilled holes to listen through, or those speaking tubes I've seen running through decks and down walls, or strange boat bits to hide behind."

"You got it."

"I hate wind and I hate water. Where's the second place?"

"The Grand Salon."

"Where half the ship is now?"

"Precisely. They can see us. We can see them. But it's not called the Grand Salon for nothing. We can sit far enough away no one can hear what we say."

"Good. The Grand Salon it is."

Mrs. Willingford and I chose a fish pink padded booth as far from Leonard's curved black bar and Walter's poker game as we could get.

Gene took our orders. I needed a drink, something poured from the bottle straight into a glass, no ice, no cherries, no nothing but booze. Mrs. Willingford smelling like *L'Heure Bleue*—the scent she wore the first time we were alone aboard the Sip o' Sea, the day I spent whining about boats and waves and icebergs until she got snippy and called me "fish bait," a day that seemed like months ago—ordered a sidecar, exactly what she'd ordered the first time we ever had a drink together in some roadhouse north of Saratoga Springs.

Waiting for our drinks, I started talking.

I was still talking when Gene brought them over. I only stopped long enough to thank him, wait until he was gone again, and continue where I'd left off.

When I finally wound down, three whiskeys later to two sidecars for Lois, she looked at me long and she looked at me hard.

"OK," she said, "the least surprising thing you've told me is about Otto Gerlinger. We'll take care of our movie director when we can. But Sam, you know we should be off this boat sometime tomorrow morning."

"I know that."

"But you might be going sooner."

I understood her immediately.

"You mean because if what I think is true, *is* true, why would the killer let me live through the night?"

"Precisely."

I'd given that one some thought. Why would they? I was their weak link now. Throwing back the last of my drink, I made up my mind. As soon as we were finished here, I was checking on Jane and Holly again—and then I was strapping on my gun. As John Wayne would do.

I'd never been a big fan of Westerns, even with all those horses running around, but who was I to resist John Wayne?

27

"Nicolas was here."

"Who?"

"The one with the long hair. Nicolas."

Curled around Jane, Holly was wearing my pajamas. In my pajamas, she looked better than I did. Holly could wear my new skivvies and she'd look better than I did.

She said, "The steward who got Walter Dew, which isn't bad, and King Barton, which is."

"What the hell was he doing here?"

"He said he wanted to know how Jane was."

"Jesus. That makes every steward onboard."

"Name someone who didn't know we were looking for Jane. Name someone who knew we didn't find her. We didn't exactly look for her quietly. Everyone knows that we found her. You'd expect them to be curious."

She had more than a point. I threw myself on a couch. "Did you tell him where we found her?"

"Of course not. Give me a break here, Sammy."

Holly was the only human on earth I allowed to call me Sammy.

"I don't like it."

"In that case, you'll like this next part even less."

"What next part?"

"The part where I tell you he asked about Olivia Powers."

"Oh shit."

"You bet, oh shit. Nicolas said if she didn't come out soon, someone had better go in. Break the lock if they had to. She could be sick. She could have done something to herself."

"Oh shit."

"I told him, someone *has* been in."

I said "shit" again, only louder.

Holly said, "Sssssh. Jane still needs her rest. If I hadn't said something, and fast, they were going in. I didn't say she was alive. I didn't say she ate anything or said anything. I just said she was checked on. They could make of that what they will. What's wrong with what I told him?"

"She's dead, Holly. Very dead. And it wasn't a broken heart or shock."

"You don't think I know that?"

"If she's dead, and someone's already been in, why didn't that someone you talked about come out screaming? Why hasn't whoever that someone is reported that Olivia Powers is stuffed in her closet with her head smashed in? Who did you say'd been in to check on her?"

"I didn't. I just said someone and left it at that. Any normal person would assume I meant it was Dr. Ken. They'd think she was OK."

"Thank whatever for whoever. We'll all deny it and you'll suddenly realize you were dreaming. Or hallucinating. And then what?"

"Then what, what?"

"What did Nicolas say?"

"He said he was real glad to hear it and he'd tell the others right away. They'd started talking about it. They were all getting real worried. Clyde wanted to bust down her door."

"And then what?"

"Then he left."

"And that was it? No trying to get a close look at Jane?"

"Of course he had a close look at Jane. She looked then just as she looks now. Like she needs plenty of bed rest and liquids."

"And that was it?"

"That was it. Except for him asking me out once we got ashore."

"Everyone asks you out."

"I know. Isn't it grand?"

I was packing heat now, namely my snubnosed Colt .38. It was shit for distance, but up close it was just peachy. Up close was how far I expected to need it.

I was now armed and looking for action. This was our last night at sea. This was the night I had to go into some kind of routine. I'd been rehearsing that routine ever since I knew it'd come to this—how I'd gather them all together, what I'd use for my opening salvo, the slow piecing together of all the facts I was sure were facts, what they all meant and who they all pointed to.

There was no police back-up, no one standing around to make an arrest. I had no idea if the guilty party would break down and confess. For all I knew, they could show up with an innocent looking satchel and just when I was reaching the big finale blow us all up.

Before all that though, if who I thought might come looking for me, came looking for me, I'd have my proof by their trying to kill me like they'd tried killing Jane and succeeded in killing Sapster. If they came looking, I also figured with a gun in my pocket I wouldn't wind up in a closet or a lifeboat or in Davy Jones' Locker.

Thanks to Mrs. Willingford, she knew and I knew I'd made myself a target. This meant I couldn't have her trailing around with me, and I told her so. That is, I told her once I found her, which was on the side deck where I'd shown her the nicks in the wood railing. They were still there and she was peering at them while I made my speech. What I got for my trouble was what I should of expected to get. She said, "Fuck that, Russo. Two of us together makes you a harder target."

I said, "You're a target too, sweetheart, because by now they'd of figured what I know you know, so two of us together makes us a juicy two-for-the-price-of-one."

"Stop talking like Bogart."

"I'm not talking like Bogart."

"You kidding? All you're missing is the lisp."

"Dammit, Lois. Go sit with your husband. Better yet, spell Holly. Jane is also a target. She got found. She didn't die. Once she's feeling up to it, she'll talk."

That one made her back up and think.

"You're right. I'll give Holly a break, let her get some sleep. But then I come looking for you."

"Good. Lock yourselves in. Don't let anyone else into my stateroom for any reason whatsoever. Except Kenneth and Otelie. Got that?"

"Gee, Bogie. I think I get it."

Back in the Grand Salon sitting where Mrs. Willingford and I had sat before, I turned my glass round and round in my hand, watched the wet ring on the table change shape, listened to the hum of Walter Dew's ongoing card game, caught the drifting smell of cigar and cigarette smoke.

Tomorrow was Thursday. They all thought sometime late tomorrow morning they'd be standing on dry land, wobbling on "land legs," waiting until the sway of the sea got out of their system. Most of 'em thought come the weekend they'd be making bets on the ponies at Hialeah. One of 'em thought he'd be racing for home in the Old Rosebud Stakes. One of 'em thought he'd be waiting in the winning circle with Joker Willingford and Mrs. Joker Willingford and their great racing mare Fleeting Fancy.

Out of all of 'em, one of 'em thought they'd be walking off the Sip o' Sea and disappearing into Miami, a big safe city. That one thought this would be the last card they needed to play in the game they were playing, the one where people and dogs got hurt but none of that mattered because to them the pot was the Holy Grail.

If I ever needed to think, I needed to think now. I had to think clearly and quickly and with the kind of purpose I'd never managed before.

What kind of a case was it where the gumshoe knew most of the plot—and it was a plot, a well planned, cleverly carried out plot, as in: a planned out act of devious cunning—but didn't know how to draw out the killer?

If this was one of Walter Dew's card games, I was holding a great hand. Spread out before me were a lot of high cards, cards that usually beat all the other cards, but in this damn game the killer had an ace in the hole.

The killer's card, the one card that could take all the chips still piled on the table, was that I didn't have a single card of my own I could call proof.

This thing ever got before a real judge in a real courtroom, which I doubted it ever would, how long before it got thrown out on its keester? If I had to guess, my guess would be not even long enough to hear an opening statement from either side.

The killer would walk.

I'd know what happened and the killer would know what happened but no one else would know like we knew. And yet: courts, lawyers, witnesses, proof, none of the usual things mattered. The truth was, it didn't matter if we never got to court. My killer wasn't going to wind up at Sing Sing playing rummy with my old pal, "Mister" Zawadzki, the interesting fellow who killed the "unclean" little girls in his care, dozens of kid killings he got away with for years. They'd never hear my childhood chum Paul Jarrett's jokes, the chum who killed a guy called Carroll when Carroll messed up drugging a race horse, the chum who came within a half inch of killing me.

Too bad. Unlike Charlie Dick, Paul's jokes were funny.

Here's why it wouldn't matter. I was sure there were

more, but off the top of my head I could think of two good reasons. The first reason was practical and I'd already thought it over and already talked about it. Without proof, they'd walk.

The second reason it wouldn't matter was ironic.

If they did lose, it would only seem like they'd lost. The truth was they wouldn't lose, they'd win.

It went like this. Maybe they'd never see the inside of a jail, but just being accused of what they'd done would mean that everything they'd done it *for* would count for nothing. It would all turn to torn tickets in their hands.

I knew my killer now. So I knew exactly what they'd do if I exposed them and lost them their shot at the golden ring. I'd get their goat. I'd be someone they'd want to hurt and hurt bad. But I also knew they'd put their life back together. They'd find some other way to get some other golden ring, maybe even a bigger brighter ring.

The killer was clever. The killer was ambitious, resilient, fast on their feet and audacious. Tell you the truth, I kind of admired the cold blooded dirty scum. You had to admire the talent if not the intent.

Within a year of walking away from the Sip o' Sea, disgraced, suspected by many, a certainty to a few, but not convicted, they'd have a new life, a new playground where they'd get the ring they'd almost caught first time round.

What I was thinking was no more and no less than this: either way, they'd walk.

When I thought about it, it made my blood boil.

Sam Russo wasn't used to his blood boiling. Sam Russo rarely got that riled. But by all the king's horses and all the king's men, I was furious now.

One way or another my killer was going to get away with everything they'd done.

That was one huge ace in the hole.

I had to think. I had to draw my culprit out into the open.

I had to get them to show their hand.

Trouble with that idea was that Sam Russo, Private Eye, was clueless. Literally.

28

"You wanna get into the game?"

"What?"

"I said... "

"Sorry. I heard you. Just didn't hear you coming."

"Oh, that. I'm light on my feet. Irma's always saying I could scare a cat. So. You want in the game?"

"No thanks, Carson. I'm playing my own game."

The look I got for that told me I was either going to find that line in one of his movies, or he was going to tell his fellow card players they weren't missing anything.

"Suit yourself," he said.

I guess being so successful at the game he played, he wasn't used to being turned down.

I said, "Good advice."

That made the lid of his left eye twitch, or maybe the lid of his left eye twitched for a living. I didn't care either way.

"You know, I've been talking to Irma."

"Oh, yeah?"

"We're stumped. We just can't figure out your part in all this."

"All what?"

"First off, why the Willingfords invited a Private Eye on a sail to Miami."

"They didn't invite a PI. They invited a friend, me."

"OK. If you say so. But you have to admit it's odd. A girl kills herself and there just happens to be a Private Eye aboard. Lucky for the Willingfords."

"Not so lucky for the girl though, wouldn't you say?"

I knew what I meant by that. Carson didn't. All I got was a quizzical look. He looked quizzical for close to a minute. And then he padded away as silently as he'd padded up.

A couple minutes later, Tommy Feather walked over. I heard him coming from the first scrape of his chair at the poker table.

"You got a second, Russo?"

"Sure. Park yourself."

Carson didn't sit down. Tommy did. Once he was down, he squirmed and I watched him do it.

"OK," he said, "it's like this. There's something fishy going on around here."

"Oh, yeah?"

"I knew that blonde, the one who jumped. I only met her on the boat so I didn't know her long, but she talked my ear off. No kidding."

Tommy made me feel old. He was twenty, maybe less. In his collected Indian way, he still walked around wide-eyed with wow. Everything was important. Everything was shiny. Oh yeah, I felt old.

"OK, so you knew her. What's fishy?"

He glanced at the poker game, slid his eyes over the bar where Leonard was keeping those drinks flowing, watched Sandrine walk into the Grand Salon, caught the stewards gliding around making deliveries, cleaning up messes.

"She wasn't right."

"Explain that."

"There was something wrong with her."

"Well, she killed herself. You'd expect if a person kills themselves, there's something wrong."

"I don't mean that. I mean she was some sweet kid but it wasn't right. I didn't believe her."

"What do you mean?"

"I don't know what I mean. I just didn't buy it."

"Buy what?"

"The situation. That she wanted to die. If that was my horse, I'd scratch it."

I waited a minute. He waited a minute. Then bounced off my couch.

"I said what I had to say. You're the shamus. It's your ride."

"Thank you, Tommy."

"Ah, it's nothin'. Just thought it needed sayin'."

Tommy Feather galloped back to his seat at the poker table.

Damn. As Jimmy Durante said: "Everyone wants ta get inta the act."

I needed a place to brood. The Grand Salon wasn't turning out that place.

Otelie Coleman was sitting on the top deck, the one I'd been sitting on with Jane when Olivia Powers suddenly screamed, I threw my book in the air, and Clara Louise had just taken a dive off the Sip o' Sea.

I'd gone there to be alone. No doubt, so did Otelie. We eyed each other with dismay.

I was the first to give in.

"OK. I'll find somewhere else."

"No you won't. We'll sit here together, Mr. Russo, get some peace with each other from all that bad business going on down below."

There was only one deckchair, the one I'd dragged up to read in. It seemed weeks ago when I did that. I sat on the deck.

We both sat quietly, dreaming our own dreams, mulling over our own worries… and, in my case, falling asleep.

"Your interesting dog, you've found her. I can't tell you how that warms my heart. Will she return to health?"

Otelie's voice jerked me out of the dream I was having. In it I was washed up on a rocky shore, coughing up water, and shivering. I'd been lying on my back, just as I was really doing on the Sip o' Sea's top deck, staring up into a cloudless sky like the sky over the Sip o' Sea, and some kid I didn't know was slowly burying me in rocks, one rock at a time.

I didn't have a mirror but I knew there was a nice fresh bullet hole in my head. It wasn't bleeding. It was just there, letting in air and letting out brain matter.

The kid was singing *Big Rock Candy Mountain*.

It took a moment to get my lips moving. "Excuse me?"

"Jane is not the nicest dog I've ever met, but she is by far the smartest."

I noticed I was getting a sunburn. Otelie was wearing a sunhat. I should of been wearing a hat. "Smart isn't the word."

"Perhaps not. Is that why someone wanted her dead?"

"What?"

"Mr. Russo, I am not a fool."

"Fuck, no. Sorry, I mean— "

"Not being a fool, I've taken note of some of the more curious things happening aboard this boat. For instance, the disappearance of the serious young actress, Miss Olivia Powers. Miss Powers is dead, isn't she?"

I gave her one of my famous stares, the one I used when someone surprised me so much I forgot every word I ever knew. I could make noises though, and I made a few now.

"I thought so. We left New York City Sunday noon. Miss Clara Louise went overboard around noon on Monday. Miss Powers was murdered on that very same day. Another young actress. Let's see now. From my calculations, Miss Powers' murder would have occurred around the time of the tropical storm, wouldn't you say?"

"Your calculations?"

"That's what I said, Mr. Russo. An obvious time to choose. All of us occupied with a suicide, a storm and the arrival of the Coast Guard. Such confusion. If I were a murderer, I should have chosen such a time. Wouldn't you?"

The woman had my complete attention.

I said, "Yes." And I meant it. If I wanted to kill someone in a confined space, and big as it was, the Sip o' Sea was still a boat, meaning a confined space.

"Now why would anyone want to kill that girl? All she did, so far as we know, was witness her friend's suicide."

"Her friend?"

"Perhaps friend is too strong a word, but on Sunday afternoon I saw our Holly and the two dead girls all together mooning over Captain Moody. Poor things. They could have asked me and I would have told them they could look like Ava Gardner and still not have a chance. He's quite smitten with a girl waiting in Miami."

"You've been paying attention?"

"Of course I've been paying attention. I'm not just a cook. Besides, anyone who works for Mrs. Willingford would do well to remain on their toes."

"Amen to that."

"Indeed."

We spent a moment in silence. If I'd ever needed to talk to someone, I needed to talk to someone now. Holly knew a lot of what I knew. Mrs. Willingford knew most of what I knew. But here was a fresh head, one who didn't need me telling her what's what. Otelie'd been paying attention.

But how could I ask her for help? I was supposed to be this Private Eye, the guy Mrs. Willingford was learning from, the guy she'd played second fiddle to, and that guy needed the help of her cook?

I had my pride.

Oh, the hell with it. I needed advice and something told me the best place to get it was from Mrs. Otelie Coleman.

I plunged. At least I began to plunge. But Otelie beat me to it.

"When I peel potatoes, when I whip cream, when I taste

a soup, I'm thinking. I've been thinking about what's going on since before that Clara Louise dove off the ship."

"Before?"

"Of course, before. You know how many times I've been on this ship cooking for the Willingfords and their guests?"

"No."

"Neither do I. But not once has it ever felt like this time feels. I felt it deep in my bones before we left, I felt it when we were hiring a whole new crew after our Holly was almost killed, and then I saw you and that dog of yours come aboard and I said to myself, I said 'Otelie, something's up else you two wouldn't be here.' You may not have known it but your Jane knew. I said, 'Otelie, you do as that dog does. You keep your eyes open and your wits about you. You watch everything. The Devil has something planned…'"

"The Devil?"

"Who else, Mr. Russo? Isn't that what you do? You catch the Devil whenever you can?"

I'd never thought of it that way, not once. Seeing it through Otelie Coleman's eyes changed everything. From one moment to the next, I knew I was through thinking I didn't have it, thinking I shouldn't call myself a Private Investigator. From now on, I was Sam Russo as well as Bogart. I was better than Bogart because Bogart was an actor. He was following someone else's script. I wasn't an actor. No one wrote my lines. No one dressed me or adjusted my lights. I was on my own and what I got myself into, I'd get myself out of.

Amazing how fast your life can change.

"That's what I do, Mrs. Coleman. I chase the Devil. And this time I know who it is."

"I thought you did. I thought you knew. But you're having some trouble getting it just right. Like the times I'm in my kitchen and everything's going fine until the last moment and I just know there's something missing, something I need to do."

"That's exactly what it's like."

"I'm a damn fine cook, Sam Russo. And you're a damn fine Devil Chaser. You'll find that something. Just you wait and see."

"I did find that someone."

Otelie whipped her head round.

"You did? Well of course you did. I knew it first time Mrs. Willingford dragged you home. She's not known to do that, it's not her way, so I knew there had to be a good reason. Does this someone know you know?"

"I'm not sure. But I think it's a safe bet they do."

"Oh my, oh my! They could kill you."

"I've thought of that. And so has Mrs. Willingford."

Otelie's black eyes got round as the pebbles on my rocky beach. "They could kill you both! You have to stop them."

"I'd like to."

"Well, let's see now. You can't call the cops."

"Nope. No cops to call."

"Only one thing to do."

"Are you thinking what I'm thinking?"

"I think I am, Mr. Sam Russo. You expose them, right in front of everyone. And you do it before they have time to kill anyone else."

"I don't have proof."

"Oh pither. Proof? Do you know for sure?"

"Yep, pretty sure I do."

"Well then, Devil Chaser, there's your proof. All the proof you need."

29

To catch our devil, I needed a plan and I needed it fast.

Best place to work out a good one was in my own stateroom and who better to suffer along through the jam I was in trying to work out the details than Holly and Mrs. Willingford?

Over the past two years Mrs. Willingford'd proved herself wily as a weasel. My friend Holly had proved herself, period.

To get into my own stateroom, I had to knock twice. Then I had to say, "It's me, Sam."

Mrs. Willingford opened the door. And slammed it fast behind me. She also locked it… again.

An hour later, I was the one slipping water down Jane's throat with the eye dropper. Jane was awake, she was alert, she was weak but not so weak I didn't get a hum.

I scratched behind her ears. I held her close. My heart hummed along with hers. And I talked faster than Clara Louise had talked, outlining a plan straight out of Agatha Christie, one I hoped they'd like and even more, refine.

They not only bought it, they jumped right in. It was the first moment of calm I'd had in days. Until they really got going.

Mrs. Willingford said, "You're right, Sam. It has to be tonight. We dock tomorrow."

Holly said, "And it has to be after dinner when the guests are busy digesting and the stewards are busy clearing away and Leonard is busy getting started for the evening."

"We're all going," said Mrs. Willingford, "Otelie as well. All those we trust will be covering every door in or out of the Grand Salon."

I said, "If we're all there, that would leave Jane alone."

"You think we'd do that?" said Holly. "She's going too. With Joker and Kenneth and your gun."

I said, "Either one of you two think this is getting stagey?"

"Of course it's stagey, Sam," said Holly, "who said 'all the world's a stage'?'"

"Shakespeare."

"Then he was a smartie. What we're doing here, Sammy, is your kind of showbiz."

"Sammy?" said Mrs. Willingford.

"Ignore her," I said.

I thought about Shakespeare and his stage for a second, went over Hercule Poirot's cases with their usual endings, all his suspects waiting in one room to be exposed as the guilty party, and got it. Holly was right. What I did was a form of show business. Every ending to every case had been one long song and dance routine but without the music and the dancing.

I found that comforting.

I was sick with nerves.

I noticed Jane's strength returning by the second. She wanted off the bed, she wanted to stand, she wanted to run. I didn't want her to do any of those things. So I held on to my dog. Under normal conditions, I wouldn't of won. Under these conditions, it was easy.

I didn't notice Holly and Mrs. Willingford rooting around in my closet until I did.

"What the hell are you two doing?"

Holly answered. "Looking for just the right outfit for you to wear."

"You've got to be kidding."

"Kidding?" said Mrs. Willingford, "as in 'not serious'? About clothes? I do not joke about clothes. Without the right ensemble, tonight might not go as well as we expect it to.

With the right ensemble, you're a star."

"Invitations!" said Holly.

I didn't get it, but Mrs. Willingford did. Immediately.

"Of course. It's our last night at sea. We'll tell them it's a Willingford tradition to hold a special soiree after dinner and everyone is absolutely required to come, no excuses. The stewards will have to be there, of course, serving drinks and canapés and party favors. Oh Holly, what a clever girl you are."

I said, "Excuse me."

"Thank you, Lois. And they're to come wearing evening clothes and... do you have party favors?"

"Good lord, yes. A Willingford without party favors? Unthinkable. Kenneth can whip up the invitations. He has the most beautiful penmanship. Hold on, I'm getting an idea, a great and wondrous idea. Oh dear god, I'm a genius. I know— !"

"Excuse me," I said.

Holly shoved aside my clutching hand, the one trying to grab Mrs. Willingford's slender white throat.

I said, "Know what?"

"We could begin with charades. Get them all in the mood. What do you think?"

Holly'd gone past speech into shrieking. "Perfect!"

At that point the both of them turned pink and smiled at each other, smiles bigger than any I'd ever gotten from either one of 'em. If I didn't already not exist, I existed even less as they threw themselves into their plans for Sam Russo's Poirot-like "Name the Killer Party".

All I could do was fume. And hang on to Jane. Jane had gone from humming to yodeling. It was looking down at my mending dog that told me what was going to gum up their works.

I did not say, I shouted: "Excuse me! But Jane is now well enough to show us who put her in a lifeboat. She can do that faster than Man o' War in a six furlong sprint."

I wish I could say I felt bad as I watched their faces fall. I couldn't say that. I wanted a quiet gathering, me doing the talking, all innocent parties surprised, the killer reacting, maybe some restraint provided by Captain Moody and his engineer, the Greek fellow Alki Kormos.

I didn't get what I wanted.

"We swaddle her," said Mrs. Willingford. "They'll all understand she's not well. As for the guilty party, they'll feel safe seeing she's restrained. Once Sam here has finished his talk and named his killer, we could unwrap Jane. Oh, it's another perfect move. Thank you, Sam. Jane will provide the final proof... if any is needed."

"The crowning touch," said Holly.

Two hours later, Kenneth's formal invitations were finished and slipped under every door or directly into a hand. In the case of the kitchen staff, the bar, meaning Leonard, and the stewards, meaning Merle, Clyde, Howard, Gene, and Nicolas, they were gathered together and told personally by Mrs. Otelie Coleman. In the case of Captain Moody and his crew, he was told to slow the ship way down to make the evening go smooth as possible. That was my idea.

The handwritten invitations looked and read like this.

In the hallowed tradition of the Willingford Family,
The yacht Sip o' Sea invites you to her
"Last Night at Sea Grand Gala."
An evening of drink and dance and games of wit.
Formal attire requested, attendance required.
And for the overall winner — a Grand Prize
Of Surprising Worth.
Tonight. The Grand Salon. 9 PM sharp.

All this was dreamed up by my girls, but that crack: "of surprising worth" was all mine.

It was sure gonna surprise someone. I hoped.

To keep things as normal as possible, and to do my best not to give away my hand, I took my dinner like I usually did—in my stateroom.

That meant Gene had to do what he usually did. He brought my food down on a fish pink tray, then took it away on its fish pink tray. All I had to do was eat it. It took everything I had to get it down.

I was spooked. Sam Russo, daring PI, had the jitters. I knew the symptoms right away. Jane and I didn't spend all that time in the middle of *Harvey* with Jimmy Stewart standing in for Frank Fay on another jag, and Josephine acting like the pro she was, to miss the signs of a big dose of stage fright.

I'd fought against writing a damn speech, one I could read at a podium. At least I won that round. No speech, no podium, no prepared notes.

They fought against my acting "normal." I won that round too. Everything had to be as it usually was or I might not pull this off. I knew what a risk I was taking. But I was counting on something I'd slowly learned as my case came together. Some people don't or won't or can't believe they can lose. Some people think they're invincible.

The killer was one of those people. I was counting on that.

To get Jane used to being swaddled so we'd all be able to hear ourselves over her hums and yodels, not to mention her trying to leap on the killer as soon as I carried her into the Grand Salon, Holly had already bound her like a papoose.

She didn't like it. She made a fuss. She tried chewing her swaddling. Nothing worked. It took some doing, but she got it. She was stuck until I unwound her, so she stopped trying to get unstuck.

I was going to pay for that later. But for now, this was my call, not hers. Right now I was the guy standing on a high window ledge hoping the wind didn't blow him off.

Gene was back to clear up. Looking at Jane in her mummy wrapping, he smiled his most winsome Monty Clift smile.

"You had us all going there, girl," he said. "You had us worried."

He got what people usually got from Jane. Silence and a glare. I got what I was hoping for. I couldn't solve the jitters like my present jitters with just a smoke and a drink. Maybe with something stronger but I didn't do stronger stuff. Not even one of Doctor Ken's pills.

But I could calm the heebie jeebies with a smoke and a drink *and* talking about the movies. If I wanted to talk about the movies, Gene was my man. He was the perfect companion to wait out the time before Holly came to collect me and Jane.

I offered him a Lucky and a light but it seemed Gene didn't smoke. Or maybe he didn't smoke on duty. I offered him a drink. He didn't drink on duty either.

I did both.

Of course, we got to talking about movies, a great way to pass the time before my own performance. One of my favorite films turned out to be one of Gene's favorite films too. We both loved Gene Tierney. We both liked Dana Andrews. We both thought Clifton Webb made one hell of a terrific decadent dandy. We were both nuts about the song played throughout the movie. Best of all, we both loved the trickery treats. When the time came for the big switcheroo, we both jumped in our seats. In short, we both loved *Laura*.

Even so, said my Gene, he liked Gene Tierney's grittier stuff better. *Leave Her to Heaven* was a study in character. Where did she find it in her to play a stone cold killer? Could I imagine my friend Holly taking it on? Or that Clara Louise?

Gene'd be great to go to the movies with.

Too bad I wasn't likely to see him again considering boats and all.

30

So here I was, just about to pull a rabbit out of a hat, or shoot myself in the foot, whichever came first, and I got one of my headaches.

Fuck it. On with the show.

Walking into the Grand Salon, I handed a mummified Jane off to Holly who sat on one of the couches between Joker and Doctor Kenneth, checked the room for Mrs. Willingford—there she was at the bar, looking like the cover of one of her fashion magazines—checked to make sure a strong but innocent party stood at every possible exit, and then checked my audience.

They were all dressed in what Mrs. Willingford demanded of them: dinner jackets for the gents and evening gowns for the ladies. Sandrine was wearing a tiara.

Whadda bunch. I could just imagine what each of 'em thought a Grand Prize of Surprising Worth was gonna be. Stock in Joker's distillery. An island he didn't need. A yearling by Joker's Wild, his best stallion back at Beeswing Farm. Backing a movie. One of Mrs. Willingford's hats.

I'd done my best with what I had in my one small suitcase. It wasn't good enough for this crowd, but all in all, I thought I looked pretty swell. I wore my fedora hat at a slant, my trench coat tied, I was packing iron, I wasn't chewing gum. I didn't get better than that.

Leonard manned the bar. The stewards wove through their people bringing drinks, offering tidbits, tidying away the usual messes people who made 'em never cleaned up themselves. Otelie kept the food flowing in. And someone, three guesses who, had done some party decorating.

If I were a guest, I might not guess this was a hanging party. Unfortunately, I think the single most important guest had an idea things weren't as they appeared to be.

Didn't matter. I knew how the first act was going to go. The second act was in the hands of our killer.

But first I had to get through my part and do it at least half as well as Jimmy played Elwood P. Dowd.

I thought they'd notice when I walked in since I walked in last. Not to mention my get-up. I'd wondered if any of 'em asked themselves if Olivia Powers would walk in after me, if Vergil Sapster was hiding behind her.

If they were, it didn't look like it. How quickly we get forgotten.

Though not Jane. Jane got a lot of ohs and ahs. After that, what they cared about was Mrs. Willingford's game of charades. They were all praying they'd win the Prize of Surprising Worth.

I took the big chair Mrs. Willingford'd saved for me. She saved it by leaving another of Kenneth's handwritten cards on the seat. The card read: *Reserved for Tonight's Grand Master*. If she hadn't, I wouldn't of been in the best seat in the house.

Funny, you can expect a thing, prepare for it, yet be caught flatfooted when it happened.

My mind went blank—until Mrs. Willingford walked over, pinched me and hissed, "It's your last chance, Sam. Wake up." Turning to her guests, she said, "Sorry. No charades. But I think you'll like the show anyway."

Then she walked back.

Mrs. Willingford was right. If I didn't run my best race, the killer got away with it.

They weren't walking away, not if I had to swallow a bottle of aspirin.

Gazing from one face to another, you couldn't hear a pin drop. If they weren't whispering, they were talking like I wasn't there. Ordering drinks, passing cigarettes… if I were an actor, I'd do a John Wilkes Booth and shoot a couple.

I didn't stand up but I did yell. I had to over this crowd. "Early on our second day out, Clara Louise, an aspiring actress, walked out of her stateroom carrying a duffel bag. A certain Vergil Sapster saw her do it. Anyone notice Vergil Sapster lately?"

I got 'em there. If they hadn't noticed before that Vergil was missing, they did now. I saw their eyes sliding around in their heads, searching for Sapster.

"On that very same day right after lunch, Clara Louise— who we all thought had slept until noon—walked across the back deck, climbed up on the railing and made a perfectly executed dive off the Sip o' Sea. She did this wearing a heavy sweater and dressy shoes. By diving, she missed the ship's propellers, but she was sure to be left far behind, too far for a ship as large as this ship to get back to her before she drowned. Captain Moody immediately sent out a distress call. Dozens of small boats heard it. He also called the nearest Coast Guard station. The small boats were there much faster than the Coast Guard.

"Clara's suicide was witnessed by another actress, already a movie star, Miss Olivia Powers, and by our opera singer, Miss Sandrine Brunetti. There was a third witness, Charlie Dick."

All heads swiveled towards Charlie, sitting quietly next to Irma Morton and Carson Kline. Carson was rapidly taking notes.

I was holding them, but not like Jimmy could. They wanted their game of charades. They wanted that prize.

Only Sandrine was angry. "Why didn't you say something, Charlie? I did."

That stirred 'em up a bit. Some questions, one or two accusations. I held up my hand. No one noticed. So I was back to yelling. "Shut up! I have a story to tell, one that's bound to tax some of your brains. Be quiet and listen."

"Is there a prize?" That was Otto Gerlinger. It would be. He wanted Joker to finance his film. That was Otto's mistake. He wasn't last on my list, but close enough to it.

He'd made himself first.

"I'm glad you asked, Otto. Yes, there's a prize. I made a few phone calls from Captain Moody's wheelhouse. Some of those calls concerned you."

Gerlinger's smile faded from eager to uncertain.

"Your name is Heinrich Bader. It's true you've directed a few unimportant films, but you made them in Germany as a decorated Nazi. You never saw Hollywood until November of '45."

Otto Gerlinger aka Heinrich Bader went dead quiet.

Walter Dew made up for that in spades. He stood up and shouted: "I'm on a boat with a fucking Nazi? You killed Clara Louise! You made her jump? Some Nazi trick, was that it?"

Bader tried, I gave him that. "Nazi trick? I am an artist, a great artist. Who is this Clara Louise that I should kill her?"

Walter was still shouting. "A Nazi doesn't need a reason to kill!"

"Sit down, Walter," said Mrs. Willingford. "Shush, Bader. Sam's got a long way to go."

"I found your medal, Heinrich. I'm still working out how you got into the country, but I know when you're leaving. I made another call. You're gone as soon as we dock."

"But my movie… I must make my movie. Is it my fault we Germans endured that silly little man?"

Alki Kormos moved up behind Otto and placed a large hand on his shoulder. Otto shut up.

"You're not leaving yet, Otto. You've got a part to play in our little drama. You invited Clara Louise aboard."

The hair over Otto's eyes rose. "But she asked me, she wheedled."

"I know. I'm coming to that. There were three actresses

on the Sip o' Sea. Olivia Powers, Clara Louise and Holly. Early on it struck me as odd that all three attended the same school, a place called the Actors Studio run by a guy called Elia Kazan. If they'd come together, each being here at the same time would make sense. They didn't come together. Holly came as a special guest of the Willingfords. Clara Louise finagled her way aboard by vamping our Nazi here. But Olivia Powers was invited by her father."

King was good. Or drunk. He sat at the bar and sipped whatever Leonard made him. The rest of 'em did what you'd expect them to do: go wide eyed wondering who her father was. Carson's pencil was flying.

"She knew who he was, but he didn't. King Barton— "

The name "King Barton" now got said in every way a name could be said. I could see how my whole act was gonna go—interrupted with every new discovery. What the hell. The more I talked, the more riveting I felt. It also helped my headache.

"King Barton thought he was inviting a little honey along for company. Olivia had other plans which she shared with a few fellow students at her acting school. Sharing her plans sealed her fate aboard the Sip o' Sea. As for King's fate, Olivia was going to expose him for driving her abandoned mother to suicide."

All King said was, "Bullshit," as Leonard poured him another whiskey.

I said, "All three Actors Studio actresses were not on the ship by accident. Holly came because she was a bona fide guest. Olivia came to confront her father. Clara Louise came because Elia Kazan cast Olivia in his latest play, one he called *Dead on the Rocks*. Clara Louise wanted that part. So Clara came to kill Olivia Powers."

"What!" screamed Sandrine. "Olivia is dead?"

"Dead as a doornail a matter of hours after Clara jumped off the boat."

The hubbub was worse than New Year's Eve in Times Square.

Toby's voice got through. "But if Clara Louise killed herself, how did she kill Olivia?"

"Not easy, but she did it. Everyone was supposed to think it was a suicide. But Clara wore warm clothes for the cold water. She dove to miss the propellers. And one out of all those rescue boats was a boat waiting just for her. In it was someone in on her plan, someone who'd get something they wanted out of helping her. In minutes, Clara Louise was getting pulled out of the water by this guy, dried off, and hidden below decks."

"Fabulous," said Irma Morton. "Carson, are you getting all this?"

"Every word, dear."

"About now," I said, "you're probably asking what Vergil saw Clara carrying early on the morning she pretended to kill herself."

From the looks I got, most of 'em had forgotten Vergil Sapster—again.

"Vergil saw her carrying a duffel bag. In it was a knotted rope tied to a grappling hook. Hanging the hook off an obscure side railing of the Sip o' Sea was one of Clara's biggest risks. One of the crew could of seen it, taken it away. But they didn't. The knotted rope was how she climbed back on board from her partner's boat as soon as she could. That must of been during the tropical storm... hard in all that wind, but not impossible. Clara was a trained dancer. With the rest of us scared or running the ship, she stood a good chance."

Like a kid in a class, Carson looked up from his notes. He said, "You're saying Clara Louise is still here. Why hasn't anyone seen her?"

"Because she's an actress. Actresses act."

The look on Carson's face, as well as Irma's, was beatific.

As a team they sighed, "Of course!" Then looked over the Willingford guests sitting on the edge of their Grand Salon seats. I knew the look. Like I'd done, they were asking themselves: which one?

Leonard was still making drinks as smooth as a piston, the stewards were still gliding among us serving Otelie's snacks and Leonard's cocktails. A smooth running team, not one of 'em missed a beat.

Captain Moody, tasked with hiring the crew, had damn good taste.

Holly was beaming at me. Mrs. Willingford looked like she liked me more than usual. Joker was holding his own. As for Jane, if we'd just let her loose, this would all be over.

I couldn't risk that. It'd all be over but over for who?

I said, "Clara Louise climbed up that rope wearing two pairs of engineering overalls... "

"Two?" said Walter.

"One on top to get messy killing Olivia with the pipe she brought from the small boat, one underneath to keep clean leaving Olivia's stateroom."

"Oh," said Walter in a very small voice.

"This was while I was in the wheelhouse listening to Commander Jackson of the Coast Guard declare her a suicide. The blonde wig..."

"Wig?" said Toby Tyrrell.

"She's not a blonde. When she dove she used a hell of a lot of bobby pins to keep the thing on and not give the game away."

"Ah," said Holly. "Good thinking."

I smiled at Holly. One of my favorite things about her was how savvy she was.

"She slipped into the sleeping Olivia's stateroom, beat her to death with the pipe, threw the pipe, the first pair of overalls, and anything else she needed to get rid of out the bathroom porthole, then she took Olivia's stateroom key—a key that should of been in Olivia's room, one I couldn't find, a missing key that told me a lot—and walked out, locking the door behind her. At this point, wearing the clean second pair of overalls and maybe another wig, she got into character before someone recognized her as Clara.

"She did all this in order to kill Olivia Powers and never be suspected because... who suspects a dead woman?"

"But why?" said Joker. "Why kill a poor girl in her acting school?"

"Simple reason, but a complicated plan. To get the star-making role Elia Kazan had given to Olivia."

Holly squeaked. "Mr. Kazan would never give that role to Clara Louise. She wasn't good enough."

"No," I said, pausing for the next uproar this would cause. "But he'd give it to Heddy Day."

For that I got a concerted, "Who?"

31

"Heddy Day!" shrieked Holly, "*the* Heddy Day from Mr. Kazan's Actors Studio! You didn't tell me that. You mean Heddy was the scary actress Olivia wrote about in her journal?"

"The very one," I said. "Vergil Sapster was Heddy's Sugar Daddy. But as a giddy 'Clara Louise', Heddy got her Nazi over there to invite Clara on this trip."

Gerlinger sighed. "What could I do? Only Nazis could work."

No one listened to him, but they listened to Holly. "Clara Louise is someone Heddy made up? Gosh. But why didn't Mr. Sapster recognize her? He was at the school too. Heddy was his mistress."

"Because she's not only a scary actress, she's a brilliant actress. There never was a Clara Louise."

"You said a mouthful there, Sam." That was Mrs. Willingford's contribution.

I said, "Holly?"

"Yes, Sammy?"

"When Sapster wasn't in town giving Heddy Day a bad time and pots of money, Heddy had someone at the school, didn't she?"

"You mean like a boyfriend?"

"A boyfriend who was also an actor."

"Gee. I wish Olivia was here. She knew this stuff better than me since she was there longer, but yes, there was an actor Heddy dated. They were quite the item until they had a fight right in front of everyone, a real humdinger, and broke up. What was his name? Something French. Alain? René? I think it was René."

"René Denman. Thank you, Holly."

Jane began to hum. If it got any louder, I'd hum along. I was learning the language of Jane. She was saying: Shut up, Sam Russo. Who cares about how and who and when and why? Just bite the killer. Bite the killer and hang on until the Miami cops take over.

Jane had a point. But I needed to try and prove all this. Half the time Poirot knew he was right, but he couldn't prove he was right. This was my half time.

Tommy Feathers was an Indian. In the movies, Indians didn't smile. They didn't laugh. They scalped innocent settlers or attacked wagon trains. Tommy wasn't a movie Indian. He smiled as he said, "And where is Vergil Sapster? You can ask him if he knew his mistress had a lover."

"Say," said Sandrine, "that's right. Where is that horrid little man?"

I said, "Hold your horses. A story like this gets told piece by piece."

Mrs. Willingford gave the Grand Salon one of her brightest smiles. "This is a lollapalooza of a story. I suggest you shut your mouths and pay attention."

"Will there be questions afterwards?" said Otto. "And a prize?"

Joker, not entirely asleep, woke himself up. "I don't abide Nazis. One more word, you're bunking in the bilge."

Heinrich alias Otto flushed and shut up.

Carson Kline, pencil poised, said, "I'm paying attention, you incredible woman, so fire away Mr. Russo."

Writers. Worse than cops.

"OK. Is everyone else following too?"

I got a couple of eager nods, a blank stare, a slow blink, and a turned head. Good enough.

"Heddy Day, a good actress, covets the role Olivia Powers, a movie star and a better actress, is getting. She decides the role will be hers if the better actress is removed."

They all nodded at that one.

"When Olivia spilled she was sailing on the Sip o' Sea to confront her ex-movie star dad on a boat— "

King Barton put down his drink. "Current movie star, thank you."

"Heddy thought: what better place than water to lose someone? Vergil Sapster, the sap, was seldom in New York. No need to worry about him. But there was the boyfriend. They staged a very public breakup."

Irma Morton had moved closer. Much closer, I was going to have to ask Carson to restrain his wife. "Why would he help her?"

"Because if her star rose, his star rose. Their breakup made Heddy look single. Without René Denman waiting near the Sip o' Sea, Clara Louise *had* to be a suicide."

"Oooh, good stuff," said Irma.

It *was* good stuff. Could Poirot do better? Yeah, he could. I kept going anyway. "Heddy created Clara Louise. She got her accepted at the Actors Studio to keep her near Olivia, but not as Heddy. I'm betting all along Clara Louise was meant to kill herself so she'd never be a suspect. I'm also betting how it was going to work fell into her lap when Olivia told the whole school she was taking a boat ride. It must of seemed heaven sent since René knew boats. When Heddy dove off the Sip o' Sea, he'd be near to "rescue" her before she really did drown. With 'Clara' jumping in broad daylight, Heddy and René could count on someone raising the alarm. Their little boat would be just another boat in a load of boats."

I popped two more aspirin, got 'em down with whiskey. "I have to hand it to Heddy. For a last minute thing, it was almost perfect."

"Damn," said Irma. "I can think of a dozen women, top of the heap, who'd kill for the fucking role, pardon my French."

"That's why Clara Louise needed a grappling hook and the rope. To climb back aboard."

"That one was risky," said Leonard, shaking up something at the bar.

"Not really. Look at the possible witnesses."

Leonard took in the specimens seated around him. "You got a point," said Leonard.

Charlie Dick was sitting by the glass door that opened out onto the main deck, one guarded by two of Moody's crew. I'd noticed Charlie from time to time. Mostly I'd noticed for a guy used to center stage, he was very quiet.

But now, leaning forward to snag a shrimp and then sitting back to slowly peel it, he said, "Fascinating tale, Russo. But after killing Olivia, why would this Heddy stay aboard? Why didn't she just climb back down her little knotted rope and putt away with her friend on his little boat?"

This is where I got to say: "Aha! I'm sure that was the plan but two things changed it. One, the storm got bad, bad enough to make keeping a small boat close enough to a big boat like the Sip o' Sea impossible. And two, because Joker told Captain Moody over there to head for the High Seas. The little boat wasn't fast enough to keep up and we left it behind. Heddy was trapped aboard."

Carson twisted in his seat. "This just keeps getting better and better. Irma! Who should play Heddy Day?"

"Not to mention, dear, also playing Clara Louise."

"Plus whoever the killer is now."

"We could get anyone!"

"Pardon me," I said, "but will the both of you shut up?"

That surprised 'em, but it didn't shut 'em up. "All right, Mr. Smarty Pants," said Irma. "When are you spilling the beans? Which one of us is Heddy Day? Love the name."

"I'm coming to that."

"I should hope so," said Joker, "it's almost my bedtime."

"Forget it, darling," said Mrs. Willingford. "You're staying until the curtain drops."

"So there she was," I said, "stuck aboard the Sip o' Sea. Maybe standing over Olivia's dead body was when she realized what good luck not leaving might turn out to be. If she'd gotten off as planned, we'd have a missing person. Heddy couldn't care less if we thought Clara Louise was a killer or a victim. What she cared about was her second character. Heddy didn't just play Clara Louise on the Sip o' Sea. She came aboard twice. Once as Clara Louise and once as the person she's playing now."

That was the revelation I'd had when I was trying to save the Willingford bacon. I'd said Holly could leave twice: once as Olivia and once as herself. Meanwhile I expected a quick sharp inhale, but Carson didn't count. As Holly said, Heddy Day was good. She might of done as well as she thought she would playing Eva in Kazan's *Dead on the Rocks*.

"She got rid of the grappling hook and didn't get caught. She went back to being her second character and didn't get caught. Until she did."

Toby Tyrrell inhaled for me. "She did?"

"She did. Twice. First by the best Private Nose in New York City. All the wigs and accents in the world can't fool my dog. So Heddy had to remove Jane. She trapped her somehow, bound her feet and threw her in a lifeboat. Jane was supposed to die there."

"Gee," said Howard, "that's terribly mean."

He got a glare from the manly Clyde for that.

"The second person to catch our killer was Vergil Sapster. Remember, Heddy Day was his New York mistress. I'm guessing Heddy didn't know he'd be on the boat. Vergil knew who she was. He told her he knew. She had to think fast." I lit a cigarette, headache or no headache. "No name's better for Sapster than 'sap'. The sap believed it when she explained she was working on a role. She lured him away, killed him quickly, and left his body in the second lifeboat."

I scanned the Grand Salon. Was I getting to my killer? I was sure getting to the rest of 'em. Hot damn, but Heddy had nerve.

Joker was wide awake. He almost looked younger. "So, the person you're talking about has killed two goddamn people on my goddamn boat?"

"Three people."

Doing the Poirot thing was turning out better than a lot of movies I'd seen. This time everyone jumped where they sat or stood.

Joker squawked. "Three!"

"I doubt the third kill took place on your yacht, Joker, but it was connected to it."

"What the devil do you mean, sir?"

"I mean our actress needed to impersonate someone else besides Clara Louise. Once Clara Louise was 'dead' someone had to be here to kill Olivia Powers. Heddy had to take a real person's place. How else to do that but kill them before they turned up for work, especially for someone like Heddy who solves her problems in a very final kind of way. One of you is that person."

Brother, I wished Bogie could of been here for how that one landed—like a Japanese shell on a Luzon beach. The worse hit seemed to be Cap'n Moody. Faced with a missing steward, he'd hired a killer without following the Willingford rules.

For the second time I'd told them the killer was among us. This time, I guess it got through.

Half of 'em moved away from the other half of 'em.

Good thing, Holly was holding Jane. Bad thing, Jane was working her way out of her wrappings. I had to talk faster.

Mrs. Otelie Coleman beat me to it.

"We dock sometime tomorrow. From all you've told us, Mr. Russo, I imagine this unpleasant person simply expects to walk off the ship and disappear into Miami."

"You got it, Mrs. Coleman. She expects to shrug off who she's playing now, meet her partner wherever he is, and get back to New York City where Elia Kazan will have to cast her in the part he meant for Olivia."

Mrs. Willingford said, "But it's not going to happen, is it Sam?"

I turned to Toby Tyrrell. Turning my head made my headache explode. "Toby, is there anyone here you never saw when Clara Louise was around?"

Toby gave that some thought. "Wish I could help ya, but nope."

"How about you, Tommy?"

Tommy didn't look like he was thinking. Turned out he was, and doing it just swell. "I've wondered about that. I've thought about it since you started talking. If one person was playing two people, they couldn't play them at the same time. The way I see it the Clara girl would get up late so she could play her other part. Same thing at suppertime. She didn't eat with the rest of us so she could be one of the— "

It had to happen. Even someone like Heddy, more in love with themselves than *The Man Who Came to Dinner*, more ruthless than *Little Caesar*, more heartless than the daughter of Mildred Pierce, had to admit when she was beat. Over by the bar, there was a sudden movement, a sudden "God damn you to hell, Russo!", and a slim figure pushing past the surprised engineer guarding the companionway that led to a side deck. The side deck led to the back deck.

Heddy was moving and she was moving fast, back towards the same deck she'd jumped off as Clara Louise.

Jane's timing was perfect. I should of seen it coming. I should of paid more attention. Jane'd wormed her way out of her wrapping. She was free of Holly and she was running not more than ten feet behind Heddy Day.

Not another word—I was out of my big important chair after her. What happened behind me, happened. All that mattered to me was Jane. Heddy could turn into a gull and fly away, I didn't care. She could mow down every big star at MGM with a Tommy gun, that was OK too. But she wasn't touching Jane. Not again.

Heddy was climbing up the same rail she dove off as Clara Louise and diving again. Or she was trying to dive, but Jane had a grip on her steward's jacket and nothing could make her let go. Heddy had to haul Jane up with her. Jane weighed a solid twenty pounds, even after half dying in a lifeboat, and she was twisting as she gripped. It ruined Heddy's balance, no way she could make that perfect dive and clear the propellers a second time.

Going over like that, she was pulp. And so was Jane.

My heart broke in my chest.

"Stop! You won't make it, Gene. You'll die and you'll kill my dog. Gene!"

But Heddy Day's "Gene" was gone, slipping and tumbling off the rail.

With her went Jane.

32

Water scared me. Deep sea water terrified me. But there it was. If it wasn't miles below me, it looked like it.

I was up and balanced on the rail looking down at a blood red wake. In it were chunks of body parts, all of 'em human body parts. Where was Jane? Nothing looked like Jane. Except, maybe, the blood.

I had no choice. I was Sam Russo. I was the guy who got my dog into another nasty mess. If we lived through this one, I promised myself I was changing jobs. There was an opening at one of Stapleton's breweries. I'd brew beer. Or maybe we could move out into the country, Jane and I. Pluck goats, milk chickens, whatever the hell people did on Staten Island farms. Jane could bite cows. Herd pigs. Whatever dogs did on Staten Island farms.

But right now, I had to dive. I had to believe Jane made it. Jane was like a cat. She had a lot more lives than I did. But even Jane would quickly drown in the briny deep with no shore for miles.

My dive was nothing like Vicki Draves diving. It wasn't even as good as Gene's try with Jane hanging on his smoky gray jacket. But it got me past the propellers. I'd of liked it if got me past one of Gene's severed legs, but you can't have everything.

So there I was, pushing away grisly bits of Gene and thrashing around in the red churning water, scared out of my wits and looking for Jane. If Clara Louise's head had been like a coconut, Jane's was no more than a spud.

Oh but suddenly, there she was, about thirty feet away

and struggling to dog paddle towards me.

She wasn't humming or yodeling, she had her jaw clamped shut trying to keep the foaming sea from filling her up and sinking her under. So did I. With two more godalmighty tries, I got her under one arm and then I was side-stroking for both our lives.

One of the few great things I'd ever done was ask Captain Moody to slow the Sip o' Sea for our Gala, to give us more time for my imitation of Hercule Poirot. Going as slow as she was, we weren't left behind as fast as Clara Louise was left behind.

We weren't Clara Louise. There was no little boat waiting nearby captained by our boyfriend René Denman. What we got were life preservers thrown at us. And the screams of Holly and Mrs. Willingford urging us on.

The Sip O' Sea may of been going slow, and Alki Kormos may of stopped her engines, but none of that mattered—the Sip o' Sea couldn't stop fast enough.

Turned out Captain Moody was thinking fast and moving fast. He lowered the ship's motor launch and jumped in to captain it towards us. So what with me yelling and Jane's letting me hold her and Eigil Moody's quick thinking, we didn't go down with Gene.

Poor Gene. A guy who liked the movies I liked, a guy I could get to like. Someone I might of called friend. Except he tried to kill Jane. Only one man did that and I still liked him. That wouldn't happen again.

And right there tells you all you need to know about talent: Heddy Day was a damn good actress.

In my stateroom, huddled up in bed, thermometer under my tongue, dog in my arms, I counted the ways.

How many times had Jane almost died thanks to me?

I'd gotten her stabbed eleven times with a hotel steak knife, all serious tries, sucked down by quick Hudson river mud maybe twice, shot at and grazed once, bound and gagged and left to die for days in a lifeboat, and now almost drowned off a yacht in the Atlantic Ocean.

That was some record.

I looked down at her. She looked up at me and hummed. I was forgiven. No. Not true. She never blamed me. For her, there was nothing to forgive.

They said a dog was man's best friend. They couldn't be more right. But was a man someone any self-respecting dog even wanted to know?

But still… this time I'd saved my dog, and this time I'd solved the damn case. Me. Sam Russo, PI. No pretending. That felt good.

People had been in and out of my stateroom from the moment I was carried in by Alki Kormos, wet and chilled to the bone. I was still holding tight to Jane. We'd been bathed, oiled, rubbed, and forced into bed where we were now watched over by a constant Holly and an occasional Kenneth.

Otelie Coleman brought her special soup. Spooning it down me, she said it would do Jane as much good as it was doing me. I said I didn't know about Jane, but I'd prefer whiskey. I didn't get any. Holly wouldn't let me smoke. I was grateful beyond words that I'd saved my dog, but my own survival didn't feel so hot.

It hurt in every way a man could hurt.

Mrs. Willingford was in and out. I had lipstick all over my face to prove it. Along with Joker (and maybe his bank account) she'd been dealing with whoever a person deals with when they're sailing into the Port of Miami with two dead bodies, one steward lost overboard, and Commander Jackson's official Coast Guard report of a young woman's suicide which wasn't a suicide, or even a murder. Clara Louise hadn't died, although she was dead enough now.

I didn't envy them. It must of been a helluva mess to

explain.

The hardest people to get rid of were Carson Kline and Irma Morton. They'd written a screenplay in record time and wanted their loose ends tied up.

Who didn't? I worked the best I could without once setting foot in Elia Kazan's Actors Studio. I never saw Heddy Day playing herself. If the cops ever found Heddy's boyfriend, I'd be surprised. René Denman was long gone. As an actor, he was already someone else, and if it turned out he had to he'd stay someone else for life.

René was one of my loose ends. The time I'd spent on Captain Moody's ship-to-shore telephone not only told me all about Otto Gerlinger but it included talking to a chatty little number at the Actors Studio. She told me five students were taking a break, not just three. Olivia Powers, Holly and Clara Louise were off on a sail. Heddy Day and René Denman had gone too, separately, no one knew where. Elia was hopping mad. Kazan was frothing at the bit to get *Dead on the Rocks* into production. He was negotiating, casting, setting up rehearsal time, and his star, Olivia Powers, the girl who was playing Eve, was off on some rich man's yacht?

I did some acting of my own on the ship's phone with the National Union of Marine Cooks and Stewards. I told 'em I knew René, we were old friends. From what was said I worked out how Heddy got aboard the Sip o' Sea as Gene, even with the Willingfords extremely careful hiring policy after Holly's adventures in the Staten Island woods.

René had once worked cruise ships as a steward. He still had his papers. When Heddy saw her chance, Captain Moody already hired all the stewards needed. Heddy killed one to create a last minute need. Which is how I knew that for Heddy Day, murder was neat and final.

To become Gene Benham, she used René Denman's papers, changing the R to a G and the D to a B. She got rid of the accent over René's é. Gene Benman was perfect.

Missing a steward at the last minute, Moody snapped her up.

Heddy had to arrive on the Sip o' Sea twice. First as Gene, settling in with the other stewards. Then slipping off for an hour or so, she quickly returned as Clara Louise. Who'd notice when Gene left or when he came back, too much fuss with all of us guests arriving, supplies loaded, luggage and a gaggle of New York City Port authorities poking around.

Heddy only had to keep it up until Clara was "dead." But Tommy Feather noticed Clara Louise never being in the same place at the same time as Gene.

It was Tommy who gave her a final review.

When it was just me and Holly and Jane, I scratched Jane's ear. "You knew all along, didn't you?"

I got back one of her looks. If she wasn't saying "Of course I did," I don't know what she was saying.

I never understand these things, but my headache—by then close to unbearable—faded away.

The Willingfords and their guests went to the races— except the dead ones and Otto Gerlinger. Heinrich Bader alias Otto Gerlinger had a clot of grim looking officials waiting on the dock to take him somewhere else.

Walter Dew was off like the favorite in the Derby, headed for the barns to take over the care of Fleeting Fancy, Toby Tyrrell right behind. Toby was only riding in the Old Rosebud Stakes but it was a big win if he took it.

Tommy Feather was faster than both of them. He had a mount in half the day's races.

Nobody won much when the Willingford mare came home with a five length lead, but I backed a real long shot Feather was riding and, for me, collected a nice little sum.

Added to my triple pay and bonus, I was a rich man.

After that, the idea was we went back to New York the way we'd come. I said not on your life and so did Holly, though not for the same reason. She had to get back fast. Elia'd lost Olivia Powers. He'd lost Heddy Day. He needed someone to play Eve and that someone was Holly.

Holly spent her time on the northbound express learning the part. I spent it finishing my book. Jane spent it in her own seat. No cargo section for her. I had to pay most of my winnings to buy her a real seat but it was worth every penny.

I did do one last thing for Holly before I left her at the door of the Actors Studio. I called Jimmy Stewart. He said he'd just finished a western. "Imagine me," he said, "on a horse. The horse kept looking back. I don't think he believed it."

Jimmy was in New York with his new wife. Yep, he said, they'd go watch Holly in *Dead on the Rocks*.

And when the press saw him there, and they would, all he'd talk about was how great Holly was.

I was in my Murphy bed, Jane along with me talking in her sleep, when Mrs. Willingford showed up in a hat I hadn't seen before. No one had ever seen a hat like that before. After we said our usual fond hello, which meant Jane had to find somewhere else to park herself, Lois handed me what seemed a small thing, but one that'd niggled since we set sail.

Why did she avoid Joker's opera singer, Sandrine Brunetti?

"Because," said Mrs. Willingford, "a long time ago we worked for the same Wichita pimp. Who knew she could sing?"

Enjoying the adventures of Sam Russo, Private Eye?

Turn the page to preview the first chapter of Sam's next case:
BLUES FOR THE DYING ...

BLUES FOR THE DYING and other books in the Sam Russo Mystery series are available from:

www.eiobooks.com

And your favorite bookseller.

Follow Ki Longfellow on the Internet:

Facebook Ki Longfellow
Twitter @KiLongfellow
Official Website www.kilongfellow.com
Sam Russo www.eiobooks.com/samrusso

I was thinking of renting some office space. I'd looked at the places on offer, two on Van Duzer Street, one so close to the Staten Island Ferry Terminal I could hear the paddles.

They all smelled like something died in 'em. From gloom was my best guess.

I'd read Chandler on the subject of Marlowe's office, dead flies, empty waiting room, and all. Compared to the three I'd seen, his sounded like a suite at the Waldorf.

I fled 'em all before something bit me.

Then I thought I'd pay for an ad in the phone book, something big enough to get noticed in the New York City Yellow Pages. Maybe a hand holding a Magnifying Glass. Or maybe a big eyeball. A few minutes of doodling, and doing a passable job—always been a passable doodler, got me into a lot of trouble growing up—I gave up on that idea too. I wouldn't call an eyeball so why would anyone else?

That left me wondering. How the hell was I was supposed to attract clients if no one knew I was a Private Eye for hire?

Detective Lino Morelli, my old pal in the Police Department, still called every once in awhile. It was the usual thing. He was in a jam and couldn't find his way out with a Klieg light. It always left me speechless. Why Richmond County didn't rip up his professional cop ticket beat the hell out of me. He couldn't find his own nose without a mirror.

After I'd said no enough times, he got the message. His calls came less and less often. I couldn't remember the last time I got one.

None of Mrs. Willingford's rich Park Avenue friends were in a jam. They all had my card. They'd been told to call me if things got hot. No one called. As for Mrs. Willingford herself, she'd sailed off on that yacht she'd married and so far as I knew had tipped over the edge of the world. I hoped not. I liked Mrs. Willingford. I liked Mrs. Willingford as much as I liked Carole Lombard. More probably, since Carole was dead. Also, Joker Willingford's wife liked me.

That left me thinking about my Murphy bed. You'd expect it would since I was in it so much.

I wanted to move the thing. If I could move my bed I could see out my only window and if I could see out the only window my one room had, it might take my mind off being alone. I didn't like being on my own. I wasn't used to solitude anymore.

The one thing I wasn't, was broke. Joker Willingford made good on our deal. I got paid that bonus he promised for cracking the murders on his boat, the Sip o' Sea, before we bumped into Miami on our way to the races at Hialeah. But even a bonus like that wasn't going to last forever.

I needed a new case.

I'd been trying to lose myself in a book. *Strangers on a Train* was a pretty good book and any other time, I'd be damned pleased to have my face stuck in it.

I wasn't pleased. I needed cigarettes. Getting up and going down to the Rexall three floors below my place seemed more than it was worth. Especially since I was still in my pajamas. I needed a drink. I had maybe a third of a pint of some cheap stuff left, but that wasn't working either. It was making me cranky.

All this was my fault. Why'd I let Jane go to Hollywood with Holly? What was I thinking? Climbing up the ladder and into the Willingford's private plane, Holly said, "Only a week, Sam. I'll bring her back in a week." Since then, I'd gotten two messages. The first was a phone call that stretched the trip out to two weeks.

I said, "Put my dog on the phone."

The second was a telegram. It said the way things were going for Holly at Warner Brothers, she wasn't sure when she'd be home.

I sent my own telegram. It said: *Jane's on a plane in two days or else.*

I knew Holly'd chew on that one. I had her there.

When the knocks hit my door, three of 'em, hard and fast, I spilled my drink on my chest.

I was off the bed and standing to one side of my door faster than Eclipse in the stretch.

I waited. Whoever was on the other side of the door waited.

The suspense wasn't killing me, but it was killing my back. You lie around a lot reading a lot of books and smoking a lot of cigarettes, and things give a little. My back was giving a lot. Not only that, but my gun was too far away to get to if whoever was out there decided to kick in my door.

Nice going, Russo. No gun, an aching back, and you're acting like King Kong is paying a visit.

I said, "Yeah? Who is it?"

"For the love of Mike, Sam, open the fecking door."

No mistaking that voice. Mickey Cates. I yanked open the door for my wild Irish friend, and when I did, he fell straight in and landed on what I called a carpet.

Mickey was shot to hell. How many times I didn't know. All I knew was he wasn't going to make it, not if I didn't get him help and get it soon.

I called the one man who couldn't say no. He wanted to. Doc Budge wanted to say no so badly he almost cried. He didn't say no but he did explain why some friend of his should come in his place instead of him. By the time the Willingford doctor got to Stapleton all the way from his cozy house in Brooklyn Heights, whatever I needed him for wouldn't need him anymore.

The sonofabitch was right. So I told him to call *his* friend, a doctor he knew who wouldn't have to take a cab, then the ferry, then a cab. This guy worked out of Staten Island's Clifton. I told Doc Budge if my friend was dead before his friend showed up, he was dead to the Willingfords. That might of been true, it might not of. All I know is he believed me.

By the time this other sawbones got there, I had Mickey in bed—mine, of course. The one not facing the window and Manhattan. I had his coat and tie off and his shirt open. He'd been shot all right but not like I'd been shot. I had three neat puckers around my heart where Paul Jarrett, a kid I grew up with like I grew up with Lino Morelli, had shot me point blank. Mickey was gut shot.

I was going to need a new mattress.

An hour later, Mickey was shot full of morphine, had the lead dug out of his belly, and was bound up like a mummy. The doctor got told by me to bill Doc Budge. I asked for his card for future adventures. Knowing my life and knowing Mickey's life, there were bound to be future adventures.

Half dead like he was, Cates was still more of a man than the friend of Doc Budge. Doctor Morrison's hand shook so bad it was me, not him, who did half the stuff that needed doing. And when we were through, I never saw someone leave my place so fast, not even Mrs. Willingford.

Mickey took the card instead of me so the poor sap would know Cates could find him. That's if Cates lived. No one, not even Mickey Cates, knew if he'd make it through the night.

I finally got dressed, hopped on down to the drugstore and brought back enough smokes and hootch to last out the wait to find out.

Then it was just me in a chair and an Irishman in my bed and a lot of quiet. As usual the phone didn't ring and no one else came knocking on my door. Lucky for the hairy moron who lived in 4-C, he wasn't home all night. I was in no mood for his drunken malarkey.

I didn't find out what happened to Cates until the sun sat like a pumpkin on the edge of my windowsill. Waiting out Mickey's struggle to live, I'd had a lot of time to think about what happened to him. I'd decided it was something to do with him and his Irish Mob up to their usual no good. This time they'd muscled in on someone not their own size. The Italians, probably. Carlo Gambino. Or Tommy Lucchese. Or Joe Bananas. Or half a hundred other vicious lugheads poking their fingers in all sorts of eyes.

I was wrong. It had nothing to do with the Irish mob. Or the Italians. Or even the Jews. It was all about Mickey's taste in women.

Mickey'd once loved a lovely young whore called Caitlin, a friend of Holly's. Caitlin didn't love him back but that didn't stop him. He took what he could get. When Caitlin was killed, I watched Mickey Cates turn into someone I wouldn't cross for all the money the Rockefellers ever stole. I was there, right in the thick of things, so I know what he could do when he got sore.

But with Caitlin dead and in her grave, I never thought the heart that beat in Cates' cold and lyrical chest could ever love another.

I was wrong about that too.

"Ah, Sam. I've done for meself this time."

"Done what?"

"I never meant to. Never again. The pain is more than a man can bear."

With the strength he had left, he grasped my hand.

"Sweet Jaysus. I swore I wouldn't bear it again. I swore on the lost life I loved so well."

"Swore what, Mickey?"

"And you'll be promisin' you won't set to laughin'?"

"Laugh? With you half dead?"

"Ah, but that's nothing. Not when ye hear the lass sing the Blues. Sammy, me boyo, you should see her standing there, her in the one light and only the piano."

"You're in love."

"That I am."

"Does she love you?"

"Well now, not so you'd notice. But I go every night and her eyes, they light like the lights of Faerie when she sees me."

"Go where every night?"

"Jimmy Ryan's."

"The basement club on 52nd Street?"

"The very one."

"And this lass is... ?"

"As black as Belfast's heart."

"She's a... "

"She isn't. Not a Belfast lass. Zara's a nigger."

The Irish had never been what you'd call tolerant of Negroes. Even now, shot up and maybe dying in my place and carrying a red hot torch for a dark skinned girl, he still called 'em niggers.

Wasn't much I could say to that, so I didn't try. Mickey was Mickey. Take him or leave him.

He squeezed the hand he still held. For a man who'd lost a gas can of blood, who'd barely made it to my door, he was strong. "I know what you're thinking."

"I doubt it."

"You're thinking t'was that brother she has, the one plays the saxophone, it was him who shot me. And why not? He hates micks more'n I hate niggers."

"So it wasn't him?"

"No, by God. It was Sweet Davy Malloy."

"Davy!"

"I'm as surprised as you are, darling man. But he'll never think to find me here."

I wouldn't count on that. I slipped the latch on my door.